THE WAY BETWEEN
THE WORLDS

THE WAY BETWEEN THE WORLDS

Alys Clare

This first world edition published 2011
in Great Britain and in the USA by
SEVERN HOUSE PUBLISHERS LTD of
9–15 High Street, Sutton, Surrey, England, SM1 1DF.
Trade paperback edition first published
in Great Britain and the USA 2012 by
SEVERN HOUSE PUBLISHERS LTD.

British Library Cataloguing in Publication Data

Clare, Alys.
  The way between the worlds.
  1. Lassair (Fictitious character) – Fiction. 2. Fens, The
  (England) – Fiction. 3. Nuns – Crimes against – Fiction.
  4. Great Britain – History – Norman period, 1066–1154 –
  Fiction. 5. Detective and mystery stories.
  I. Title
  823.9'14-dc22

ISBN-13: 978-0-7278-8097-0 (cased)
ISBN-13: 978-1-84751-391-5 (trade paper)

Except where a
described for tl
publication are
is purely coinc

All Severn Hou

Severn House l
the leading inte
are printed on

l [FSC],
titles that
e FSC logo.

MIX
Paper from
responsible sources
FSC® C018575
www.fsc.org

Typeset by Palimpsest Book Production Ltd.,
Falkirk, Stirlingshire, Scotland.
Printed and bound in Great Britain by
MPG Books Ltd., Bodmin, Cornwall.

For Richard.
"When you look up, there shall I be;
When I look up, there shall you be."

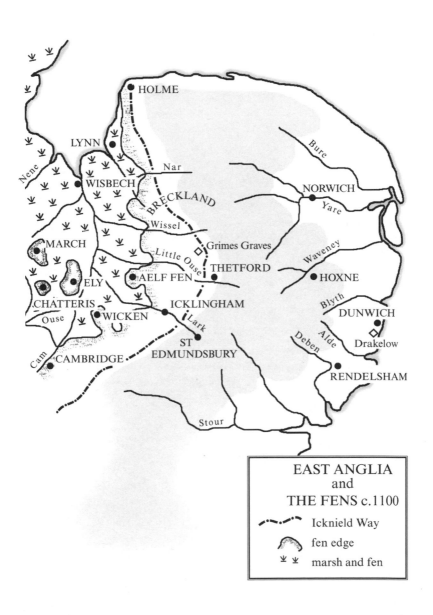

EAST ANGLIA
and
THE FENS c.1100

-·-·-· Icknield Way
🝔 fen edge
⅄ ⅄ marsh and fen

ONE

ome to me! I need you!

C The words brought me awake, shaking, trembling, sweat on my body although the night was chilly. I had been dreaming. It was the same dream; the one that had come to me twice already. Each time it had been more powerful; more frightening. This is what I dreamed . . .

I am standing by water. I can hear it, but I cannot see it, for there is a thick, white mist that swirls up around me from the cold, moisture-soaked ground. I am in the fenland; that I know without a doubt. I was born in the fens and, until recently, spent my entire life there. This place of my dreams, however, is nowhere I recognize.

There is something out in the mist, something that terrifies me . . .

When I first had the dream, I had no idea what it could be; it was shapeless, nameless. The second time, I sensed a being close by me, but whether it was human I could not say. This third time, I caught a glimpse of the horror that haunts me: I saw a dark figure, shadowed and ominous, indistinct save for its malice, which sought me out and drilled into me like an iron point.

I had no idea what it was, but I knew it was evil.

That night there was an additional factor: the voice. As my fast, alarmed heartbeat gradually slowed, I steeled myself and tried to recall exactly what had been said. Said . . . No, that wasn't right. Those summoning words had not been spoken; they had been put inside my head. I knew that was so because when I tried to decide if a man or a woman had been responsible, I realized I had no idea.

A repetitive dream meant that someone – something – in the spirit world was trying urgently to reach me. In my three dreams, that thing had become increasingly insistent and threatening. I gave a small whimper of fear. As I lay there in the dark, I had never felt more alone.

It was a great novelty for me to sleep by myself. Until that year – it was the spring of 1092, and King William, son of the Conqueror, had been on the throne of England for four and a half years – I had slept in a small cottage with at least one and as many as eight other people. In my home village of Aelf Fen I had lately lived with my healer aunt, Edild, in her tiny, fragrant house that, between us, we always kept neat and tidy. Before that, I had lived with my parents, my brothers and sisters and my beloved grandmother, who died last year. Both my sisters now lived elsewhere: one with her husband and family in another village, and one in the abbey where she is a novice nun. The eldest of my three brothers married last summer, and he and his bride will share the family home until he can build a dwelling just for them.

As for me, I was on my second visit to the house of a sage who has decided, for reasons I still do not dare to think about, to take me on as his pupil. When first I learned of his existence, I was told that Gurdyman was a wizard, and sometimes, when some demonstration of his extraordinary powers leaves me horrified and fearful, I think that word described him best.

Life with him is totally different from everything I have previously known. To begin with, he lives in the busy, bustling town of Cambridge, the streets of which are crammed with every rank and level of society, from lords in fine, richly-coloured wool, velvet and gold, to abject beggars who crouch on corners and hold out their mutilated limbs as they plead for charity. In addition to the indigenous population, Cambridge lies on a river that brings the merchant ships right into the town, where they tie up along the broad stone quays. You can buy the produce of the known world in the market, and the chatter of languages spoken by all the foreign captains and sailors makes you think that the Tower of Babel must be right here in the town.

Let me describe Gurdyman's house. It is quite astonishing; a most unlikely place to live. It is hidden away in a maze of dark and narrow little streets that twist and turn around the market square. You turn right, right again, left, right, right, left . . . Or do you? Actually, it's easier to find your way than to describe it, for certain landmarks such as a small pot of lavender on a doorstep serve as prompts. Even so, I still get lost quite frequently. I sometimes entertain the thought that the house is deliberately hiding itself.

Once you have located the right alley, you come to a flight of shallow steps leading up to double doors, set within an arch of well-shaped stones. Inside the house, the twisting and turning intensifies. You take a few paces along the hall, then a smaller passage leads off to the right. If you take it, you go down steps, turn left, along a few more paces, turn left again and descend a steep, narrow stair that seems to take you right down into the earth. Bowing your head to get beneath a low arch, you emerge into Gurdyman's workplace, in a vaulted crypt below the house. I had been here for some time before I realized that this crypt isn't actually beneath Gurdyman's house; the dwellings in this alley sort of fold together, and Gurdyman's house is woven into the spaces between those of his neighbours. When you're down in the crypt, it is the neighbours who walk about over your head.

Back upstairs in the hall, you walk on and come to the space that serves as kitchen, eating room and storage area. It is not large, and the furnishings – table, two stools, various cupboards for pots, platters, cups, knives and food – are crammed against the walls, kept clear of the small cooking hearth in the middle of the room. A steep little ladder against one wall leads up to an attic room.

Beyond the kitchen, the twisty-turny house springs its final surprise. You turn left under an arch and find yourself in a small, square courtyard enclosed by high stone walls and open to the sky. Here Gurdyman has a table, a chair and a bench, and whenever it is not actually raining or snowing, he likes to sit out here, often very well wrapped, deep in thought, a quill, penknife, ink and scrap parchment by his side in case he needs to record some brilliant idea. He says the greenery – a vine, a rose and a large bay tree in a big earthenware pot – is a solace.

He seems to live mainly in his crypt, where he has a low

cot. The attic room is mine alone during the time that I am
with him. When I first appreciated this, I was very embarrassed
because I was quite sure he had moved out for me. But no,
he assured me; the room indeed used to be his sleeping
chamber, he explained, but when he came to think about it,
he realized that of late he usually slept in his crypt.

My attic room has stout stone walls on three sides and a
little square opening in the wooden boards of the floor where
the ladder comes up. On the fourth side, there is a series of
three arched windows that look out over the courtyard. In
summer, I shall be able to smell the herbs and flowers that
Gurdyman is growing down there; they are as yet little more
than delicate green shoots, for it is early in the spring. Now,
when it is cold at night – and usually it is – I roll leather
blinds down over the windows to keep out the chill. I have a
wide bed with a feather mattress all to myself – I still can't
believe my luck – and it is made up with linen sheets and
soft, warm woollen blankets. Across it I drape the beautiful
shawl that my sister Elfritha made for me and I feel as
pampered as a queen.

That night, the night I heard the summoning words, for the
first time I wished I was not alone. Luxurious it might be, but
I would have given almost anything for the comfort of knowing
that someone else of my family slept close by. I lay wide
awake, afraid even to try to sleep again. I made myself think
about that recurring dream. I repeated those words: *come to
me! I need you!*

After quite a long time, my fear lessened and curiosity stirred.
Who could have appealed to me? Who, among my family and
friends, was so urgently requesting my help? I wondered what
aid this person believed I could give. I was learning to be a
healer – or at least I had been until my studies with my aunt
began to be interrupted by my visits to Cambridge – but surely
anyone wanting a healer's skills would call on Edild rather
than me. What else could I do? I was just starting out on my
work with Gurdyman and, again, who in their right mind would
summon me when Gurdyman lived in the same house? Perhaps
this person didn't know about Gurdyman. Or perhaps they did

but he was far too grand and fearsome for whatever small task they had in mind. If they were summoning me, it had to be a small task: if nothing else was certain, that was.

For what remained of the night, I lay worrying at the problem. Then a faint glimmer of light penetrated into my little room around the edge of the leather blinds, and somewhere in the town I heard a cock crow. I slipped out of bed, drew my gown on over my shift, tidied my hair and put on a clean white coif and, my shoes in my hand, went backwards down the ladder and crept along the dark hall to the passage that led down to the crypt. Gurdyman, I knew, was an early riser; that is, on days when he slept at all.

I found him standing before his workbench, quite still, his arms crossed and a look of intense concentration on his face. On the bench, a glass vessel rested on an iron tripod and beneath it a flame burned. Some liquid in the vessel was giving off pale blue steam and it smelt vaguely of irises.

I said tentatively, 'Gurdyman? May I speak to you?'

He spun round, and for a moment his bright blue eyes gazed blankly at me as if he had quite forgotten who I was and what I was doing there. I was used to this and simply waited. Then he shook his head a couple of times as if to clear away whatever had been preoccupying him and said, 'Of course, Lassair.' Taking in the fact that I was dressed ready for the day, he added, 'Morning already!'

'Have you been up all night?' I was sure he had and, even as I asked the question, I was moving over to the small table where he habitually kept a flagon of small beer and a little food. I spread butter on a piece of rather dry bread, cutting a slice of rich cheese and adding it to the bread. Handing it to him, I watched as absently he took a bite and began to chew.

'I almost have it,' he muttered, half to himself. 'Today I shall try one or two further variations to the formula, then we shall see.' Turning to me, he gave me a brilliant smile and said, 'Oh, yes, we shall see!'

I smiled back. I was glad to see him eating, for I knew that he often neglected himself. I did not expect him to tell me what he was trying to do. He was, after all, the master; I was only the young and very inexperienced pupil.

'I thought that today we could begin on our study of the rudiments of alchemy,' he said, still chewing. 'I plan to begin by showing you some of the materials that are employed and the symbols that represent them, proceeding to a demonstration of a simple purification process.'

'Oh—' Half-excited, half-alarmed, I did not know how to respond.

'But you have come to me on another matter, I see,' he went on. 'You asked to speak to me; please, go ahead.'

I had already decided on what to say, and now, as quickly and succinctly as I could, I told him about my dreams and the summoning words that I had received the previous night. He did not interrupt and when I had finished, he said thoughtfully, 'Hmm.'

I waited. After a moment, he said, 'You are afraid of whatever lurks in the mist.'

'I am,' I agreed.

He looked straight into my eyes. 'Do you feel you must obey the summons, for all that you do not know from whom it comes?'

'Yes.'

'Then you do not believe that the fearsome entity in the mist spoke the words, for if you did you would not even contemplate replying to whoever is calling for you, never mind answering the summons.'

I had not thought of that. 'No, I wouldn't,' I said slowly. I did not know who had put those words inside my head, but in my heart I knew it was someone close to me. As I heard them, it was almost like listening to my own thoughts.

Gurdyman finished his bread and cheese, drained his mug of beer and wiped his mouth and his fingers on a clean white napkin. Then he said decisively, 'For the moment, let us put aside the dreams. If this message is as urgent as you believe, then it will come to you again.'

I did not like the thought of that. The three dreams I'd had so far had shown a distinct escalation in their power to frighten me, and I dreaded what might come next. But Gurdyman was still speaking, so I made myself listen.

'. . . a list of those people who you think might have cause to ask you to help them,' he was saying. 'Your family, naturally, and your friends in Aelf Fen. Sibert, for example.'

Sibert was indeed my friend, and I could well believe that it was he who had summoned me. We had shared danger before and knew we could depend on each other.

'Who else?' Gurdyman had reached for a sharpened quill and a scrap of vellum, and was busy writing as he spoke. 'You have healed many people, Lassair, and perhaps one who you treated successfully wishes to ask for your help once more.' Watching over his shoulder, I saw him write, in beautiful, even letters, *former patients*, followed by a question mark.

I contributed one or two more suggestions, for I had relatives whom Gurdyman did not know about and it was always possible one of them needed me. Then, when his questioning expression elicited from me no further names, he rolled up the ragged piece of vellum, put it aside and said, 'Now, to work.'

Even as I went wide-eyed into my first lesson in alchemy, I did not forget about the dreams and the summoning words, and I knew Gurdyman did not either. It was one of his habits, I was discovering, to outline a problem, note down all the details and then turn his mind to something quite different. He had an idea that the mind, given a problem to solve, was quite happy to get on with it while the body was engaged in other tasks. I spent the day taking from his hands bottles of strange liquid, fragments of various metals, hunks and chunks of materials, repeating after him their strange names: caustic lime, nitre oil, vitriol, borax, burned alum. Then came a bewildering assortment of receptacles and instruments: alembic, crucible, retort, receiver and even a skull. He unrolled a fresh piece of vellum and instructed me to write out the names and the corresponding symbols. Later, I knew, I would have to commit it all to memory.

Late in the day, Gurdyman consulted his astrological charts and announced that the Sun was in Aries in the Eleventh House and both the ascendant and Mars in Gemini in the First. He gave me a thoughtful look. 'Your sun is in Gemini, as are your Mercury and Venus,' he observed, 'and your Mars and

Jupiter in Aries. You are air and fire, and you totally lack earth and water.' I wondered rather apprehensively how he knew. My aunt Edild had once cast my birth chart, but it was highly unlikely she'd ever shown it to Gurdyman. He stared at me thoughtfully for a few moments then, smiling, said softly, 'I have just the thing.'

My first experiment in alchemy consisted of grinding some dried leaves and flowers in a pestle and mortar, mixing them with water and then heating the liquid in a still over the bright flame of an oil lamp that Gurdyman called a wick. I watched as the liquid turned to steam – Gurdyman said this process was known as vaporizing – and then, entranced, I saw tiny droplets begin to collect in a separate vessel that he called the receiver. Finally, when all was finished and the glass vessels had cooled down enough to touch, he extracted a drop of the new substance and held it out to me to sniff at. It smelt delicious; like summer flowers with the sun on them.

'One becomes two, two becomes three and out of the third comes the one as the fourth,' he intoned. Then, his distant expression softening into a smile, he said, 'We took flowers and water, and we turned them into this sweet perfume.'

My mouth was open in surprise. I said, somewhat dimly, 'Oh.' Then, recovering a little wit, I added, 'What did you mean about this being just the thing?'

'You are air and fire. We used fire to harness water and the product of the earth.'

'The flowers?'

'The flowers. With our materials we made a substance – perfume – that belongs to the air. Do you see?'

I was not sure that I did. 'I *begin* to see,' I said cautiously, 'but there is very much that is far beyond my understanding.'

He beamed. 'Then you truly have put your feet on the path of learning, for wisdom is as much recognizing what we do not know as what we do.'

I wasn't entirely sure I understood that, either.

I was exhausted when at last I went up the little ladder to my bed. I hoped I would sleep so soundly that no dream would penetrate, and for much of the night that must indeed have been the case.

The dream returned soon after dawn; I know that because when it released me from its claws and I woke up, light was just beginning to illumine the sky.

That night's dream was the worst of all . . .

I am back in the mist again, trying to find my way over waterlogged ground because the dreaded *something* out there is after me. Then, suddenly, there are other people around me – fleeing, like me, from this nameless terror. An old man helping a weak old woman; a mother trying to hurry along three little children while clinging tightly to the mewling baby in her arms. Big men armed with staves drive us along, urging us on. The water under my feet seems now to be much deeper, so it is a great effort to keep wading on through it. Then the terror truly catches hold of me: the water is rising faster than we are moving, and it is going to overwhelm us.

Panicking, I do not know what to do. Should I remain with the throng of people? Would it be safer to be in a crowd, so that we could all help each other?

I turn away from the hurrying masses, slip beneath the outstretched arm of one of the men herding us along and hurry off over the marsh. I hear a scream and, spinning round, see a huge wave rise up and engulf the ground where I had just been standing. The people have vanished.

I whimper in terror. Then I run.

The light is poor, and swirls of mist float around my feet, but somehow I am able to leap from tussock to tussock, and soon I know I have left the others a long way behind.

Then a great, dark figure looms up directly in front of me, so abruptly that it is as if he has risen up from the deep places of the earth. He is huge, towering above me. His face is deadly pale, his wide, thin mouth a red gash in the white skin. His teeth are long, sharp and pointed, and bared in a snarl.

I try to scream, but I am struck dumb and no sound comes out of me. Then he raises both arms high above his head and I see what he holds: an enormous battleaxe, a thunderstone, worthy of some great god or chieftain out of the old tales. Its single blade curves round in a vicious semicircle, its bright, keen edge dripping blood. He swings it around a couple of times and then brings it down so swiftly that it sings through the air . . .

I woke up crouched in the corner of my bed, soaked in my own sweat, screaming as if I could never stop. I was making so much noise that the summoning words had to be repeated before I heard them: *come to me! I need you!* And even as they rang inside my head, it was as if I was still dreaming, for I had a sudden vivid vision of a wild and desolate place where the wind howled like a tormented spirit and old, rounded hills seemed to pace along a dim horizon. There were the ruins of some ancient building – pillars, huge stone slabs with strange markings on them – and, hollowed into the side of a low mound, a dark, narrow space like a grave or a crypt. I thought I saw a lifeless body, crouched foetus-like down in the earth . . .

The vision left me almost as quickly as it had come. I fell forward on to my pillows and buried my head under my arms.

Gurdyman must have heard my screams, for quite soon I heard him puffing his way up the ladder. His head appeared through the gap in the floorboards and, with one swift look at me, he levered himself up into the attic and hastened across to me. I had already discovered many things about him: he is highly intelligent and extremely learned; he has a phenomenal memory; and his powers, the depths of which I had only just begun to suspect, leave me nervous with awe. Until that early morning, I had not appreciated that he has a very kind heart.

He did not speak at first, just held me in a warm, close embrace, one hand stroking my hair as if he were soothing a scared animal. Then, when my sobs finally ceased and the racking hiccups that followed were becoming more and more infrequent, he said quietly, 'The dream again.'

'Yes,' I whispered.

'Tell me.'

I hesitated, for I did not feel I could make myself go through it again so soon.

'Lassair, child, it was a dream,' he said. 'In itself it cannot harm you, and to give in to your fear and try to close it away in the back of your mind will only empower it. Get it out into the good light of dawn, and we will watch as it dissipates.'

I knew he was right. My aunt Edild has sometimes had to help people whose dreams make them afraid to sleep, and she says much the same thing. She also says that a dream that recurs means a message that you ignore at your peril, but I tried not to think about that just then.

I took a deep breath, clutched at Gurdyman's warm hand and told him everything I could remember.

When I had finished – and I was quite relieved to find that the retelling had not reduced me to my previous pitiful state – he got up and crossed back to the top of the ladder. Turning, he gave me a bright smile. 'Well done,' he said. 'You have been very brave, and you deserve a good breakfast, which I shall prepare.' He set off down the ladder. 'Come down when you are ready,' his voice floated back up, 'and we shall decide what you are to do next.'

Do next? I had hoped that, having done as he had bade me and told him, I would be allowed to forget all about this strange business and get on with my studies. Now, as I got out of bed and swiftly drew on my outer garments, I had a nasty feeling that was not to be.

We ate our meal – of bread, honey-butter flavoured with cinnamon and a slice each of last night's apple bake – and Gurdyman gave me a hot, spicy drink that tasted slightly bitter. I wondered if he had prescribed a mild sedative and thought I would be quite glad if he had. The food was plentiful and tasty, as always in Gurdyman's house, for, when he remembers to eat, he eats well. When we had finished, he looked at me and said firmly, 'Lassair, it is clear to me that whoever or whatever is trying to contact you will not give up. You have two choices: either endure these dreams, which will become more and more terrible, or go and find out who is summoning you and what they want of you.' He studied me gravely. 'You are not without courage, and you have a degree of resourcefulness,' he mused.

'You think I should search for whoever's calling me?'

He gave a small shrug. 'It is what I would do. But it is your choice, child.' He gave a slight smile. 'If you do not, I fear I shall have to speak to my neighbours and explain why my young pupil wakes them up with her screams.'

I felt my face blush. 'Do you think they heard?' I hissed.

'It's no use whispering now, child,' he said with a laugh. 'The damage was done at dawn.' Relenting, he added, 'Don't worry. My neighbours are used to hearing strange noises from this house. I doubt that anyone will mention it.'

I doubted it, too. From what I had observed, Gurdyman's neighbours preferred to restrict their dealings with him to a stiff little bow of the head and a polite good morning. It can't be easy, living cheek by jowl with a wizard.

I knew what I was going to do. I think I'd known since I first heard those urgent words, the dawn before this one. Someone needed me and, although I was still young in the healing arts, already I had learned that when people called out to you with such an appeal, you did not turn away.

I fetched the piece of vellum on which we'd listed my family and friends and spread it out. 'Most of the people I know live in or near to my village,' I said, staring down at the names. 'I'd better start there.' I let go of the ends of the vellum, and it rolled itself up again. 'It's still early. If you can spare me, Gurdyman, I'll set out straight away.'

TWO

The spring day was overcast but mild, and I made good time. On the road out of Cambridge, a young ginger-haired lad driving a cart loaded with logs stopped and gave me a lift, offering to take me as far as Wicken. There he would go straight on for Ely and I'd set off to the north-east, to Aelf Fen. He was inclined to be flirtatious, obviously wondering if a quick fumble behind a hedge might be his reward, but I put on my most demure demeanour and told him I was going to visit my sister in her nunnery. When I got down, I felt bit guilty and gave him half the meal I'd packed for myself. He seemed happy enough with that instead and gave me a cheery wave as he clicked to his horse and drove off.

When I reached the village, to my great joy the first person I saw was my father. He is an eel fisher, and he was busy on a channel that was full of water after the spring rains. On seeing me, he leapt right over the slowly sliding, green water and embraced me, breaking off almost instantly to look anxiously into my face.

'Is anything wrong?' he asked. 'You are well? You're not in any trouble?'

'I am fine, Father!' I said, laughing. 'I'm very well, working hard but enjoying it, and as far as I know not in trouble of any kind.'

He let out his breath in a *phew* sound. Then, grinning, he said, 'Don't know why I should assume the worst, just because you've come home on an unexpected visit. I'm right glad to see you, Lassair.' He hugged me again, this time bestowing the gentle kiss on my forehead which he has been doing ever since I can remember.

I felt bad that I hadn't told him straight away about the dreams and the summoning voice. In that moment of reunion, I just wanted to enjoy being with my beloved father, without spoiling it with matters of so dark a nature. 'Is all well with you?' I asked him.

'Aye, as you'll observe, it's a good season for the likes of me.' He indicated his lidded wicker basket, and I could see through the gaps in the weave that it was full of writhing eels. 'After the cold and the endless rain last autumn, and that terrible storm we had at the equinox, it's a great relief to have good catches again.' He grinned. 'The eels kept themselves safely tucked up deep down in the mud, but they're emerging now that spring's here and there's a bit of warmth in the air.'

'And everyone else? How are they all?'

'Your mother's well, praise the good Lord, and the family too.' For a moment his face clouded. 'That is to say, Alvela's been poorly again.' Alvela is my father's sister, Edild's twin, and she lives up in the Breckland with her flint knapper son Morcar. Alvela is one of those women poorly equipped to deal with life's hardships, and she frequently suffers from bouts of ill health.

Had the summons come from her? Was it she who had put those urgent words into my mind?

'Is she very sick?' I asked. Sick enough to send out that desperate plea? I added silently.

But my father smiled. 'No, child, she's not. She's had a congestion of the lungs and was finding it hard to get her breath, but Edild's gone up to Breckland to care for her and she'll soon be on the mend.'

Oh. Not Alvela, then.

'Come on.' He bent down and slung the leather handles of his basket over his strong shoulder. 'We'll get on home, and you shall see for yourself that the rest of them are thriving.'

My mother greeted me with her usual loving smile, apparently unsurprised to see me. I wondered if that could mean it had been she who summoned me, and I was about to ask her when she said, 'I'm so glad you're here, Lassair, there's something I've been planning to ask of you when next I saw you.'

So it *had* been my mother! Feeling the relief flooding through me, I said with a smile, 'Well, you managed to get your message through to me!'

Her face went blank. 'My message?'

I knew I was wrong. Just to make quite sure, I said, trying to speak lightly, 'You haven't been calling out to me, then? Saying, *come here, I need you*?'

My mother gave me quite a stern look. 'Now why,' she said, 'would I do that? Silly lass, you're far too far away in Cambridge to hear me, even if I shouted at the top of my voice!'

I forget, sometimes, how very literal my mother is.

My baby brother Leir came up to me, his arms opening in a silent plea to be lifted up and cuddled, and I readily obliged, burying my face in his silky fair hair. I shouldn't really refer to him as a baby any more, for he is five years old now and, as my protesting arms were informing me, growing into a well-built and strong boy. 'Did you summon me, little brother?' I whispered to him.

He gave me a soggy kiss and said, echoing my mother, 'Silly lass!'

I put him down.

The long working day was drawing to its close now and presently there came the sound of footsteps outside. The door opened and my other brothers came in, the elder one, Haward, with an arm around his wife's expanding waist, the younger, Squeak, trotting behind but pushing them out of the way when he saw I was there. He rushed at me and, in a thirteen-year-old's version of Leir's greeting, flung his arms round me and swirled me round in a circle. He, too, was growing strong.

They all asked what I was doing home, and I found ways to ask all three if they had any reason for wanting to see me. Squeak looked puzzled as he answered, and merely said, very sweetly, 'I *always* want to see you, Lassair. I miss you when you're away.'

Haward, with a glance at his wife, said that they'd needed advice from Edild a couple of weeks ago because Zarina had fallen and they'd feared for the baby, although all was well. Zarina took my hand and said, 'I'd have been just as happy to consult you, Lassair, but you weren't here,' which I thought was very nice of her.

As we all sat down to the evening meal, I remembered that my mother had said she had something to raise with me. 'You didn't tell me what you were planning to ask me,' I reminded her.

'Didn't I?' Her smooth-skinned, plump-cheeked face creased briefly into a frown. 'No, I didn't. It was just that I thought, next time you were here, you might tell us a story. It's half a year now since Granny Cordeilla died, and we haven't had a tale since.' She looked at me worriedly. 'It's not too soon?'

Slowly, I shook my head. I had known since Granny died that sooner or later this moment would come, for she had passed on to me the role of the family's bard, the one whose job it is to memorize the family bloodline and to learn all the tales in its long history, retelling them regularly so that nobody forgets who they are and who their ancestors were. Granny knew perfectly well that, of all her children and grandchildren, I was the one with the God-given facility to remember the

stories. She knew, too, that I loved them and that repeating
them whenever I was asked would be no hardship.

'It's not too soon, Mother,' I said to her with a smile. 'I'll
tell you what: if I am excused clearing up the platters and
mugs, washing them and tidying them away, I'll tell you all
a story this very night.'

I went to stand outside in the warm spring night. Inside the
house, the family were busy arranging seating for us all, and
I knew the best place for the storyteller, beside the fire, would
be reserved for me. My mother had promised to prepare a cot
for me; although I lived with Edild now, and could easily have
slipped across the village to sleep there that night, Edild was
away and I would be alone. Normally, I would not have minded
in the least, but just then I feared my powerful dreams. If I
found myself back in that nightmare landscape of mist and
blood and I was all by myself, I was not sure how I would
endure it. When my mother had said *why don't you sleep here
tonight?* I had willingly accepted. But now, in the immediate
future, there was a very important task ahead of me. I turned
my mind to storytelling.

I don't know what prompted my choice of tale. Granny
Cordeilla once said that the story chooses the teller, and that
if you open your mind and simply wait, the spirits of the
ancestors will prompt you. I composed myself, closed my
eyes, shut off the constant steam of my thoughts and filled
my mind with the intention of making my parents, my brothers
and my sister-in-law happy with a good story. For a while
nothing happened, and then, with a smile, I knew which story
I was going to tell.

'I tell my tale in honour of my grandmother and predecessor,'
I began, looking round at the circle of faces in the firelight,
'for it concerns her namesake, the first Cordeilla, child of Lir
the Magical and his wife Essa.' I glanced at my mother with
a secret smile, for her name too is Essa. 'Now last born to
Essa and Lir were twin girls, and their names were Cordeilla
and Feithfailge. They were identical in every way, born of one
flesh divided and one soul that was shared between two.

Cordeilla was the elder, but only by a matter of moments, and it was said that the babies were born with their little fingers entwined.'

I heard a soft gasp from Zarina, sitting curled up against Haward, one hand on her swelling belly. I calculated swiftly: I had recognized that she was pregnant late last summer, not long after her wedding to my brother, and I reckoned she had a month or so to go until the birth of her son. I knew the child was a boy, although I would not have dreamt of telling her so.

'Now Cordeilla had a secret strength that her sister did not share,' I went on, 'and, although she always lay right beside Feithfailge, her mouth to her sister's as if she was breathing some of her power into her sibling's frail body, Feithfailge did not thrive and she died soon after her birth.'

Out of the corner of my eye I saw Haward hug Zarina, and he whispered something, smiling reassuringly. I caught his eye and he gave me a quick frown, as if to say *fine choice of tale this is for a pregnant woman to hear!*

I wanted to reassure him, but that was not my role. When I was acting as bard, I was no longer his younger sister. The ancestors were with me, in me, and their demands overrode any niceties. One day, I promised myself, I would explain that to him.

'Although Cordeilla was still only a tiny baby –' I picked up my tale –'nevertheless she grieved for her twin and would not be comforted, until Essa wrapped her up in her dead sister's blanket and laid her on the spot where Feithfailge lay buried. A change came over Cordeilla, and it was said by the Wise Women that she absorbed her dead sister's essence from out of the ground, thus comforting herself; ever after, Cordeilla was both twins, the dead Feithfailge and the living Cordeilla, and it was said that she lived her life for both of them.'

Little Leir opened his mouth to say something – probably to ask a question, for these matters would be hard for a child to understand – but my father put his hand softly on his son's head and gently shushed him. 'Lassair is bard tonight,' I heard him whisper, 'and not the sister who you treat with the familiarity of family.'

My father recognized the role I had adopted, then. But he was the son of one of one of the greatest bards of recent times, so he would.

'Cordeilla was the Weaver of Spells,' I went on, 'and her son Beretun became a cunning man of wide renown, whose pupil Yorath fell in love with him, for all that he was more than twenty years older, and she wed him and was ever after known as Yorath the Young Wife. Their second son Ailsi was twice wed. His first wife was Alainma the Lovely, and she was as beautiful as any of her northern ancestors, with long golden hair, eyes light blue like the dawn sky and a loving smile that she bestowed on all those that she loved. She gave birth to a child, but it died, and Alainma died with it. Ailsi's grief was terrible, and he lived alone for twenty-one years, rejecting every appeal by his family for him to abandon his solitude and go back to live among his kin.'

Again, I saw Haward hug Zarina close to him. I saw the glint of tears on her face. My tale was sad, I knew, but so were all the old stories. Death was always close, as it always will be.

'Ailsi grew thin and bitter in his solitude, and his family gave up trying to help him, for all they got for their pains was a curse and a harsh cry of *leave me alone!* His sister Alma stopped arranging for comely and suitable women to pass by his lonely house, for he was not to be tempted out of his sorrow, no matter how fair, rich or shapely the woman. And then one day Alma had an idea: supposing she could somehow make Ailsi laugh, might that not break the icy tomb in which he had sealed himself?

'Now Alma had a new friend, an heiress of considerable means who, orphaned and alone, had recently moved into the village. Her name was Livilda, she was tall and gauche, she had a face like an amiable horse and she only had one leg.'

There was a giggle, swiftly stifled, from Leir, as presumably he imagined what a horse-faced woman with one leg would look like.

'But Livilda had a great gift: she could make people laugh. Alma's life had not been without sorrow and, as she grew old, she suffered greatly from pains in her joints, but Livilda could always cheer her up. She would imitate one of the village characters or she would recount some small happening in her day's round, often making herself the butt of her humour, ridiculing all her defects from her protuberant eyes and her long nose to her single leg.'

I could hear Leir wriggling, and I knew the question he was burning to ask. 'I expect,' I said, 'you're all wondering what happened to the other leg? Well, I'll tell you: Livilda was sitting in church one day when she was a little girl and there was a great tremor in the earth, so violent that the church walls began to crack. Everyone rushed outside, and only just in time, for the cracks grew wider and wider and, before everyone's horrified eyes, the walls began to sway and huge stones tumbled to the ground. Now Livilda had been naughty and disobeyed her mother; she had a new kitten and she had smuggled it into church with her, hidden in her pocket. Now, horrified, she realized the kitten had escaped. With no thought for herself, she raced back inside the church, found the kitten crouched in a corner and swept it up. She was almost outside again when a huge stone fell on her, trapping her leg and crushing it beyond repair. The village healer gave her a seda- tive and sent her to sleep, and when Livilda woke up, she had one leg and a neat stump.'

A very soft voice – Leir's, I thought – whispered, 'What happened to the kitten?'

'Both Livilda and the kitten made a good recovery,' I went on. 'Now, to return to Ailsi, Alma decided to take Livilda to meet her lonely brother. At first he tried to bar the door to them, but he caught sight of Livilda doing her impression of a heron, standing on one leg and darting its beak into the water after fish, and something very strange happened, something that he hadn't experienced for twenty-one years: he began to laugh. To begin with, it sounded like the creaking of an old door that needs its hinges oiled, but then, as he began to remember what laughter felt like, the sounds became free and joyful. He ran outside, caught hold of his loyal sister with one hand and grasped Livilda's shoulder with the other. "You look like a horse and you move like a deformed chicken," he said to her, "but you have just worked a miracle. You are many years younger than me, for I am an old man now, and you probably have a husband; if not, will you consider marrying me?"'

I looked round at my audience. Six pairs of eyes were fixed on me and, behind them, I saw the small, upright figure of my granny, siting in mid-air in the place where her little cot used to stand. She gave me a nod of encouragement and mouthed, *go on, then! Don't keep them in suspense!*

I gave her a grateful look and said, 'Livilda had never been called a worker of miracles before and it rather tickled her fancy, so she told Ailsi she didn't have a husband and would marry him, adding that, because he was indeed so old, they'd better not waste any time. They were married within a month and, to put the crown on their unexpected happiness, Livilda gave birth to three healthy children, all with the right number of legs.'

I paused. Tempting as it was to go on with Livilda's tale – she's always been one of my favourite ancestors – there was another strand to the tapestry of our history that I wanted to finish with. 'Now I will return,' I said, altering my tone so as to sound less frivolous, 'to Luanmaisi, most powerful of Wise Women, who was sister to Alma and Ailsi. She walked with the spirits –' there was a soft exclamation from Zarina – 'and they taught her their ways, taking her between the worlds to encounter beings of other realms. It is the great mystery of our bloodline that we know not how, when or where she died, although it was said among the wise that she left this world and did not return. What is known is that she disappeared into the mists of the fenland one autumn day, just after the equinox celebrations, and that later she bore a daughter, Lassair the Sorceress, child of the Fire and the Air.' Like me, I thought, but I did not say it aloud. 'We do not know what became of Lassair either, for her thread of the tale is shrouded in mystery and we do not even know who fathered her. It was, however, strongly believed,' I added, lowering my voice to a whisper, 'that she was half-aelven.' There was another gasp; in fact, several gasps. I glanced across at Granny's corner and she shook her head, mouthing: *enough, now. Always leave them wanting more.*

Thanking her with a small bow, I straightened up, looked round my audience and said, 'As to what might have happened to Lassair the Sorceress, and what did happen to the children of her uncle Ailsi and his one-legged wife . . . I shall tell you another time.'

There was a gratifying chorus of groans and one or two comments pleading for more, but I shook my head. I saw Granny silently clap her hands, smiling her approval, and then she gently faded away.

All in all, I thought that my foray into storytelling hadn't gone too badly.

THREE

I slept surprisingly well, waking only after everyone had left for the day's work to find my mother busy kneading bread, her sleeves rolled up to her elbows and the strong muscles of her forearms working hard. It was only when I was fully awake that I realized I hadn't dreamed. Or, if I had, I'd forgotten. Perhaps the spirit who was trying so hard to attract my attention appreciated that I was already doing my best.

My mother looked up from her bread-making and gave me a loving smile. 'It's good to see you back in your old home,' she remarked. 'I'm sorry I couldn't make up a bed for you in your old spot, but as you'll have seen, Haward and Zarina sleep there now.'

I was lying in the space once occupied by Granny's little cot. No wonder I'd slept soundly and dreamlessly; she'd been looking after me. I sent her my silent thanks, and for an instant seemed to see her wrinkled old face with its deep, dark eyes smiling benignly at me.

'Zarina looks well,' I said, getting up and wriggling into my gown, then bending down to roll up my bedding. Floor space was always limited in our house, and I found it hard to believe I'd slept through the family rising, eating their swift breakfast and setting out for work. I must have been exhausted.

'Yes, she does,' my mother agreed, and I turned my thoughts back to my sister-in-law. 'Edild has kept an eye on her, but in truth the girl's so healthy and strong that there's really no need.'

I paused in folding up my blanket, remembering the vivid sense of a new life that I felt emanating from the bump in Zarina's belly. A little boy, a healthy child, who would grow well and be a joy to his family . . .

'Enough daydreaming, Lassair, and please get out of my way – I'm busy, even if you're not.' My mother's voice cut across the pleasant vision of a small boy with his mother's dark looks and his father's sweet nature, and I felt her elbow dig me, quite hard, in the ribs. With a smile, I tucked the bedding away beneath my parents' bed and asked her what I could do to help.

The morning flew by. I enjoyed working with my mother; we were very well used to each other's ways and performed a multitude of tasks with barely a word. It did me good to have her strong presence. She is a big, broad, fair woman, and being with her tends to ground you and root your feet in the good earth. Since I'm both water- and earth-lacking, perhaps being with my mother provides the firm earth element I do not have. By noon, I was feeling invigorated and ready to proceed with my mission.

My father was working right out by the open water that day, too far for him to return for the midday meal, and he had taken both Squeak and Leir with him. Haward was out on the strips of land that the family work up on the drier ground behind the village, and he, too, had taken his noon meal with him. Zarina still worked for her crusty old washerwoman, and she alone came home to eat with my mother and me.

All the time I'd been going about the day's jobs with my mother, I'd been thinking who could have sent me those summoning words. I seemed to have run through everyone in my family, so it was time to think about my friends. Having helped my mother clear away the meal, I left her having a well-earned but brief rest and went through the village to my friend Sibert's house.

There was nobody at home.

I thought I knew where Sibert would be. Unless it was one of his days for working for Lord Gilbert, lord of our manor, he would be out on his family's strips close by the road that leads to Thetford. I took the short cut over the higher ground, pausing to pay my respects to the ancient oak tree that stands up there, and, among the many people working away on the land, soon spotted a familiar figure.

'I heard you were home,' Sibert greeted me as I approached. He hadn't even turned round.

All of a sudden I felt convinced that it was Sibert who had called out to me for help. We have been close at times over the years; once I saved his life, and, later he'd returned the favour. I know his deepest secret, and I have never told a soul. Mind you, that is largely due to my fear of what his uncle Hrype would do to me if I did; Hrype is not actually Sibert's uncle but his father, and that is the secret. I understand that Sibert doesn't want to talk to me about this, and I respect that, much as I'm burning to know how he feels. I think the fact that I restrain my curiosity is one of the reasons Sibert likes me.

'How are you?' I asked, moving round to face him as he worked down the long row of onions, pulling up endless weeds. The bank that bordered the strip was just behind me, and I sat down on it.

'All right,' he admitted grudgingly. 'I'll be glad to see the last of these bloody onions.'

For the second time that day, I pushed back my sleeves, fastened my hair under my coif and set about lending a hand. 'And your mother?'

'She's all right too.'

'Hrype?' I never know whether to refer to him as *your uncle* or *your father*, so I usually call him by his name.

'Hrype's away, so I have no idea.' Sibert straightened up and fixed me with a glare. 'What's all this about?'

I thought briefly. I decided there was no harm in telling him and so I did.

'A summoning voice?' he repeated, smiling. 'That sounds dramatic. Are you sure it's calling on you for help? Maybe

it's got the wrong person and it's after old Gurdyman. He'd
be a lot more use to anyone than you.'

'If you're going to insult my admittedly limited powers to
do anyone any good,' I said calmly, 'you can finish the onion
bed by yourself.'

He straightened up, a hand to the small of his back, and
grinned at me. 'Only joking. I know you're a fearsome magician these days, as well as a brilliant healer.'

I was used to his teasing. We went back to our weeding.
'So Hrype's away?' I said after a while.

'Yes.'

'Where is he?'

'No idea.'

'When's he coming back?'

'Don't know.'

This was going to be hard. I weeded on for some time and
then said, 'Sibert, I know we've been making light of this
voice I've been hearing, but it's actually quite important. I'd
like to talk to Hrype, so if you have any clue as to where he
is, I'd love to know.'

He stopped weeding. Bending down to look into my face,
he said quietly, 'It *is* important, isn't it? I can see it in your
expression.'

'Mmm,' I agreed. We were both standing upright now, eyes
on each other's.

Sibert said, 'I don't know for sure, because my – because
Hrype does not confide in me.' There was pain beneath the
abrupt words, and it told me much about my friend's relationship with the strange, difficult man who fathered him. 'But I
overheard him speaking to my mother, and he said there's
someone who concerns him – a priest, I think. My guess is
that he's gone to find out more about the man.'

'*Concerns* him?' It seemed a rather general term. 'What
does that mean, exactly?'

'*Exactly*, I couldn't say.' Sibert's tone was angry. 'They
thought I was asleep, and in any case they were muttering.
Mother said did he – Hrype – really have to go, because
she's always fearful and nervous when he's absent, and
he said yes he did, because—' Sibert frowned. 'I thought

he said, because this man who I think is a priest is a threat
and very powerful.'

I thought about that. Hrype is a cunning man, full of magic,
full of a very special sort of force. Had he meant this priest
was a threat because of the religion he represented, which
in the eyes of many – especially its own clergy – stands firm
in its opposition to the old ways? It seemed very likely.

Could it be, then, that it was Hrype who needed me? That,
faced with the problem of a zealous priest determined to route
out the last vestiges of the old ways, Hrype had summoned
me to help him? For a few delicious moments I almost let
myself believe it. Then reality struck me like a shower of rain
in the face, and I returned to earth.

Still, this talk of a *very powerful* priest was the first lead I
had uncovered. I was determined to follow it up. 'Do you
think your mother would know where Hrype is?' I asked
tentatively.

Sibert had gone back to his onions. 'Why not stop pestering
me and go and ask her?'

As I hurried back to the village, I hoped I would find that
Froya had returned. Also that she'd be prepared to tell me
where Hrype had gone; Froya is a very distant figure, and with
her there is always the feeling that she is so busy fighting
off her inner demons that there is little of her left over for
anyone else. I do not suppose for a moment that she is easy
to live with, and I admire Hrype for his loyalty to her, especially when he loves another woman so deeply. (His relationship
with my aunt Edild is another secret that I keep to myself.)

In the end I never got as far as tapping on Froya's door, so
I didn't find out if she was there. As I clambered down the
bank that leads off the higher ground and on to the track
through the village, I heard my mother calling out to me.

She was far from calm and serene now. Her cap was awry;
her face was red and full of anguish. She ran up to me, grabbed
my hands in both of hers and said, 'Oh, thank God you're
here! Where have you *been?* Have you heard?'

'I was out on the upland talking to Sibert,' I replied, feeling
my heart thump with alarm. 'What is it? What's happened?'

My big, brave mother seemed to sag, and for a moment I supported her not inconsiderable weight. Then she forced herself to stand upright and said, 'There's word that a nun has been found murdered. A knife to her throat, they say, or possibly she was strangled.' She frowned, then shook her head violently. 'Oh, I don't *know* – the story is confused.'

A nun. I felt very cold.

'Who brought the news?' I demanded. It could all be just an ugly rumour, a salacious tale to relieve the boredom of country life.

'The peddler from over March way – he's brought a consignment of pins and we've all been crowding round him; I haven't seen a package of pins since last autumn. Oh, *oh* –' my mother's eyes filled with tears – 'and I never got mine! I forgot all about them when he told us!'

I put my arms round her. I already knew, but I thought I should ask anyway.

'He's from March,' I repeated. 'That means he'd have journeyed past—' I hesitated. Perhaps if I didn't put it into words, it wouldn't be true.

But my mother was nodding. 'Yes, yes, I know! He was there two days ago, and the news was spreading like fire in a hayrick. The dead nun's from Chatteris!'

Chatteris Abbey is a small foundation of Benedictine nuns, neither very wealthy nor very important. There are perhaps twenty nuns there, maybe twenty-five. And one of them is my beloved sister Elfritha.

I heard the echo of those desperate words. *I need you!* I braced myself to face the horrible possibility that they had come from my sister.

We hurried home again, and the news must have reached even the outlying lands of the village, for all the family were back.

My father said firmly, 'We have no reason at all to believe that anything has happened to Elfritha. She is one of a score, so the chances are slim.'

Slim, perhaps, but they could not be discounted.

'I thought she'd be safe in her convent!' my mother sobbed. 'Life is hard and full of many dangers, and it was my one great consolation, when she went away to shut herself up with the nuns, that she'd be *safe!*'

'She probably is perfectly safe,' my father said. I thought he sounded less certain than he had before.

There was only one way to find out. Someone would have to go to the abbey and ask. Dreading that this was indeed the answer to the mysterious summons, I said, 'I will go to Chatteris. I'll set out straight away, and I ought to get there tomorrow.'

There was a chorus of protests, mainly from my father and Haward and mainly to the effect that I ought not to go off travelling alone when there was a murderer about. I held up my hands, and my family fell silent.

'It makes sense for me to go,' I said calmly. 'For one thing, any of you would have to get Lord Gilbert's permission to leave the village, whereas he doesn't know I'm here so I'm free to come and go as I like.' It was a rare luxury for people like us, and I was not surprised to receive one or two envious glances. Lord Gilbert believed I was in Cambridge; he had given permission for me to go and study there because, as Edild and Hrype had explained when they went with me to present my case, the more I learned, the more use I would be in the village. Lord Gilbert undoubtedly believed I was being taught further healing methods. Neither my aunt nor Hrype mentioned the other skills that my new teacher possessed in such abundance, and I certainly wasn't going to.

'For another thing,' I went on, 'I'm used to travelling and I know how to look after myself.' I tapped the knife I keep at my belt.

I could now protect myself in other ways, too; Gurdyman had already taught me many things besides the first rudiments of alchemy. But I did not think it wise to reveal this to my family.

There was a short silence. Then my mother looked at my father, and even from where I sat I could read the appeal in her eyes.

'So I am to risk the safety of one daughter in order to set your mind at rest concerning another?' my father muttered. He turned his eyes from my mother and looked at me, and I read such love in his face that I felt tears smart. I blinked them away and gave him a smile.

'You truly are prepared to do this?' he asked.

'I am, Father.'

He sighed heavily. 'My heart misgives me, and I want more than anything to go with you,' he said. 'But I cannot.' His eyes fell, and I had a strong sense of his sudden hatred for his lot: if he followed his powerful desire to look after me, he would risk his livelihood, his home and the well-being of all the other people who depended on him.

It was not easy for people like us.

I went over to him and laid a hand on his shoulder. 'I will be quite safe, Father,' I said quietly. 'It is, as you say, most unlikely that Elfritha has come to harm. As soon as I know she is safe, I will send word.'

His only answer was to take hold of my hand and squeeze it, so hard that it hurt.

I set out for Chatteris while there still remained some hours of daylight. The sky was clear and the weather continued to be mild; I had no fear that a night in the open would do me any harm. My mother packed food for me and a leather flask of small beer, and Zarina rolled up a light blanket. I was dressed for travelling, having journeyed from Cambridge, and had my heavy cloak with its deep hood. The leather satchel that I always carry contained the personal items that I would require, as well as a freshly-replenished basic stock of medicaments. A healer is always a healer, wherever she is, and must be prepared to give aid whenever she is asked.

We said our goodbyes inside the house. It seemed sensible not to make a big public display, which would have got people talking. I didn't think anybody had taken any particular notice of me so far; I was dressed sombrely and from a distance probably looked just like everyone else. There was no need to suspect Lord Gilbert had been informed of my presence in the village.

I embraced my family and, with the impression of their loving kisses still on my cheek and the sight of their anxious faces before my eyes, slipped out of the house and quietly left the village. I saw no one except in the distance, and none of those still working the fields and the fen edge took any notice of me. Soon I had left Aelf Fen behind and, as I trod the road that would curve in a long loop around the southern edge of the fens and then north again to Chatteris, I could have been alone in the world.

I made good time, setting my feet to a marching rhythm and humming to myself to keep my spirits up. I told myself that my sister couldn't possibly be dead, since she had called out to me for help. I didn't allow myself to consider that the sort of summons I had received could equally well have been sent by a dead spirit as a living one. I kept saying to myself, *Elfritha is safe! She's safe!* and the words wove themselves into the pattern of my footsteps. After a while I thought I saw a familiar shape out of the corner of my eye: perceiving my need, Fox had come to keep me company and was silently pacing along beside me.

Until I realized this, I hadn't let myself face my fear of the coming night. With my animal spirit guide at my side, my dream – if it came – would not be so terrifying.

When at last the light began to fade, I looked around for a place to sleep. I had passed the landward end of the Wicken promontory now and taken a short cut that I knew across the marshes to the north of Cambridge. Some years ago I'd had to find a similar safe path from the island of Ely to the mainland, and I'd discovered that it's actually quite easy to do if you're in the right frame of mind. I think it's part of being a dowser, and that's a skill I've had most of my life. It seems that, in addition to being able to find underground water and lost brooches, I can also trace the line of the firm ground through the fens.

Now, not wanting to settle for the night out on the marsh – it's far too wet, for one thing, and you'd wake up very soggy – I turned southwards and was soon clambering up a steep bank to the higher, drier ground. Presently, I came to an outlying hamlet. It was almost fully dark now, and the small group of mean-looking dwellings showed no lights. I made out the ragged shape of a tumbledown hay barn and crept inside. The hay was old and smelt a bit musty, but I heaped it up against the most solid-looking of the walls and reckoned that, with my blanket and cloak, I would be snug enough.

I decided I could risk a little light, so set a stump of tallow candle on a patch of ground from which I'd carefully removed all the stray bits of hay, and struck my flint. The warm, yellow glow showed that the barn was even more dilapidated than I'd thought, and I thanked my guardian spirits for a fine night. I opened the pack of food and ate hungrily; I hadn't realized how famished I was.

I had almost finished when I heard a low growl from out of the shadows. Alarmed, I raised the candle and saw a black and white bitch slowly advancing on me. She had a wall eye and held her head turned slightly to one side so as to look at me out of the good eye. I spoke some quiet words – Hrype had taught me how to disarm angry animals – and she gave a soft *wuff*. I twisted off a small piece of the dried meat from my food pack and held it out to her. She walked slowly up to me and, with a gentle mouth, took it from my fingers. I smoothed my hand over her head, still speaking the spell, and soon she came to lie beside me. When I finally curled up to sleep, it was with the wall-eyed bitch at my back and, as I closed my eyes, the last thing I saw was Fox pacing to and fro in front of me.

I don't know whether it was my fatigue or the presence of my two animal companions: either way, I slept without dreaming. However, when I woke at first light I heard the echo of those words ringing in my head: *come to me! I need you!*

With a new urgency driving me on, I got up, packed up my little camp, brushed the hay from my clothes and, with an affectionate farewell to my wall-eyed bitch, set off again.

Quite soon I came on a busy road leading roughly north-westwards, and I guessed it was the route leading out of Cambridge that skirts the fenlands to the west. I cadged a ride with an elderly woman driving a small cart pulled by a mule and laden with brushwood, advising her on how to treat the stiffness in her poor, twisted hands in exchange. I gave her a small bottle of Edild's remedy, explaining that she must rub it into her joints each morning and evening. She looked at me sceptically, but I just smiled; the remedy would work, I knew it.

She dropped me off close to where the ferries run across to Chatteris, on its little island. Feeling increasingly apprehensive, I walked the last half a mile and waited at the fen edge until a boatman tied up at the quayside. We bartered for a while and then settled on a fare, and he rowed me over the water to my destination.

I'd visited the abbey several times before. The nuns of Elfritha's order keep themselves to themselves in general, although they do have a small infirmary where they treat outsiders, and their refectory hands out food from time to time. Not that the food is anything to get excited about: vowed to poverty as they are, the nuns eat very plainly and very sparsely.

My boatman was a taciturn man whose face wore a permanent frown, and I was disinclined to ask him if he knew about the murder. If the news was bad – I was praying as hard as I knew how that it wouldn't be, even though I appreciated that not being bad for us meant it was bad for some other family – I didn't want to hear it from a grumpy boatman.

The crossing did not take long. I paid my fare and clambered up on to the quay, stopping at the top of the stone steps to take in the view. There were two or three rows of shabby dwellings, undoubtedly housing those few families who managed to survive on the island, either by ferrying people to and from the abbey or by providing fish and other basic necessities to the nuns. In the distance, the track wound away through some fields and a bit of sparse scrubland before eventually losing itself in the muddy, marshy margins of the surrounding fen. The abbey dominated the scene, although in truth there wasn't much to dominate and it wasn't much of an abbey. Its high walls were interrupted by a pair of stout gates facing the track, and above them could be seen the roof-lines of the various abbey buildings, tallest of which was the church. I knew from visits to my sister that there was also a huddle of buildings around the cloister, consisting of refectory, chapter house, dormitories, infirmary and one or two others whose function I was not aware of. Chatteris was a pretty desolate spot, and it had always come as a surprise to discover that my sister and her fellow nuns were by and large a happy, cheerful lot. Perhaps that was the reward you got for giving your life to God.

I realized straight away that the mood was very different from on my previous visits. There were clutches of locals huddled together, muttering and looking around them with fearful glances. Everyone seemed on edge, and one or two people stared suspiciously at me. Having no idea of what dangers might lie before me, I didn't want to be conspicuous. Pretending that I needed to adjust my small pack, I stopped at the entrance to a dark little alleyway leading off the main track and prepared my defences.

Hrype told me that it's actually quite easy to become invisible. You don't actually do so, of course – or, at least, he might be able to, but such high magic is far beyond me. It's a matter of taking the time to study the scene – what sort of mood predominates, how the local people look, how they wear their clothes, how they move – and then slowly and steadily thinking yourself into looking just like them. You can, of course, make small alterations to your clothing if you like, but it's more a question of *feeling* like the rest of the crowd. That day, I could see that people were moving furtively, keeping their heads down, glancing over their shoulders as their fear got the better of them. When I was ready, I stepped out into the street and merged with them. I hope it doesn't sound arrogant if I say that I don't think anybody recognized me for the stranger I was.

I had noticed already that the abbey gates were closed. This was a blow: I had expected to walk in like I usually did and ask the gatekeeper nun if I could see my sister. I wondered what I should do. I had a perfect right to enquire after Elfritha, and surely many of the anxious people standing outside the gates had come here for the same purpose. I was on the point of stepping out from the place where I had paused, beneath the shade of a stand of alders, but some instinct held me back. I am learning to trust my instincts, and it is as Gurdyman, Edild and Hrype all tell me: the more you listen to these inner promptings, the better they will work for you.

I tried to work out why I should keep hidden. If Elfritha was unharmed, then surely it did not matter if it became known that I was there? But if she was the murderer's victim – *she's not, she's NOT!* I cried silently – then it might be a different matter . . .

I stood in an agony of indecision. Finally, I could bear it no longer. Any answer, even the one I so feared to hear, would be better than this terrible uncertainty. I took a deep breath, squared my shoulders and was about to step out in the open when firm, strong fingers grasped my arm and a big hand went over my mouth. There was a harsh whisper in my ear – *'No, do not show yourself!'* – and I was pulled backwards, deeper into the shady space under the trees.

My heart thumping, I twisted my mouth free of that hard hand and turned round to face my assailant.

FOUR

It was Hrype.

'What do you think you're doing?' I hissed angrily. 'You've cut my lip!' I put my fingers to my mouth and held them up, bloody, right in his face.

'I am sorry, Lassair,' he said softly. 'I had to stop you, but I hope you know I did not mean to hurt you.'

I muttered something, still cross with him. Then, my curiosity piqued, I said, 'Why did you have to stop me? Don't you understand why I'm here? A nun's been killed and this is Elfritha's abbey!' In case he had missed the point, I added in an anguished hiss, *'She's my sister!'*

For the first time the reality of the situation hit me. Perhaps it was because, now that I was no longer alone, I could let my defences slip a little. I felt tears form in my eyes, and I brushed them away.

He must have seen, for he took hold of my hand and gave it a squeeze. 'I know,' he said soothingly. 'We will find out what has happened as soon as we can, although I do not believe—' He stopped.

He did not believe what? That Elfritha was the murderer's

victim? I turned to him, words of urgent appeal bubbling up, but he shook his head. 'Do not ask,' he said, 'for as yet I cannot be sure.'

Suddenly, I felt faint. I saw big black spots before my eyes, and I thought I was going to vomit. Hastily, Hrype pushed me down to the ground and made me put my head between my knees. 'Take deep, slow breaths,' he commanded.

I kept seeing Elfritha's face. Sweet-natured, gentle, and by far the nicer of my two sisters, Elfritha would have made a wonderful wife and mother to some lucky family, only from a very young age she knew she belonged to the Lord. I have never told her, but from the day she left to enter Chatteris Abbey, there has always been a bit of a hole in my life.

I was feeling better. I raised my head – slowly – and looked up at Hrype. 'What do you suggest we do?'

He lowered himself down to sit beside me and, leaning close so that he could speak very quietly, said, 'There are things I must tell you.' He paused, gathering his thoughts. 'There are – rumours, of a fanatic of the new religion who has not the tolerance of some of his fellows.'

Yes, so Sibert had suggested. I did not say so aloud. It had been, I supposed, only a matter of time. We who still honoured the old ways were open-minded. I, for example, had developed a growing love for the saviour god of the Christians, and I understood how appealing it was to believe you had a loving, stalwart friend constantly at your side, encouraging you always to do the good thing – one who, whilst he was sad when you let him down, was ever ready to forgive if you were genuinely sorry. But our tolerant attitude did not appear to be shared by the priests of the new religion, who seemed to take the view that they and only they were permitted to know the true nature of the god of us all and reserved the exclusive right to approach him. This, I guessed, was how they had been able to make themselves so very important to the people to whom they ministered. It had been shrewd, I reflected, to tell the people that their god was all-powerful and ever-present, but so mysterious that his word could only be read by those vowed to his service, who would pass on to their flock only as much as they felt the flock ought to know.

God may well be powerful, I mused, but it seemed to me that the true power rested with his priests. And, for all that they said King William was irreligious, even pagan – although I do not understand what people mean by that term – it was all too apparent that the priesthood's hold on the consciences of men was steadily tightening . . .

'A fanatic?' I prompted Hrype, who was deep in thought and frowning.

'Hmm? Yes. He is newly arrived at Chatteris. He was the confessor at Crowland, shut up out there with the monks on their lonely, muddy island, but the monastery was destroyed last year. They are rebuilding it, of course,' he said with a faint sigh, 'but for the time being, their priest has been moved to Chatteris. He is acting like the new broom of the old saying, sweeping vigorously into secret corners that it would be better to leave alone.' Hrype paused. 'I have been investigating him. I did once encounter him, for I had . . . business at Crowland some time ago.' He clearly did not want to elaborate, and I wasn't going to ask. 'I needed to find out more, however, so I spoke to some of the serving men at Crowland, and I have learned much about this priest. He is utterly single-minded in his faith, and he does not baulk at using the most rigorous methods to persuade others to obey his god.' He gave a brief, rueful smile. 'They said at Crowland he was as hard on himself as on any of those whose souls were entrusted to him, for he fasted regularly and burdened himself with a heavy wooden cross slung around his neck as a constant reminder of his Lord's suffering. He is – a powerful man.'

That, from Hrype, was praise indeed. When he uses the word *power*, he is usually referring to the sort of power possessed by men such as him: magic power. It seemed odd, at first, to hear him refer in this way to a Christian priest, but, thinking about it, I realized that the men of high position in all religions must have a certain amount of magic, if by that you meant the ability to communicate with beings invisible and generally undetectable to the rest of us. In the mass, the priest communes with his god on behalf of the flock, or so we are told.

'His power is a threat to our kind?' I whispered.

Hrype glanced at me. 'Yes, I believe so. This man does not like competition. He wants the hearts and souls of the people turning just one way, and he will not tolerate any suspicion of loyalty to a far older faith.'

He spoke in general terms, but I sensed there was more. 'I believe that you think there is a more personal danger,' I said slowly. 'Something closer to – to us? To your family and mine?'

He nodded. 'Yes, I fear there may be. I am not sure yet. It is why I am here.'

'I thought you had come because the murdered nun may be – may be—' I could not make myself say her name.

He took my hand and held on to it. 'We will find out soon, Lassair, I promise. But we must be very careful if we approach the abbey. I can't explain yet, but as soon as I know the truth concerning what is happening, I will tell you more. That, too, is a promise.'

I believed him. Hrype knows better than most men that a promise is binding. 'Very well,' I said. 'Then, as I said some time ago, what do you suggest we do?'

He grinned, a swift expression, there and gone in the blink of an eye. 'We will go together down to the abbey gates and join all the other anxious friends and relatives,' he said. 'We will pretend to be father and daughter, for I would prefer it if we were not recognized as our true selves.' He studied me. 'You have already shielded yourself quite well,' he observed, 'for your aura is dimmer than usual and not typically yours.' I was unreasonably pleased at his praise. I was not yet sure what my aura was and had no idea what it normally looked like, but I was sure that to have altered it, even by a little, was quite an achievement. 'But you can do much better,' he went on, dashing my moment of self-congratulation. 'Listen, watch and learn.'

After a rather intense few moments, Hrype and I left the shady shelter of the alders and set off for the abbey gates. I kept shooting quick glances at him; I could hardly believe what I had just witnessed, and I wished with all my heart that I could look at myself, to see if I'd had the same success. He still had Hrype's features, build and height – he *must* have! – and he still wore the same garments, but he was totally different. His face was twisted into an expression quite unlike anything it usually adopted, he had rearranged his long hair, and he had bent and somehow folded his body and his long limbs so that he seemed to scuttle across the ground like a hunchback. As for me, he had got me to draw my hair back tightly and rearrange my coif so that it covered my forehead as far as my eyebrows, then to place a dark fold of my cloak over it so that it looked a little like a nun's headdress. Then he told me to imagine I had very short, bandy legs and a pain at the base of my spine. He made me concentrate so hard on this that quite soon I really did have a pain, and the only way I could alleviate it was to walk in a bow-legged waddle. I felt fat, although I knew there was no way I could be . . .

We were close to the muttering group outside the gates now. 'Not long, daughter, until we find out,' a thin, reedy voice with a hint of the complaining tyrant said, close by me. Whoever that old man was, I reflected, I bet he led his poor daughter quite a dance.

After a moment, I realized that the old man was Hrype.

He had a stick in his hand – where had that come from? Had he picked it up in the alder grove? – and now he was using it to force a way through to the gates. 'Make way,' he cried in his squeaky elderly man's voice, 'make way! My old legs have had a long walk today and will not support me much longer, and I would have tidings of my daughter from these wretched nuns before I collapse!'

One or two people muttered in agreement, saying that it was cruel of the nuns to keep people waiting for the news they were so desperate to hear. 'Here you are, Grandad,' one burly woman said, 'you come through here to the little side gate there – it's that one they'll open, I'll warrant, when finally they make up their minds to tell us anything.'

There were more mutterings. 'Three days ago it happened, or so they say, and all we've heard are rumours! For shame!' someone said.

'Tell us what we have come to find out!' someone else shouted.

Hrype raised his stick and banged it on the wooden panels

of the gate. *Bang, bang, bang.* I wanted to stop him, for it seemed folly to draw attention to ourselves after we'd gone to the trouble of altering our appearances. But then I understood: making us conspicuous was part of the disguise, for a man with something to hide would lurk in the background.

Several other men had joined Hrype and were also thumping on the door, which was not that sturdy and was already beginning to show cracks in the panelling. Someone within must have realized, for abruptly there came the sounds of bolts being drawn back and a key turning in a lock. The door opened to reveal a tall, broad-shouldered nun with a hatchet face and very piercing blue eyes. She wore the black veil of the fully professed, and the heavy bunch of keys clanking from a cord at her waist indicated her seniority.

'Stop that,' she said. 'You will break it down.'

'We want news of our womenfolk!' a man behind me cried. 'We know there's been a murder, and we all need to know our women and girls are safe!'

'One of you will be disappointed,' the nun said calmly. 'We have been praying for the soul of our dead sister, but now that we have done what we can for her, for the meantime at least, you may come in and speak to the sisters.'

There was a general heave in the direction of the doorway, which was quite narrow. I feared some of the slighter people might be crushed, and the big nun must have had the same thought. 'One at a time,' she said in the same calm, quiet yet utterly commanding voice. Raising an arm in a deep, black sleeve, she pointed to where a row of older nuns stood before the abbey's church. 'Proceed to the sisters over there, and give the name of the nun you wish to enquire about.'

'I want to see my daughter, not enquire about her!' a woman yelled.

The big nun nodded. 'Naturally. As soon as the kinsfolk of the dead woman have been identified, if they are here, we shall speak to them and take them apart for solace. Then the rest of you will all be able to see your kinswomen.'

She stepped aside, and we filed into the abbey. As we crossed the courtyard, I felt sick with nerves. Supposing it was Elfritha? What would I do? How, oh how, was I going to be able to tell my parents she was dead? As if Hrype felt my anguish, he reached out and took my hand.

We approached a small, plump nun whose elderly face was deeply creased with laughter lines but which now held only grief. Her eyes were red with weeping. Leaning towards us, she said quietly, 'Which nun do you wish to enquire about?'

Hrype nudged me, and I opened my mouth to speak. My voice wasn't there. I coughed, swallowed and tried again. 'The novice Elfritha,' I whispered. I was about to add that she was my sister, but then I remembered nobody was supposed to know Hrype's and my identity. 'We are friends of the family,' I said instead, 'here on their behalf.'

For an instant the little nun's face fell, and I thought she was about to cry. Then – and I am sure she saw my reaction – she reached out, took my free hand in both of hers and said, 'No, no! Elfritha is unharmed.' Then she beamed, so widely and so genuinely that it was like the sun coming out from behind the clouds. 'God be praised,' she added, and I muttered an *Amen*.

I was hardly aware of Hrype helping me away. One of the other nuns was shepherding us along, around the corner of the great church rising high above us and into a cloistered space on its right side, where the community were waiting. At first I couldn't see Elfritha, and I thought wildly that there must have been a mistake and she was dead after all, but then there was movement in the still, silent group of black-clad figures: someone in a novice's white veil pushed her way through and my sister took me in her arms.

While Elfritha and I were still tightly embraced, I felt hands on my arms and Hrype was pushing the two of us, none too gently, into a dark little corner where a narrow passage led off the cloister. 'We mustn't be seen talking together,' he hissed.

Elfritha raised her head, an astonished expression on her face. 'But—' she began.

'Hush!' Hrype pushed us further along the passage. 'Lassair, we must go. Arrange to meet your sister later, somewhere we shall not be observed.'

Elfritha was clinging on to me, tears streaming down her

face. 'I don't understand,' she said. 'Why can't you stay? I hoped someone would come, Lassair, and I'm so glad it's you, and I—'

I know Hrype well enough to appreciate that he wouldn't have given his order if it wasn't necessary; strange he may be (he is), but he understands about love, and he would not have separated me from Elfritha had he not felt he must.

'He is right,' I said gently to my sister, wiping her tears away with my fingers. 'When can we meet? Are you free to come out of the abbey?'

She shook her head in puzzlement, then shrugged. 'Well, yes, I suppose so. I'm often sent to collect flowers and plants for the herbalist, so I could say I'd been told to go out and gather something later on today . . .'

I realized she would be in trouble if anyone uncovered the deception, and it touched me that she should put loyalty to me above obedience to her superiors. 'Be careful,' I warned her.

'I will.' She gave me a quick smile. 'I'll meet you this evening after vespers, on the path that leads down to the left of the quay – water pepper grows down there, and I'll pick some. Don't worry, Lassair, everything's so confused at the moment that I'm not likely to be challenged. I can confess later.' Her face clouded. 'It's horrible,' she whispered. 'Oh, I keep picturing her—'

'Later,' Hrype interrupted firmly. 'Come, Lassair.'

I gave Elfritha one last hug and turned away. Hrype grasped my hand and pulled me along, out into the crowd of nuns and their relatives in the cloister. He paused here and there, stopping on the fringes of several of the little groups. I guessed his intention was to confuse: had anyone been watching us, they would not have known which of the nuns was associated with us.

Why was he so wary? Was it because of this fanatical priest? No doubt he would tell me in his own good time.

Once we were outside the abbey gates, Hrype melted away. He was there beside me one moment, still in his crusty old man's guise, and then when next I looked he had gone. I knew

better than to try to find him. He would be back at the appointed
time, I knew. I was not at all sure what 'after vespers' meant,
so I would have to keep an eye on the abbey church and look
out for the nuns emerging.

That, however, was not my main concern. I had undertaken
to inform my family as soon as I knew Elfritha was safe, and
now I turned my mind to how I should go about it. I went
down to the quayside, planning to see if anyone might be
heading off in the direction of Aelf Fen, but then I realized
this wasn't wise. Hrype was going to some lengths to keep
our identity secret, and all his good work would be undermined
if I sent a message straight to my family. Even if I persisted
with the pretence of being no more than a close friend, I
couldn't send a message without naming my family and my
village. It seemed prudent not to allow either to become known.

In any case, it was highly unlikely anyone would be going
that way. Instead, I asked around to see if there was anyone
bound for Cambridge, and soon I found a family of parents
and two little children, returning to the town having ascertained
that the husband's nun sister was not the murder victim. They
were, understandably, jubilant and readily agreed to my
request. I told them where to find Gurdyman's house and gave
them this short message: *please send word to the eel catcher
that his daughter is safe.*

Gurdyman knew what my father did for a living. He might
not know which daughter the message referred to, but that
didn't matter; I would explain when I saw him.

The wife smiled at me. 'You, too, have had good news,
then,' she said.

Not wanting to elaborate, I simply said, 'Yes,' then thanked
them again and hurried away.

I watched the abbey from the shelter of my alders for the
remainder of the afternoon. I saw the nuns file into church
and then out again. I did not see Elfritha emerge, but that
wasn't surprising, for she was going on an imaginary, clandestine errand and would not wish to attract anyone's attention.
I slipped out of my hiding place and hurried along to the
quayside.

I did not see her at first. I made my way along the quay, now deserted, and after perhaps a quarter of a mile, I heard someone whisper my name. Turning, I saw Hrype and my sister, concealed behind a stand of brambles, the brilliant green leaves of which shone in the dim light.

I went to join them. Hrype said solemnly, 'Now, Elfritha. Please tell us who it was that died, and what happened.'

Elfritha thought for a few moments, and then began to speak. 'The dead nun's name was Sister Herleva,' she said quietly. 'She hasn't – she hadn't been at the abbey very long, only six months or so, but already we were good friends. She was young and light-hearted, and inclined to be silly. She was often in trouble for giggling, but she didn't seem able to help herself. She loved life, and there was a radiance about her that made others happy just to be with her.' My sister's voice shook, and she took a steadying breath. 'Three days ago – no, four – she didn't appear for compline. That's our last office, just before we go to bed. It wasn't the first time she'd missed an office, and we didn't think much about it beyond being sorry for her because she'd be in trouble again and have to do a more severe penance than last time.' She paused, her eyes cloudy with sorrow. 'But she wasn't in her bed the next morning, and then we knew something had happened. The nun who comes round to rouse us saw the empty bed, and she turned away without a word and hurried off. Later we noticed that all the senior nuns were busy searching for Herleva, and then word went round that she'd been found.' She gave a sob, quickly suppressing it. 'She was lying behind the stable, and they discovered a big lump on the back of her head. Someone said there was patch of blood staining her veil. She was a novice,' she added absently, 'so her veil was white. There was a deep cut in her neck and a lot more blood and they – they're saying there was a pool of vomit beneath her head.'

The poor girl. She must have realized what was happening, and her fear had brought that violent reaction in her guts. I found myself hoping fervently that the blow to her head had knocked her unconscious, so that there had been no awareness of the knife in her throat that took her life. If her assailant had hit her hard enough, it probably would have done. She might even have been dead before the cut; it depended on how much blood had come out of the wound. Edild had taught me that living bodies spurt blood from wounds, whereas it only seeps from someone whose heart has ceased to beat.

But I was thinking like a healer, not as a loving sister. Elfritha, beside me, was trembling with distress, and I hadn't even offered her a word of comfort. I took hold of her hand. It was very cold, so I wrapped her in my arms, trying to soothe and reassure her with my body warmth.

Glancing at Hrype, I saw that he was frowning, apparently deep in thought. Elfritha went to speak again, but I touched her cheek and, when she looked at me, shook my head. Hrype does not like to be interrupted when he is thinking.

After what seemed like a very long time, he nodded and said, 'Very interesting.' He added something else, which could have been: *it is as I thought.*

But whatever he thought, he wasn't going to share it with us. When this became clear, Elfritha – who, unlike me, is not used to his ways – looked indignant. 'Is that all you have to say?' she asked.

'Yes,' Hrype replied. 'Come, we must get back. You should return to the abbey before anyone misses you.'

Elfritha picked up her bunch of water pepper and – side by side, with Hrype silently following – we went back along the quay. We saw her as far as the abbey gates, where she and I said our farewells. 'We are holding a vigil for Herleva,' she said, 'and I doubt I shall be able to see you again.'

'I understand, I'll come back when—'

But Hrype, his expression abruptly sharpening, interrupted. 'The dead girl is not yet buried?'

'No. Father Clement is away and will not be here until the morning. He's our new priest; he was appointed back in the late autumn, just before Christmas. He sent word that he was fully occupied elsewhere but was praying earnestly for the dead sister and all of us.'

Father Clement. I memorized the name. I was going to make some comment – to ask what sort of a man he was, whether he would be able to reassure and solace the nuns with his presence – but I happened to glance at Hrype. And his expression alarmed me, for it was dark with menace.

Then I realized. Father Clement was Hrype's fanatic of the new religion.

FIVE

Hrype and I found a sheltered spot to spend the night. I had a hundred questions I was desperate to ask, but I knew I must leave him in peace until he was ready to speak to me. He had promised to tell me as soon as he knew the truth, and I knew he would. What I didn't know, of course, was how long it would take him to find the truth out. We built a small fire, for the sky was clear and the night was growing chill, and he made us a hot, spicy drink. He shared his food with me, for I had finished mine, and then we settled down to sleep.

I was warm enough, for our camp was beneath a bank where brambles grew thickly and we were out of the light wind that gusted intermittently. So much had happened that day that I forgot to be afraid to fall asleep. My reward was to be sent such a fearsome nightmare that I woke sweating and sobbing with fear. As I came up into consciousness, I saw that strange, wild landscape with the low hills, and the ruins with the grave-like hollow. For an instant I thought I saw a huge bull come roaring up out of the ground, his eyes wild with anger and fear, his nostrils flaring. I heard the words again. This time, they were slightly different; they said: *where are you? I need you!*

Even while I was still suffering from the horrors induced by my dream, part of my mind was recognizing that, if the summoning voice was still calling out to me, it couldn't have been Elfritha's.

I dropped my face into my hands and wept.

Hrype tended me in a distant sort of way. He seemed to perceive without my telling him that I'd had a bad dream.

Knowing him, he'd probably had a quick look inside my mind and seen the images for himself. He poked up the fire and made me another drink, and I guess it must have contained a mild sleeping draught, for I knew no more until I woke to thin daylight.

Hrype had gone. So efficiently had he covered his tracks that he'd left no sign of which path he'd set off on. In fact, had I not seen him beside me in the night, I wouldn't have known he'd been there at all.

I did not waste any time wondering where he'd gone and what he was up to. Hrype is a mystery, and such is the sense of deep power that emanates from him that you question him at your peril. He is, I honestly believe, a good man, although in truth good and evil are not really terms that you apply to someone like him.

He had left me food and drink, so I sat there and made myself finish everything before I got up. I was still feeling disturbed, for the dream had shaken me. When I felt I was as fully restored as I was going to be, I rolled up my blanket, packed up my belongings, straightened my clothes and my hair and put on my coif. Then, ready to face the day, I set off.

I had been thinking hard as I ate my breakfast. Father Clement, according to Hrype, had set himself the task of eradicating the old ways. It would be an uphill struggle, I knew. Laws were always being passed – *no one is to dress the wells*; *nobody must worship false idols in the form of the old gods*; *the singing of charms and the wearing of tokens and amulets is not allowed*; and many more – and the sheer number of these prohibitions showed the strength of the ancient traditions and how much faith the populace had in them. People took the sensible view that what had worked for their parents, grandparents, great-grandparents and so on was good enough for them. They might be happy to attend church and worship the Lord Jesus and his awesome father, but when trouble came, as it invariably did, in the form of sick children, barren wives, fields that did not produce crops and animals that failed to thrive, the people placed their trust in the old beliefs, and who could blame them?

This Father Clement would keep his eyes and his ears

constantly open for what he would see as the devil's work. He was the priest of Chatteris Abbey, where you'd imagine there would be little in the way of heretical murmuring. Among the nuns, that was . . .

Suddenly, I knew why Hrype had been so careful not to let the two of us go into the abbey in our normal guises. It had been for his own sake, of course, for he was pursuing Father Clement and would not wish to be recognized. But it had been just as much, if not more, for my sake: I visited my sister whenever it was permitted, and we always talked non-stop for the duration of our allotted time. She would tell me about her life in the abbey – which, incidentally, she loved, or had done till her best friend was murdered – and then I'd answer all her eager questions concerning the family, the village and my healing work with Edild. And, on my last visit, I revealed to her some of the milder topics on which I was receiving instruction from Hrype and Gurdyman.

I would have trusted Elfritha with my life, and I did not suspect for an instant that she would have told her priest what her younger sister was up to. But what if someone had overheard? Usually, we walked together out of doors in the cloister when I visited, but the last time it had been very wet and we'd sat with the other nuns and their visitors in the parlour. It was unlikely but, I had to admit, possible that our quiet words had attracted the attention of someone else – a nun or one of the relatives – and that, in an excess of religious zeal, they had told Father Clement.

If that was true, then I could be in danger.

As I walked along the quayside towards the abbey and the settlement around it, I wondered what would happen if I was right and Father Clement really *was* eager to find me. The problem was that to many churchmen, anyone whose religious beliefs differed in the smallest degree from their own was guilty of heresy. Once someone had set him or herself apart in this way, other accusations often followed. When life was cruel, it was natural to want to put the blame on someone, and sooner or later the cry would go up that the misfortune had happened because a witch had uttered a curse. Much of Edild's and my work as healers consisted of providing charms and remedies for people who believed they had been cursed. Neither of us truly believed this was possible, but Edild's view was that to prescribe a 'magic' rabbit's foot or a mild herbal concoction would do no harm. Quite the opposite, in fact; we usually found that the cure was effective simply because the patient believed it would be.

We were on the fringes of Christian society, my aunt and I. So, come to think of it, were Gurdyman and Hrype, but they were inconspicuous compared to a pair of village healers, and, anyway, I reckoned they could both look after themselves. My fear, when I made myself face it, was that I would be the subject of Father Clement's attention simply because, although I dutifully went to church from time to time, I also practised what he would call pagan rites. If he was as fanatical as Hrype believed, then undoubtedly he would see me as a heretic. At best, I might have to do several years' penance. At worst – and I knew there were precedents – I could be put to death.

The sensible thing would be to quietly get off the island and go back to Aelf Fen or Gurdyman's house, then avoid Chatteris Abbey until either the fire went out of Father Clement's belly or he went away again. Don't think I wasn't tempted: of course I was. But I knew that if I slunk away, the dreams would go on tormenting me and, for all that I now knew it wasn't Elfritha's, that voice would give me no peace. I could not for the life of me see how my night terrors could be connected with the murder of a novice nun, but I knew as well as I knew my own name that they were. Instinct again, but, as I have said, I was learning that my instincts were almost always accurate.

Having made up my mind, I felt better. The first thing I must do, I decided, was to find out as much as I could about the late Sister Herleva. Discovering where she came from, and whatever it was about her that had driven someone to kill her, would be a good start. The obvious person to speak to was her best friend, my sister, but Elfritha was the one person I couldn't seek out, for if I did so someone would probably remember who I was and I could be putting myself in danger. I would try not to enter the abbey at all, I thought; instead, I would keep my eyes open for some local person – a tradesman, a craftsman – who had dealings with the nuns without being of the community. If I was lucky, encouraging this person to talk would be the easy part. Murders were a rare occurrence, especially in abbeys, and this one would be the talk of the area for weeks, probably months, to come.

I went back to my hiding place under the alders, made myself comfortable and waited.

Presently, a fat, red-cheeked countrywoman puffed in through the abbey gates, two large half-barrels suspended from a wooden yoke that rested on her broad shoulders. I stood up to see better and saw that each barrel contained what looked like small, round cheeses, each wrapped in white cloth. My hungry stomach gave a growl at the thought of a fresh, tasty cheese, and as I reached in my leather satchel to find coins, I realized I had the perfect excuse to catch the old woman's attention.

She stayed for quite some time inside the abbey. I hoped she was busy gossiping. When she emerged, I slipped out from the trees and followed. I waited until she was some distance down the track that led to the settlement to the east of the abbey, then increased my pace and caught up with her.

She was happy to sell me a cheese, putting down her burden to rest as she did so. She perched her ample buttocks on the bank beside the track, and I sat down beside her. Not wasting a moment, I said, 'I hear there's been a murder at the abbey.'

As soon as she turned to me, eyes wide in wonder and an expression on her face that told me she was just dying to tell the latest news to somebody, I knew I'd chosen well. 'Yes, my dearie, so there has!' she began. 'It's one of the novices, a pretty, plump, chatty little thing, quite my favourite because whenever she was on kitchen duty when I delivered my cheeses, she always gave me a drink and a crust to help me on my way. She and her friend, they were about the only ones who had time for a weary old soul like me.' Her face fell momentarily. I did not believe her, for Elfritha had many good friends among the nuns, both novices and the fully professed, and I was quite sure most of them would have had the charity to give their cheese woman some refreshment.

'What was her name?' I asked, although of course I already know.

'Sister Herleva,' the woman said. 'She was from over beyond Lynn way, from some place up on the coast. She hadn't been with the nuns long – let me see, I reckon it was last summer she came, maybe autumn. It's – it was taking her a while to settle down to convent ways, and I did wonder if she'd stay. They don't let them take their vows, you know,' she added confidingly, leaning towards me, 'if they don't think they're ready. Sometimes they never are and then they go out again.' She smiled in a self-congratulatory way. 'I know a lot about nuns, me. I've been taking my cheeses to Chatteris Abbey these thirty years, and not much gets past me.'

'No, I'm sure it doesn't.' Flattery seemed a good idea. 'They say her throat was cut,' I said, dropping my voice to an intimate whisper.

The cheese seller put her mouth close to my ear. 'She was hit on the head and her neck was slit from ear to ear,' she whispered back. She looked swiftly up and down the track, but there was nobody in sight. 'There's something else,' she hissed. 'I shouldn't be telling you this. No one's supposed to know, not even the nuns themselves, but I had to visit the herbalist on account of she wanted some of my sage and I overheard her talking to the abbess.' She paused, undoubtedly for dramatic effect, then said, 'Poor little Herleva was poisoned!'

I remembered Elfritha mentioning the pool of vomit. I'd thought perhaps Herleva had been sick because of her terror. But poison! How extraordinary, that she'd been poisoned, then hit on the head, then had her throat cut. Had the poison not been sufficiently potent and the blow to the head not hard enough? Poor little Herleva, indeed. Somebody had been utterly determined that she should die, even if it took three attempts.

'Surely she was very young, for someone to hate her so much?' I said, opening my eyes wide and trying to sound naive.

The cheese seller patted my hand kindly. 'Oh, there's reasons enough to kill a person other than hatred,' she said, 'as I fear you'll come to understand, my dearie, before you're much older.'

'But what could they possibly be?' I asked, genuinely wanting an answer. Herleva was young, kind, gossipy and a novice nun. Why would any of those things make anyone want to kill her?

The old woman shook her head. 'No use asking me, dearie. I came to realize years ago that the ways of this wicked world are beyond my comprehension.'

She levered herself to her feet and raised her yoke back on to her shoulders, wincing as she did so. 'The lass would have been poor, so it can't have been theft that made someone do for her. Nor love, come to that, since the nuns are chaste, or meant to be!' She laughed shortly. 'Your guess is as good as mine, dearie. Now, I must be getting on my way, or I won't be done afore dark.'

I stood up too. 'I hear there's a new priest here,' I said. I was interested to see if the woman would have an opinion on him, and I wasn't disappointed.

'*Him!*' She spat on the ground. 'Yes, we've a new priest all right. I don't know how he is with those nuns, but I can tell you, dearie, he's as tough as they come with the likes of us. Hard as rock, he is. Rigid in his ways, with no time for excuses and explanations. A sin's a sin, and that's that.' She leaned closer, dropping her voice. 'We don't much like him, I can tell you that. He's got no heart, see. Like my son says, he wouldn't piss on you if you were on fire.' She nodded, as if to emphasize her words.

'I see.'

'Don't tell anyone I said that,' she added, her face suddenly anxious.

I patted her broad arm. 'Of course I won't.' On impulse I reached in my satchel and took out a small pot of Edild's remedy for stiff muscles. 'Use some of this on your shoulders before you go to bed tonight,' I said, pressing it into her hand. 'It'll help the pain.'

She looked at it, then up at me, giving me a kind but almost toothless smile. 'Thank you,' she said simply. 'It's good to know there's some fine, Christian folk left in this wicked world.'

Then she waddled away.

*   *   *

It was time for me to leave Chatteris. So thoroughly was my curiosity aroused that if I stayed, I knew I might be tempted to throw caution to the winds and try to go into the abbey and seek out Elfritha. She had been Herleva's friend. She would know, if anyone did, the secret reason why the poor little novice had died. She might not realize she knew, but I could, I was sure, winkle the information out of her if I asked the right questions.

No, I must not even think of going into the abbey.

My footsteps had taken me back along the track that led to the gates, but I made myself turn aside and return to the alder grove. I sat down on the grass, eyes fixed on the abbey before me. Herleva had died in there, her body left behind the stables. Was there any point in going to inspect the place? The body had long been removed, and no doubt the blood and the vomit had been cleaned away, so the answer to that was no.

Nevertheless, I just didn't seem able to tear myself away.

I heard voices from the direction of the quay. Turning to look, I saw a big, lithe, broad-shouldered man dressed in black, accompanied by a short, round little man in the coarse wool habit of a monk. The tall man was quite young; perhaps only twelve or fifteen years older than I was. He walked with an athletic stride, his shoulders flung back and his back straight. There was a sense of power about him that did not come solely from his physical presence.

He was almost at the abbey gates now. I drew further back into the shadows and stared at him. His face was tanned, as if he spent much time out of doors, and rather lean, the jaw square. The mouth was wide and mobile, the light eyes set deep beneath thick, fair brows. His hair – also fair, with coppery highlights – was worn long and looked very clean, and his robe was newly laundered.

I realized what a very handsome man he was.

He was talking to his fat companion. Straining my ears, I tried to make out the words.

'. . . should arrange to bury her as soon as we can, Brother Paul, for the weather grows warm.'

'They will miss her, sweet child that she was,' panted the monk, who was having to hurry to keep pace with the tall man's long strides.

'They will indeed.'

'Shall you – er, I don't like to make suggestions, but shall you mention after the service her kind nature and how everyone really liked her, her being so gossipy and friendly and all?'

'Oh, I think so,' the tall man said with a sad smile. 'Frivolous characteristics, perhaps, in one who believed she had heard God's call to enter his service as a nun, but then the poor child did not really have any gifts that the Lord would truly value.'

I supposed that he was right, strictly speaking, but it seemed unkind, especially considering how poor Herleva had met her death. Perhaps there was little use for her light-hearted sort of cheerfulness within the walls of a convent, although on my visits to Elfritha I had always been surprised at how much laughter the nuns seemed to share. Herleva probably would never have been a senior nun, perhaps not even a very good one, but the world was a sorry place for most of its inhabitants and it seemed to me that this tall, black-clad man was being unnecessarily harsh in his judgement of the dead girl. He must—

Then I knew who he was.

I would have realized sooner, I'm sure, had I not been preoccupied with my thoughts about Herleva. For one thing he was dressed in black and accompanied by a monk; for another, the monk had referred to what he was going to say about Herleva.

I crept to the very edge of my hiding place, intent on getting a better look at him. He had his back turned, for he was speaking to the hatchet-faced nun who had opened the door to Hrype and me the previous day. Now she was bowing to her visitor, straightening up to stand back and usher him inside with a wave of her arm.

The monk scurried in first, the tall man following.

Just as he was about to move out of sight behind the abbey's high walls, he turned.

I knew he could not have seen me, for instantly I drew right back, crouching low to the ground so that I was entirely hidden behind the lush spring undergrowth. *He did not see me*, I repeated silently. I knew I shouldn't have done it, but I couldn't help myself: I summoned my fledgling power and sent out a feeler in the tall man's direction.

In return I got such a violent shock that it threw me flat on my back. Terrified that he had heard the thump as I fell, I got to my knees and parted the leaves to peer down at the abbey. To my vast relief, he had gone inside and the gate was closing behind him.

Hrype had said he was a powerful man. If I had ever doubted it, I did so no longer. I had felt that fathomless, light gaze turn in my direction, and for the blink of an eye it had felt as if searing beams of white-hot light had raked over me.

Whatever his beliefs, whatever he was, Father Clement was a man to be reckoned with.

A man, I was forced to admit, to be feared.

SIX

I made my way back to Cambridge.

I felt so low and dispirited that I would much rather have gone home to my family. I was very tired, for I had spent two nights sleeping out of doors and, although the weather had been mild enough, I had not been able to relax sufficiently to allow the deep sleep that restores. I had been so worried about my sister, and that anxiety had taken its toll. It was a vast relief to know that it was not Elfritha who had been so horribly, violently murdered, but the dead girl had been her friend and I knew she grieved for her. I wanted to go to my sister and comfort her, but I couldn't.

As if all that wasn't enough, there was also the legacy of my dreams. I kept seeing images – the mist, the dark figure, that strange crypt-like hollow in the hillside – and the sounds of the visions rang inside my head. I heard that restlessly moving stretch of water, waiting, lurking, somewhere beyond my sight. And, of course, those words were always with me.

My family would have given me their love and their support. But I needed something more than that: I wanted someone to help me untangle the mystery into which I had been drawn. Hrype would have been capable of advising me, I was sure,

but he had disappeared without a word. He might have gone
back to Aelf Fen, but it was by no means certain.

And that was why I went back to Gurdyman.

I knocked on the door of the twisty-turny house just as dusk
was falling. I had been travelling since morning and I was
worn out. Gurdyman let me in, took one look at me and, with
a shake of his head and a quiet 'Tut!' led me along the passage
to the open courtyard. He must have been sitting out there in
the evening light, for when he gently pushed me down so that
I was sitting in his big chair, the soft cushion on the seat was
still warm from his body. He disappeared back inside the
house, returning presently with a tray of food. I started to say
something, but he held up a hand.

'Eat first, Lassair.'

I wolfed down good white bread and cold meat, two small,
spiced savoury pies and then three little sweet cakes, flavours
of honey and cinnamon mingling deliciously in my mouth.
Gurdyman handed me a fine pewter cup, filled to the brim,
and I drank deeply. It was some special concoction of his own
and, although it was cold as I swallowed it down, quite soon
it seemed to spread warmth through my body. For the first
time in days, I began to relax.

He was watching me closely. As I leaned back in his chair
– he was perched opposite to me, on the bench he usually
made his visitors sit on – he smiled. 'That's better,' he
murmured. 'Now, first I must tell you that yesterday I received
a message that I was to send word to the eel catcher that his
daughter was safe.'

'Oh, I hope you didn't mind! I'm sorry I couldn't tell you
more, but—'

Again, he held up his hand to silence me. 'No need to
apologize, child. Now I know that your father is an eel
catcher, for you have told me all about your family. The
message that his daughter was safe could have applied to
you or to either of your two sisters. I guessed the message
came from you or, at least, was concerned with your mission,
and I was content to wait to find out more. I found a reliable
lad – one I have employed as messenger before – and I

dispatched him to your village. By now, your family will be aware of the good tidings.'

Until he told me that, I hadn't appreciated how heavy a burden I'd been carrying. That I knew Elfritha was safe but my parents did not had been hard to bear. I met Gurdyman's bright eyes. 'Thank you,' I said softly. 'You cannot know what that means to me.'

'Oh, I think I can,' he murmured. Then, switching moods as fast as a blink, all at once he was businesslike and brisk. 'Who was in danger, Lassair, and is now safe?' He narrowed his eyes, studying me intently. 'Not you, I think, for the shadow still hovers over you.'

Shadow? I did not want to think about that. So, trying to keep to the point and make my tale as clear and succinct as I could, I told him of my arrival at Aelf Fen to find my kinfolk safe and well, and of the news of the murder of the Chatteris nun. I related how I'd hurried off to Chatteris and found Hrype already there, and then our discovery that it was Elfritha's friend who was dead, and I revealed how they said she'd been killed. I explained that Hrype had disappeared during the night and how, this morning, I'd spoken to the cheese seller and learned a little more about poor dead Herleva. Finally, slightly ashamed of myself, I told him that I'd been afraid for my own skin because the fanatical priest might know all about me and be on my trail.

'He is powerful, this Father Clement,' I whispered. 'Hrype said he was and, now that I have encountered him, I have faced his force myself.'

Gurdyman didn't say anything for quite a long time. I was feeling drowsy and, taking advantage of the fact that I was sitting there so still, Gurdyman's black cat jumped lithely up on to my lap and made himself comfortable. His name is Abraxas, and he is very handsome. Stroking his smooth and luxuriant fur sent me deeper into my self-induced trance. I was on the point of falling asleep when at last Gurdyman spoke.

'What of the dreams, Lassair?' he asked.

'I'm still getting them,' I said shortly.

He was not satisfied. 'Is the content the same? And the summoning voice, does it speak the same words?'

'The content is much the same. I still see that strange scene with the low hills and the grave-like pit in the side of the mound, and also there's an enormous bull that seems to rush at me out of the earth.' I hesitated. 'But the words have changed. The voice still says *I need you*, but before that it's now *where are you?*'

There was another long silence. I could have been mistaken, but I was pretty sure I'd seen a sudden flare of interest in Gurdyman's eyes when I mentioned the bull. Vaguely, I wondered why. I should have been alert, fascinated, bursting to ask him all sorts of well-thought-out questions, but I was just too tired. Scenes and events from the long day floated through my mind, slowly merging with dreams. Then I felt Gurdyman's hand on my shoulder, shaking me gently.

'Go to bed, child.'

I did as he bade me, dropping Abraxas to the floor and stumbling inside the house. I made my preparations for bed – they were even more perfunctory than usual – and very shortly I was tucked up in my little attic room. The last thing I saw before I closed my eyes was the light of Gurdyman's candle down in the courtyard. I wondered how long he would stay up but, even as the thought went through my mind, I was asleep.

It was late next morning when I woke, if the sun through the open shutters was anything to go by. I felt rested and refreshed, and I had slept without dreaming, other than an absurd bit of nonsense about a cat climbing a ladder and offering me a piece of cheese, which I did not take seriously and certainly did not see as portentous in any way.

I descended from my little attic and made myself some breakfast, then went along the passage and down the steps to the crypt. Gurdyman was busy at his workbench and barely looked up as I entered. He was bending over his apothecary's scales, an open jar in one hand and a tiny silver spoon in the other. He put a very small amount of some brownish substance into the pan of the scales, frowned at it and added some more.

He corked the jar and returned it to its place on the long row of shelves on the far side of the cellar. 'That will do,' he said. 'I shall finish it later.'

'Can I help?'

'Yes. But, as I said, we'll do it later. For now, there is something I must ask you and, depending on your answer, something it seems I must tell you.'

I felt a shiver of alarm, for his tone was grave and his face, usually so full of light and humour, was set in serious lines. He drew out two wooden stools from beneath his bench and, sitting down on one, waved a hand to the other. I perched on it and, my heart beating hard, waited for him to speak.

'In your dream you say there was a bull,' he began. I'd been right, then, when I thought I saw my mention of the bull pique his interest. 'Tell me exactly what you saw.'

I closed my eyes and tried to recapture the image. 'The scene is a lonely, desolate place, and I can see a line of low hills out on the horizon. The light isn't good – it's misty, or perhaps it's getting dark. Close to me there's a ruined building, and somehow I know it's very, very old. There's a pillar and some huge slabs of stone with carvings on them. I see a—' I paused, wondering how best to describe the crypt-like hollow. 'There's an opening in the side of an earth mound, a bit like a grave.'

'And what of the bull?' Gurdyman prompted.

'The bull is suddenly right in front of me,' I said. 'I don't hear him approaching, which is odd because he's really enormous and he's wild with fear and very angry. It's – it's sort of as if he's been there all the time but I wasn't able to see him until someone decided the time was right.'

Gurdyman nodded. 'As if a curtain had been drawn aside,' he murmured.

'Yes, exactly like that!' I exclaimed. Only, surely the bull couldn't have been concealed behind a curtain, or I'd have heard it bellowing and stamping . . .

'Describe what it looked like,' commanded Gurdyman.

'It was just a bull,' I said lamely. 'A very big one.'

I thought I heard him sigh. 'How was it standing? Was it facing you?'

I screwed my eyes tight shut, trying to remember. 'No,' I said after a moment. 'It was turned slightly to my right, and its head was thrown back.' Then I recalled something I had quite forgotten. 'There was a man there!' I cried, my eyes flying open and going instantly to Gurdyman. 'Or I thought there was – he was in the shadows, and he wore a weird cloak with a deep-blue lining that had stars all over it!'

Gurdyman closed his eyes, and his lips moved as if he was praying. Then he looked at me, a smile on his face. 'Lassair, it is as I thought,' he said, still smiling. 'I do not yet know why you were sent this dream vision. There has to be a reason – there always is.'

'Is it connected with the words in my head?' I asked eagerly. 'Can you tell me what it's all about, Gurdyman, and who it is who is calling out to me?'

He put out a hand and grasped mine briefly. 'Perhaps.' He seemed to retreat into himself for a moment. 'Yes, perhaps.' Then he withdrew his hand, settled himself more comfortably on the stool and said, 'I told you just now that there was something I might have to tell you, and the time has come for me to do so.' He glanced around his cellar, eyes lingering here and there.

'This house of mine holds many secrets,' he murmured. 'Some of them you will come to know about, Lassair; some will remain hidden. I will reveal one of them to you now, for it seems to me that the moment is right.' He paused, and I sensed he was reluctant to go on. It was with some effort that at last he began.

'There has been a settlement here for a very long time,' he said. 'Many centuries ago, men recognized that its location was readily defensible, for there is an area of higher ground which overlooks the place where the watery, dangerous fens can be crossed at their south-eastern corner. Later, the invaders from the south crossed the Narrow Seas and made this country part of their vast empire, although they never subdued the north to their will. They built a great wall there, marking the limit of their territory. They would have said, I have no doubt, that it was to keep the barbarians out.' He smiled faintly. 'They made roads across the length and breadth of the land, and their soldiers were ever marching up and down, to and fro, on the move all day and by night resting in the forts that their engineers put up along the roads. They built such a fort here, in the same place where a fort had stood before, and a settlement grew up around it. At first only soldiers lived here, but in time the merchants came too, for the river connects the town to the sea and trade developed swiftly. In the fullness of time, men brought their wives and their families, and a rich society developed such as we see here today. But to begin with this was a man's world: a hard, tough world of soldiers, merchants and traders.'

He stopped, eyes again roaming around the cellar. Then, drawing a breath, he went on. 'Wherever the soldiers went, their god went with them, for their lives were comfortless and full of danger, with death always at their shoulder. Their god was a god of light, of hope, who made a blood sacrifice for mankind in order to nourish the good earth and allow men to live.'

'Like – like Jesus?' I asked tentatively.

'Like him, yes, but then throughout man's long history, many religions have worshipped such a figure: a god who died for them and rose from the dead.'

'Why did the soldiers choose this particular one?'

'Because his worship was organized in a way that appealed to the mind of a fighting man,' Gurdyman replied. 'The soldiers of the southern empire lived under rigid military discipline, and the rules were firm and unbreakable. In this religion, worshippers were divided into ranks, just as the soldiers were in their everyday lives. The lowest rank in the religion, that of the new initiate, was a Raven. He went through various ordeals and, if he passed them, became a Nymph. The ordeals increased in severity, and some of them were both very painful and truly terrifying. If a man was brave and steadfast, eventually he could progress to Soldier, Lion, Persian, Runner of the Sun and, finally, Father, although few men rose to that high degree and many, indeed, were content to remain at a lowlier level.'

'They'd be foot soldiers rather than officers,' I suggested.

He smiled, pleased at my understanding. 'Yes.'

Persian. Runner of the Sun. Silently, I repeated the exotic names to myself. 'Did they have churches?'

'No. They worshipped in caves – *spelaeum*, in their own

tongue. In places where a natural cave was not available, they would construct an underground chamber. Always, wherever the god was worshipped, there had to be fresh water nearby in the form of a spring or an unpolluted well. The men of the south were habitually clean, Lassair, for they bathed frequently and used the occasion as a social event, going from baths of cold water to hot water and steam, and employing servants to scrape the dirt from their skin.'

I smothered a laugh, finding the idea of communal bathing both absurd and faintly embarrassing.

'They never approached their god without first performing a ritual cleansing,' Gurdyman was saying. 'Together they would enter the sacred space, going down the steps until they were inside the earth, and there they would bathe and dress in clean robes before proceeding into the god's presence.'

His voice went on, calm, even, soothing, almost hypnotic, and images flashed through my mind. A cave. Going down the steps into an underground chamber. A town that had stood there for centuries. A house with many secrets.

Then I knew what he was telling me.

'This cellar was a place where the soldiers gathered to worship!' I burst out.

His eyes met mine, and I saw that he was smiling again. He put a finger to his lips to hush me.

'*Wasn't it?*' I hissed.

I knew I was right, even before he answered. The crypt seemed to be teeming with the presence of unseen men and the air was full of magic.

Gurdyman stood up and moved across the stone flags of the floor. It always surprises me how light on his feet he is, how silently he moves, for although he is short he is not a small man. Now, however, he almost seemed to hover above the ground . . .

We had been sitting beside the workbench, which stood against the far wall to the right of the steps leading down into the crypt. Beside the steps was Gurdyman's low cot, and the opposite wall was covered in shelves that groaned under the weight of bottles, jars, rolls of parchment, scales, lamps, ink, quills and all the other tools of Gurdyman's work.

The fourth wall was covered by a large, heavy hanging. I had never given it much attention, for whatever pattern or scene was once depicted on its generous folds has long been obscured behind the smoke and the fumes and the occasional clouds of noxious humours that frequently fill the crypt. It is now a uniform dark-grey colour, and if you accidentally brush against it, clouds of ancient dust fly out.

Gurdyman walked up to it. He paused before it and, turning to me, beckoned with his finger. I got up off my stool and slowly approached him.

He took hold of the hanging with both hands. With a powerful tug, he pulled it down from the wall.

When I saw what was behind it I gave an involuntary cry and stepped hastily backwards, for in that first instant I truly believed that living, breathing creatures were lungeing towards me.

There was a man: a broad, strong-looking man dressed in a soldier's short tunic. He wore a cap that rose up in a softly-pointed cone, and a wide cloak flew back from his shoulders as if a fierce wind blew. It was red, and the lining was deep blue, like the twilight sky, and spotted with brilliant points of light that seemed to shine like the stars. His right leg – it was thick and very well muscled – was extended, tense with the effort of keeping his balance, and his other leg was bent at the knee and pushed down hard into the shoulder of an enormous, pure-white bull. His dagger was thrust into the creature's throat, and he was in the very act of sacrifice: the bull's life blood – vivid red, glistening as if it had only just begun to flow – spilled out and pooled on the ground.

The painting was extraordinary, and it throbbed with life.

'Behold Mithras.'

I did not know who spoke the words. It might have been Gurdyman, but it didn't sound like his voice.

There was a long silence. I stood awestruck, and eventually I felt Gurdyman take my hand and lead me away.

'This house is on the spot where, many years ago, a rich merchant built himself a fine dwelling.' It was Gurdyman who spoke; it was some time later that day and we were sitting in the sunshine in his inner courtyard. I still felt very odd; it must have been past the time for the midday meal, but I had no appetite. My stomach was tense with – nerves? Excitement? I was not sure.

'We know the merchant must have been a wealthy man,' Gurdyman went on, 'because he built in stone. As you will be aware, child, there is very little stone in this area and it has to be brought in from elsewhere.' He glanced up at the clouds floating across the blue sky. 'He could also afford to choose a location well away from the bustle and the stinks of the quayside,' he went on, 'which must have pleased him, for no doubt he had quite enough of that during the working day.' He smiled happily at me. 'Imagine him, Lassair, coming home at the end of a long, hard day. Tonight is special, for a very select group of men will make their quiet way to the house later for a ceremony. They will meet up here, then one by one they will descend the steps and prepare themselves, washing carefully and dressing in their ceremonial robes. Then they will go into the cave, and there the god will welcome them into his presence.'

'I felt him,' I breathed. 'I'm sure I did, I—'

Gurdyman held up a hand, and I knew I was not to say any more. 'I believe you did, child,' he said softly.

We sat in silence for some time. I heard a blackbird singing, and the sound seemed far too normal for a day when something so extraordinary had happened. As if the blackbird thought so too, abruptly the song ceased. After a while, I said, 'How do you know, Gurdyman?'

'Hmm?'

'How can you be so sure about the merchant and the – and what he made down there?'

Gurdyman smiled. 'You do not doubt what I say, then?'

'No!' It hadn't even occurred to me. Deep within myself, I knew that all he had said was right.

'Good,' he murmured. Then: 'As to how I can be so sure, there are ways, Lassair.'

The word seemed to hang in the air. 'Ways?' I repeated in a whisper.

'The barrier that divides time can be crossed, you know,' he said softly. 'If one has the courage to try.'

Out of nowhere I heard my own voice, relating the tale of my ancestor Luanmaisi and her daughter, my namesake. 'Luanmaisi walked with the spirits,' I murmured, 'and they took her between the worlds to encounter beings of other realms.'

My mind detached from the present and I remembered what else I knew. I seemed to hear Granny's voice: *Luanmaisi learned much powerful magic from the spirits and the elves, and it was said that her daughter surpassed even her mother. Both women were shamans, healers and shape-shifters. Luanmaisi's animal spirit was the hare: solitary, independent, representing immortality and symbol of the corn spirit, a fighter who will always ferociously defend his own territory. Lassair's was the silver fox known in the northlands: clever, adaptable, cunning, able to move unseen. Fox has great magic in his pelt, and his element is fire . . .*

I wondered now if it could be possible that either mother or daughter, or even both, became sufficiently great shamans that they left this world and went into another one, where they existed still.

Gurdyman's eyes were on me, demanding my attention, and they seemed to bore into mine, as if he was trying to get inside my head. 'She was of your blood, this woman?' he asked.

I nodded. 'She bore a daughter, although nobody knew who the child's father was. The daughter was called Lassair.'

Gurdyman beamed widely, as if something had just been proved to his enormous satisfaction. 'Hrype was right about you,' he observed. 'Child, so much awaits you!'

'Will I do it?' I asked in an urgent hiss. 'Will I cross the barrier and go between worlds?'

I thought for one wonderful, terrifying moment that he was going to answer me. But then he smiled very kindly, reached out to pat my hand and said, 'Not today.'

And as if a vast door had slammed on a room full of golden light, suddenly the magic that had been humming and thrumming in the air was shut off. We sat, a round old man in a shabby robe and a thin girl who looked like a boy, on a spring day in the sunshine, and somewhere above us, unconcerned, a blackbird sang.

*   *   *

I was dreaming . . .

I am up in that wild country where the humps of low hills march steadily along the horizon. I am very afraid. Someone is after me. The giant with the axe? I do not know, but the urge to flee, to run till I can't run any more, is quite irresistible. My feet keep stumbling, the soles of my boots caught in something tacky, and I realize it is blood. I cry out loud, and my voice is swept up in the bitter wind that whirls and swirls, sending dark clouds flying across a low orange sun.

I have to find a place to hide!

I am in that strange place where the ruins are. Beside me, the open grave pit beckons. I would be safe in there, wouldn't I? I bend and creep inside, but the soft earth crumbles around me, falling on my face, in my eyes, in my mouth, and I forget about having to hide and scream because I think I am being buried alive. Then there is a figure in a cloak with a knife in his hand, and he leaps on the back of a bull and slits its throat, and the blood spurts over me, warm, pulsating with each beat of the mighty beast's dying heart . . .

I woke up.

I was lying on the floor of the crypt beneath Gurdyman's house, wet with my own sweat, hot with the fever of my dream and yet shivering with cold. Gurdyman was crouching over me. He had a thick blanket across his shoulders, and he removed it and wrapped it tightly round me. It was warm from his body. I realized I was sobbing and, with an effort, made myself stop.

I looked up into his kindly, concerned and – I had to admit – fascinated face. I understood something about Gurdyman then: he would always look after my welfare, but his overriding interest in me was because he recognized some potential in me that as yet neither of us fully understood.

I was a little disappointed. But it was better to know, then I would not expect more than he could give.

'You have been sleepwalking,' he said. He moved away from me slightly, going to sit down on his low cot. 'Clever of you,' he added in a light tone, 'to have negotiated both the ladder down from the attic room and the dark steps into the crypt without mishap, but then it's said that sleepwalkers rarely come to harm in their own houses.'

'How did you know I was down here? Did I – did you hear me screaming?' I was very embarrassed to think that again I'd woken him with my noise.

'I did, but I was already on my way to find you. I had dozed off in my chair out in the courtyard.' That was why he'd been wrapped in the lovely, warm blanket. 'There was a disturbance in the air, and that was what woke me.'

A disturbance? I wondered what that meant. Had the power of my dream shaken the whole house? The idea scared me.

He was watching me, his expression unreadable. 'I think you had better tell me what you saw,' he said softly. 'The spirits do not send a dream of such resonance unless they seriously expect you to pay heed.'

I drew a deep breath, gathered my courage and then made myself go back to those awful scenes. I spoke even as I thought; I knew that if I hesitated, I might not dare put them into words.

'Tell me more about this pit,' he said when I had finished. 'You have seen it before, I think. With an occupant, as I recall.'

'Yes, that's right. It – the body isn't there any more. It was empty when I – when I went inside.'

'Is it close to the ruined building?'

I pictured it. 'Yes. It's beside a structure that looks like a hearth, and there's a stumpy, square pillar nearby with marks carved into it.'

Gurdyman was nodding even before I had finished speaking. 'Yes, yes, it all fits,' he muttered. Then he looked down at me and gave me a beaming smile.

'You know this place, don't you?' I whispered.

'I believe I do,' he agreed. 'The terrain that you describe is familiar to me.' He paused, frowning, and I sensed his attention had momentarily gone far away. With a small shudder, he brought himself back. 'I told you yesterday about the soldiers' religion, Lassair. These same soldiers were sent to guard the great wall that their emperor ordered to be built up in the north, and there they made the caves where Mithras was worshipped. Everywhere they went, they kept their god close. I told you too about the ordeals that the men endured in order to progress to higher degrees. Fire was frequently required, and sometimes the ordeals involved being buried alive in order to be reborn into a better, more refined state. I think you saw a certain Mithraeum on the great wall. You saw the hearth, and you saw the altar: what you described as a short, stumpy pillar. The hole in the ground where you tried to hide was the ordeal pit.'

I looked at him. 'Have you been there?' I whispered. He must have; it was the only explanation.

His expression was enigmatic. 'I have seen the place,' he said.

'It is surely a long way to travel,' I persisted. 'Did you—'

He held up a hand. 'Enough, child,' he said, mildly but firmly. 'It is not for you to enquire.'

For a moment I felt the very edge of something . . . some great force that existed within him but that usually was kept well concealed behind the genial facade. It frightened me. I wrapped the blanket more closely around me and seemed to feel myself shrink.

When he spoke, his voice was as friendly and cheerful as ever. 'I wonder,' he mused, 'why you should be sent this image so insistently.' He looked at me, his face creased in a frown. 'Is it possible that one of your kin lives there in the north?'

'No,' I said, without hesitation. I knew the full tally of my kinsmen and women – it was part of my job as the family's bard to memorize not only the past generations, right back to our first occupation of the fen lands, but also the details of the living.

'Could anyone be visiting the region?'

'No. None has any reason to be so far from home.'

As I spoke my mind was distracted. A suspicion was beginning to grow, at first no more than the first tiny patch of cloud that will later bring a storm. Nerving myself, I stared at him and said, 'What is there up there, where you say this Mithraeum is? What sort of a place is it?'

'It is border country, a place where two kings fight for possession,' he replied. 'Both men wish to reinforce it to protect their own land.'

My small cloud was waxing steadily. 'Is there danger there?'

'Oh, yes.' He looked grim. 'I fear that there is.'

'Could – might a man be hurt there? Could he be injured, if there was fighting?'

'Yes, child.'

Such a wounded man, far from home and friendless, might need a place to hide. A place deep in the earth where, like a wounded animal, he could lie and lick his wounds. Call out, perhaps, to someone he loved. Dream of her; send his essence to appear in her dreams . . .

I knew then who I had seen lying in that pit. I knew who had called out to me, who had said, again and again, *come to me*, and then, *where are you? I need you!*

Half of me wanted to sing and shout with joy because he had not forgotten me. In need, perhaps in pain, it was I to whom he had called out in his despair.

The other half was plunged into an abyss of dread because he was hurt.

SEVEN

He had been in the north country for twelve long months, and he longed with all his heart and soul to leave.

He longed for her, too. For that slender but tough girl with the watchful, wise eyes who had flashed so briefly into and out of his life and yet left such an enduring impression in her wake. The total amount of time they had spent together might have been brief, but what had happened to them on the island of Ely seemed to him to have linked them in some way.[1] He hoped – he was almost sure – it was the same for her.

Even before the terrible thing had happened, he thought of her constantly, and he felt that he carried her with him, inside himself. Once he had seen her in a flash of waking vision. He had been jubilant, full of the thrill of battle, the blood lust still on him. He thought he heard her call out to him, and then he saw her. She was pale, her face tense, and the scar on her cheek that she had won when she fought side by side with

[1] See *Mist over the Water*

him had stood out livid white. She was in danger – he knew that, although he had no idea how he knew – but in the same instant that he felt the stab of fear for her, he understood that she was stronger than her opponent and would not die.

He lay in his secret place, the pain from his wound so severe that he knew he would not sleep. He understood that he must keep his mind occupied, for if he did not, he might give in to the despair and the loneliness. Death was lurking; if he did not fight it, he could easily succumb. Slip into its kindly embrace. Wasn't he already lying in his grave? This was what could so very easily happen, if a man proved himself too useful to his king . . .

Enough, he told himself firmly.

He tore his mind away from the present and went back to the day when it had all begun . . .

One of the many problems besetting King William II was that which his mighty father had always said to avoid if at all possible: fighting enemies simultaneously on two fronts. Early in the fourth year of his reign he sailed for Normandy, where the ongoing problem of his younger brother, Duke Robert, had broken out once again, with Robert nibbling away at William's possessions in the region and going so far as to besiege the castle of one of William's loyal barons. On arrival William immediately outbid his brother for the support of the barons and the services of the mercenaries, who abandoned Robert and flocked to William. Robert had no option but to come to terms with William, resulting in a treaty to which both brothers signed their names.

William, however, was not given long to savour the victory. Word reached him while he was still in Normandy that King Malcolm of Scotland had invaded northern England, advancing across a wide front and pushing on determinedly until the local inhabitants organized themselves sufficiently to drive the Scots back. William raced back to England, where he hastily gathered a large army and sent them north, some by sea and some travelling overland.

It was by then September, and one of the worst early autumns men had ever known. It was cold, it was wet, and the wind blew with a steady, brutal, unvarying force that drove people half-mad. William's army, making what haste they could to shore up the northern border, suffered appallingly. Those in the land-army were beset by severe cold and by hunger that had many soldiers weak from near starvation. The ship-army fared even worse, for the equinox brought gales of such strength that their ships foundered and sank and almost all the men perished.

What remained of William's army found King Malcolm calmly waiting, in an area of Lothian south of the Forth that was English to its very bones. Malcolm was the aggressor, but William, far from his power bases in the south and with half his army dead, was in no position to use force. The two kings negotiated a settlement: Malcolm agreed to become William's vassal, giving him his allegiance as he had done to William's father. Such support was not lightly given, and William well knew it. In exchange, he offered to return to Malcolm the twelve English townships that the Scottish king had held under the Conqueror, as well as an additional gift of twelve gold marks, to be paid annually.

As he oversaw his army's preparations for setting out on the long road southwards, William was already planning what to do next. Among his plans, handing either the gold or the towns over to King Malcolm did not feature at all.

He was far from satisfied with the outcome of the recent foray. It was true that, with the loss of the ship-army, his forces had been severely weakened and he had been in no position to fight. Nevertheless, to have been forced to make such concessions to the Scottish king – even ones he had no intention of honouring – had amounted to a grave loss of face.

What was needed, the king decided, was a major fortification of the borderlands between England and Scotland. An area of land that was securely under English control, with strong castles and inhabited by Englishmen who would live and work there, would keep the Scots at bay back on their own side of the border. In addition, the men who settled up there would provide a fighting force if Malcolm tried to invade again.

William turned the scheme over in his mind. After some more careful thought, he decided exactly how his plan should

be carried out. He also knew who would be the first man he
would summon to aid him as he set it in motion.

Rollo Guiscard had been in the border country in the summer
when King Malcolm pushed south into England. Rollo knew
that he had managed to impress King William more than once
and the king now appeared to regard him as one of the more
able of his spies. William recognized and appreciated intelligence and subtlety, both of which he saw in Rollo. Accordingly,
before leaving for Normandy early in 1091, the king had secretly
summoned Rollo to a meeting attended by just the two of them
and issued his instructions. Rollo was to watch the northern
border and, should any advance be made while the king was
out of England, instantly send word.

Rollo had fought his way through the various skirmishes of
the midsummer, emerging almost unscathed; the discomfort
of a minor wound had been more than compensated for by
the awareness of a job well done.

Now King William needed Rollo's services once more. A
summons was sent, via one of the few of the king's messengers
who actually knew where Rollo was. Rollo was good at melting
into the background: when, as now, he was with a group of
dirty, tired soldiers grumbling as they prepared for their long
journey, he was indistinguishable from the next man. At other
times, his temporary identity as a merchant, a soothsayer, a
dutiful son on his way to visit his sick father, or even a monk
or a priest, would be equally convincing.

Slipping away from his companions, Rollo smartened
himself up, groomed himself and his horse and set out to meet
his king.

The conversation between the king and his spy took place
in a quiet spot away from the king's encampment, and the
only eyes that observed the two men together were those of
the king's close guard. The king's short, strong body was
covered by a plain cloak, his reddish fair hair concealed beneath
its hood.

'You have done well, Rollo Guiscard,' the king observed
as Rollo rose from his bow.

'Thank you, My Lord King.'

The king's broad, ruddy face creased into a smile. 'I was right, was I not, to fear an incursion while my back was turned?'

'Yes, absolutely right.'

'Right, too, to have sent you here as my eyes,' the king went on. 'Few men would have so quickly appreciated what Edgar Aethling was about when he came racing up here, sore because I had just booted him out of Normandy.' He nodded sagely. 'But you did, didn't you? You guessed he would persuade Malcolm that the time was ripe to invade the north of England.'

Suddenly, the pleasant expression was gone, wiped away, and a look of fury filled the king's face. 'He had the king's ear, curse him, for the man is married to Edgar's sister. Curse her too!' He added a string of oaths, his red face glowing scarlet. Then, calming himself, he went on: 'Thanks to you, word reached me before too much harm was done. Now, we have a *treaty* –' he put heavy, sarcastic emphasis on the word – 'and all is right with the world, is it not?'

Rollo, fairly certain the king did not expect an answer, did not provide one.

But for a soft creak from the expensive leather of the king's boots as he paced restlessly to and fro, there was silence for some time.

Then William stopped and turned to face his spy. 'I have another task for you, Rollo Guiscard,' he said softly.

Rollo bowed. 'My Lord King?'

'England is open to such attacks all the time the border is weak. There are tracts of land where no men live, Rollo, and there the tough and ruthless border barons seek to make their own petty kingdoms.'

I know, Rollo thought. *All the details were in my report to you.*

'I shall stamp my authority on these lands,' the king went on. 'I shall first take Carlisle, for it lies all but abandoned, and if I do not seize it, Malcolm will.' He had resumed his pacing, one fist repeatedly punching into the opposite palm, but now he stopped and once again faced Rollo.

'I will take my army into the north-west next spring,' he

announced, 'as soon as the roads are fit to travel and the days begin to lengthen. In the meantime, I want you to go there and discover how the land lies. Who holds the town, if any man does, what the fortifications consist of, how many men may be drawn up against me.' He went on talking for some time, succinctly outlining his plans.

'I understand, My Lord,' Rollo said when he had finished. He guessed there was more to come and, after a moment, the king spoke again.

'I have heard tell of a man they call Hawksclaw, although his true name is Thorwald. He is, they say, of Norse descent, and he seeks to carve out his kingdom from other men's lands, as did his forefathers.'

Rollo, too, had heard of Thorwald, known as Hawksclaw. The name was whispered along the border country with a mixture of fear and awe.

'It may be that the territory I aim to stabilize in the north-west is not of concern to him,' the king went on, his tone soft and thoughtful, 'but I will not take the risk.' His pale eyes shot to meet Rollo's. 'You know what I want of you.'

'I do, Lord.'

'Good,' the king murmured. 'Very good.' He reached beneath his wide cloak and untied a small bag of soft brown leather from his belt. From inside it came the chink of coins. He handed it to Rollo. 'Take this on account,' William said. 'You will be rewarded in full when this business is over and done with.' His eyes still intent on Rollo, he added softly, 'I do not forget my debt to those who serve me loyally and efficiently.'

'As I well know, My Lord King,' Rollo agreed. His service to the king was slowly and steadily making him a wealthy man.

Believing the meeting to be over, Rollo prepared to be given his leave and the king's traditional parting blessing to those in his favour. But the king made no move; instead, he said, lowering his voice, 'When your task in the north-west is complete, there is something else.' He beckoned Rollo closer, and then spoke right into his ear.

As he listened, Rollo's eyes widened and he felt a stab of fear.

The king finished speaking and stood back. He was watching

Rollo closely, as if gauging his reaction. 'My Lord King, that is . . .' Rollo sought for the right word. 'Astonishing,' he managed.

'Astonishing, yes,' the king agreed grimly, 'but true, nevertheless. Or so I am told.'

'And so many died,' Rollo murmured, his whirling thoughts concentrating on the human tragedy.

'It was treason,' the king said sharply. 'The result could have been far graver than it was. The intention is perfectly clear.'

'Indeed so, My Lord,' Rollo agreed hastily. He squared his shoulders and faced his king. 'What would you have me do?'

As the king told him, Rollo felt something deep inside him tremble with atavistic dread.

After the king had led his army away on the long road home, Rollo covered his tracks, melted into the background and, leaving the Forth behind him, set off south for Carlisle. He had plenty of money – the king had made sure of that – and he completed his brief list of purchases in a string of small towns and settlements along his route. Nobody would recall a man who bought a modest amount of food, or a single blanket, or a warm winter cloak, but a gossip with nothing better to do might repeat the tale of someone who splashed out a bagful of coins all at once and bought out the shop.

He already had a good horse. Strega was a bay mare, nondescript and with no memorable markings, and she was neither particularly tall nor of noticeably fine breeding. She was, however, tough, strong and virtually unshockable. She and Rollo had been together for some time, and he had chosen her name in memory of the powerful witch women out of the legends of his native Sicily.

As he grew near to the lands around the great firth that divided Scotland from England, he stopped to disguise his appearance. He was deep in the northern forest, the autumn was well advanced and he had not seen a living soul for over a day and a half. He darkened his blond hair with a mixture of mud and ash, drawing it back off his face and fastening it with a length of twine. Stubble grew long on his chin, and he darkened it to match his hair. Then he took from his pack the stained and torn tunic that constituted his poor traveller's disguise, covering it with an equally ancient and travel-stained cloak.

As he began his exploration of the district, he set up a series of refuges. Working almost exclusively alone, as he did, he only had himself to rely on and, if he encountered danger, he had to be sure there was somewhere to hide. In a modest-sized town some distance from Carlisle, he paid out rent in advance for a tiny room in a busy inn, speaking briefly to the proprietor – in truth, far too busy a man to be very curious – and describing himself as having family business in the area which would often take him away for several days at a time. It was not likely he would ever need it, but there was no way of knowing. Better to have a room he never used than to need such a bolt hole and not have one. Then he set off into the wilds of that sparsely-populated border country and found an abandoned farmstead, where he made a shelter in an old barn. He discovered a scatter of ancient ruins and spotted a place where he would be protected from the weather. In each place, he left supplies of basic foodstuffs and containers of fresh water. Elsewhere, he sought out tracts of woodland where the trees grew close together and the pine needles lay in a deep carpet. In an emergency, he knew he could survive in such places, even with winter coming on; he had done so before. He memorized each location, making quite sure he could find the places again if he needed them.

When he was satisfied that he had done all he could, he set off for the populated areas and, for the first time in weeks, re-entered the world of men.

Through the deep quiet of the winter months, Rollo set about discovering everything he could of the area which the king wished to fortify and make his own. He found a land fed by one broad river and many tributaries, creating a boggy terrain that would be difficult to negotiate unless you knew the safe paths. As he stood one December morning, gazing out over a wide expanse of waterlogged ground, frost and patches of ice slowly melting in the weak sun, he thought of

Lassair. She had found the firm ground across the fens from Ely to the mainland, and in so doing had saved their lives. In a sudden stab of loneliness, he thought he would have given almost anything, just then, to have her by his side.

Ruthlessly, he pushed her to the back of his mind. She wasn't there, and he was incapable of summoning her.

The ancient town of Carlisle was the focal point of the region. William's plan was sound, for a fortification there would enable his soldiers to guard the major road out of western Scotland. But Carlisle was, Rollo discovered, in ruins. Destroyed by the Danes two hundred years ago, it was still a place of half-collapsed walls and devastated dwellings open to the elements. The biting wind howled through the many open spaces like a demon, and a man more susceptible to the power of the spirits would have been fearful.

Rollo, in the guise of a poor merchant, put up in a dirty, tumbledown inn beside the road leading out of the town to the north. He feigned an injury to his leg, an excuse that enabled him to remain there for two weeks, hobbling around and asking discreet, careful questions. There were rumours of a powerful, brutal lord who had designs on the town, and the few inhabitants were very afraid that his arrival would turn an existence that was barely tolerable into something far worse. If the lord deemed you unimportant to his schemes, they said, you would be lucky to escape with your life.

The lord, as Rollo had already guessed, was referred to by everyone as Hawksclaw. Nobody knew much about him, other than that he lived in the wild lands to the north-east, in what some said was a ruined castle. They whispered, wide-eyed, that he had no wife but kept seven women captive, one for each night of the week, and by them had a gang of bastard sons as cruel and ruthless as he was.

Listening to the tales, believing perhaps a third of what he was told, Rollo recognized what he must do. He knew that many of the English did not like their new Norman masters, and he could well appreciate why not. But here in the north-west, if the alternative to William's rule was a ruthless, lawless brigand who made up the rules as he went along, then surely the choice was obvious. Rollo's own attitude, had anyone

asked him, was that at least William's firm hand kept the
country peaceful. William did not care what men believed,
what they thought, which god they worshipped; as long as
you worked hard, kept the peace and paid your taxes, in all
likelihood the king would leave you alone. Moreover, he would
fight off the country's enemies, as a king should.

Such were Rollo's thoughts as, step by careful step, he made
his plans to kill the man known as Hawksclaw and so leave
Carlisle and the north-west safe and ready for the king's arrival.

It should have been foolproof. So thorough had Rollo's preparations been that he believed he knew his enemy's routine down
to every instant of the day. Hawksclaw was not a hard man
to read: he was a bully and a braggart, and he kept his men
obedient to him through brutal cruelty. Rollo had formed the
opinion, after having watched the man's stronghold for a week
or more, that the removal of their charismatic but vicious
leader would be the end of the threat posed by this particular
private army. Hawksclaw's men, he believed, would creep
away once he was dead. It did not seem likely that any of his
sons would assume their father's mantle. They numbered not
the 'gang' that the people of Carlisle had claimed but in fact
only three, one of whom was a boy and one crippled. The
remaining son looked as if he had suffered too much from his
father's casual brutality and appeared to be a weak, indecisive
man.

Rollo slipped into the stronghold for the final time late one
night. It did indeed look like a ruined castle, but the days of
its strength and power were long gone. The outer walls were
breached in several places, and the wooden gates had been
repaired many times, latterly in what appeared to have been
a half-hearted fashion. Rollo's previous forays had enabled
him to memorize the interior layout, which consisted of a
central yard – foul with mud, ordure, puddles of yellowish
water and dozens of animals, from scrawny hens to skinny,
disease-ridden wolfhounds – surrounded on three sides by
rows of two-storey buildings made mostly of wood. These
structures were, in general, crudely made, filthy dirty inside
and slowly falling apart. On the lower level there were stables,

a small forge and several storerooms, most of them half-empty. Above were a series of dilapidated alcoves that stood open on the side facing the yard, the only privacy for those within provided by flimsy wooden shutters or badly-cured animal skins. One corner of the stronghold was built of stone, and it was here that the lord had his private chambers. They were on the upper floor, reached by a wooden staircase that led up from the yard. There was a wide hall, in the centre of which a fire burned in a circular hearth, and, off to one side, a bed chamber. The whole place stank like a midden built over a latrine.

There were usually a handful of dispirited men hanging around and sometimes more; Rollo had once counted fifty. It appeared that not all of Hawksclaw's fighting force were permanently billeted with him, which made sense because, for one thing, the lord would not have to feed them all if they did not live with him, and, for another, if they were spread out, there was less danger that every one of them would be wiped out in a single attack. Sometimes Rollo had seen a group of woman, huddled together, one of them looking fearfully over her shoulder and another sporting a swollen, weeping black eye.

It was clear from the demeanour of Hawksclaw and his men that they felt sufficiently secure in their lonely stronghold not to fear attack. The place was minimally guarded, and it was easy for a man of Rollo's experience to slip in and out unseen by the pair of young men – little more than boys – who habitually leaned against the gates and bragged to each other of their prowess in the saddle, in the field of combat and, most frequently, in the bed of whichever of the women they claimed to have most recently forced themselves on.

On that last night visit, the two young guards had been replaced by an old veteran with a huge beard and a long scar through one eye. He had made himself comfortable, slumped down in a corner out of the wind, and appeared to be fast asleep. Passing him silently, Rollo slipped through one of the wider breaches in the walls and, for a few moments, stood in the deep shadows looking out across the yard. There was not a soul, human or animal, to be seen. He made his soft-footed way up to the chamber where Hawksclaw slept. There was a gaping hole in the stone wall, inadequately covered by a torn piece of leather, and sufficient moonlight came through for Rollo to see quite clearly. He approached the pile of animal skins that served the lord for a bed and stood for a moment looking down at the sleeping man under his thick blanket. Even in the relaxation of sleep, the face was cruel and hard. His mind cool and detached, Rollo killed Hawksclaw as he slept.

He was on his way out of the room when he heard a faint sound. Spinning round, he saw a girl spring up from the floor on the far side of Hawksclaw's bed, where she must have been hidden from view, curled up and asleep. She was naked, her body sinewy and slim, her small breasts firm and high. Long black hair flowed down her back, and her dark eyes were blazing. She sprang at Rollo, and he felt a searing, burning pain in his chest, about a hand's breadth above his heart.

He grabbed the handle of the knife and pulled it from her hand, biting his lips against the cry of agony as the steel was wrested out of his flesh. Instantly, her hands were at him, her fingers scrabbling for his eyes, and he grabbed her wrists, forcing her hands away. She tried to kick him in the groin, but he sensed the attack coming and, grasping her around the waist, flung her to one side so that her flying feet found only empty air. He knew she would kill him if she could.

Among his victims, no woman yet featured. He did not wish to kill one now, even a wild demon like her. Bunching his right hand into a fist, he hit her on the side of her head, and she went limp. He carried her across to the bed and laid her beside her dead lord. The night was cold, so he was careful to cover her well with the heavy woollen blanket.

For a moment he stood staring down at her. He had not hit her hard, and already she was stirring. He turned and left.

The wound in his chest became inflamed, and he believed he would die.

While he was still able to travel, he'd put many miles between himself and Hawksclaw's stronghold. He did not believe the dead man's followers posed any serious threat to the king's plans to take the area, but they were more than capable of taking lengthy and agonizing revenge on the man who had killed their leader. If Rollo were to be caught, death, when it at last came, would be nothing but a relief.

He had made his way to the most desolate of his refuges, a mystifying ruined building like nothing he had ever seen before. It was rectangular in shape, not very large, and at one end were three squat pillars. The site was overgrown, and chunks of stone lay all over it. There were the remains of a hearth, and, beside it, a pit dug into the earth. The building must once have been underground, for even now, although open to the wide sky, it lay beneath the surface of the surrounding land. It was reasonably safe to have a fire there – by day at least – and by using dry fuel it was possible to keep the smoke to a barely visible minimum. Rollo had adopted the pit as a sleeping place, lining it with dry leaves and dead grass and building up the earth in front of it so that, once within, he was sheltered from the wind and the rain. He took to setting many of the stones that littered the site into the fire during the day, and then placing them in his pit when he extinguished the fire at nightfall. Some nights, when the temperature did not fall too dramatically, he was quite warm.

In the depths of his sickness he cried out to her. But she did not come.

He realized, as slowly he began to recover, that it was his own careful preparations that had saved him. His refuge was too far away from Hawksclaw's stronghold for any of the dead man's men to have hunted him down, even if they had tried. And his foresight in making ready a safe, sheltered place to lie up in had kept him from freezing to death when, helpless and wracked with fever, he had lain in his pit and longed for Lassair.

In time, he had begun to understand that he would live.

Now, he knew he could not go on hiding. His wound was healing – though in the absence of any professional attention it had closed in a ragged, bumpy line that itched and prickled. It should have been stitched, he knew; he had other scars on his body that, although the result of far graver wounds, had mended cleanly thanks to careful stitching. But he had baulked at sewing up his own flesh. His only remedy had been a small bottle of lavender oil; Lassair had told him it helped fight infectious humours. He wondered now if it had saved his life, reflecting that if so, it was the second time she had held him back from death.

Now that his strength was returning, he knew he must hasten to send word secretly to the king, to inform him that the potential threat in the north-west no longer existed. Hawksclaw was dead and, without his leadership, Rollo did not believe that wretched, ragged band of old men in their lonely, tumble-down compound stood much of a chance of stopping a man like William.

And then, after he had located one of his network of reliable men and dispatched his message, there was the matter of the other command that William had issued to him . . .

Rollo had deliberately not thought about it until now. It was so different in kind from any challenge he had faced before that he was wary of it, to the point of being fearful. He was used to flesh and blood men – or women, he thought ruefully, remembering the girl in Hawksclaw's bed – who came running at him with sharp steel in their hands trying to kill him. His world was a fighter's world, and he was content that his talent for the silent, secret work of the killer spy had been recognized by his king, and that William was putting him to good use. But this other business was nothing like either a clean, open battle or a clandestine assignment.

In his heart, Rollo knew that he did not want to do this job. It was so far outside his experience that he was not sure even how to begin, never mind bring it to a successful conclusion. And the whisper of the unknown force that seemed to be involved frightened him; he would not have said that he was superstitious, but for this terrible thing to have been achieved, the power involved must be awesome indeed . . .

His thoughts were getting him nowhere. He did not have a choice, for the king had given him a mission and he had accepted it. He would have to do his best, and if that wasn't good enough he would probably die.

With a heavy heart, still feeling weak and far from well, he got up very early one morning, packed up his belongings and carefully went over every inch of the place that had been his strange refuge. When finally he turned his back on it and walked away, it would have been all but impossible to see that any man had been there.

He trudged off along the line of the ancient wall that snaked away eastwards across this narrow neck of England. He had left Strega in the care of a man in a small and isolated village some miles away, and until he reached the place, he had no choice but to walk. His pack had rarely seemed heavier, and it was only willpower that kept him going. The weather was milder – spring was well advanced now – and for a fit man the march would have been a pleasure. Rollo, as he very soon realized, was very far from fit.

As, eventually, the lonely hamlet came into view, Rollo hoped fervently that the stable boy had taken good care of Strega, for she and Rollo had a long ride ahead of them.

He would travel on towards the east until he reached the sea. There were still some twenty-five miles to go, across the wild north country which his pursuers would know so much better than he did. Twenty-five miles to cover, during which he would be alone and vulnerable to attack. He would have to employ all his skill, using not only sight and hearing to detect a possible threat, but also that strange extra sense that seemed to be there when he most needed it. If Strega was well fed and well rested, as indeed she ought to be, then she would be eager to run and, with any luck, they would reach the sea by nightfall. He would find some busy, bustling port in which to lose himself, and he would have the luxury of a good hot meal, perhaps even a wash, and a comfortable bed to sleep in. Then – and his soul began to sing at the thought – at long last he would turn south and leave the desolate, dangerous north behind him.

His next destination and his next mission lay just ahead of him, in the near future. The fact that what the king had ordered him to do was as dangerous, in its way, as a whole troop of murderous brigands with revenge in their hearts, he did not allow himself to think about.

One thing at a time. And he still had to get to the coast . . .

EIGHT

My huge joy at the realization that it was Rollo who had been calling out to me made me walk on air for two whole days. Then, as I woke on the third morning from a deep and dreamless sleep without the merest suspicion of words spoken inside my head, I was hit with a sudden sense of dread, so profound that for a moment I felt physically sick.

He had been in terrible danger. He had been hiding in some frightful pit once used in the initiation rites of an ancient religion. He had been wounded, sick, desperate. I had seen him, and I had heard him call out to me, many times. Now the dream visions had gone and the words had ceased.

I was awfully afraid I knew what that meant: Rollo was dead.

I put my head in my hands and wept.

Gurdyman was kind, in the sense that he told me quite brusquely that I had no proof and should not plunge into despair without good cause. I felt I had reason enough, but the determination in his bright eyes made me wonder if I was right. Instantly, Gurdyman spotted my moment of doubt.

'You must keep busy, child,' he remonstrated gently. 'Moping about here and thinking the worst will avail neither you nor this Norman of yours.' I had told him quite a lot about Rollo, although, as so often with Gurdyman, I felt I was revealing things he already knew. He had a way of slowly nodding his head as I spoke, as if to say *yes, yes, this I am aware of*. The mere mention of Rollo's name had been enough, for Gurdyman seemed to know all about the Guiscard family. To my relief, although he referred to Rollo as my Norman, I had the distinct impression that he did not view the Guiscards as ruthless and brutal conquerors. On the contrary, he seemed to have a certain respect for them.

He was right, of course, and I did indeed need to keep

occupied, but just at that moment I was at a loss to know what I ought to be doing.

'I need some supplies,' Gurdyman announced, getting to his feet. 'Many of the bottles on the crypt shelves are almost empty, and there are some items which even our apothecary has run out of. Come, child –' he reached for his stout stick – 'we shall step out in the sunshine of this fine morning and walk down to the quays, where, with any luck, we shall be able to find some merchant who has fortuitously just taken delivery of the very items we require.'

I fetched my shawl and we set off. Knowing him as I was coming to, I was pretty sure that he was right and a boat with a cargo of rare and exotic herbs, spices and oils would just be tying up.

We emerged into the marketplace, where the food stalls were already doing brisk business. Making our way through the maze of little streets and alleys on the far side, soon we were stepping out on to the road that leads up to the Great Bridge. On the far side, I could see Castle Hill, and at its foot men were busy on the site where the new priory was being built. We remained on the south side of the river, turning to the right just before the bridge and heading off down the long quay.

Presently, Gurdyman raised his stick and pointed to a long, sleek boat which was just manoeuvring up to the quay. A sailor stood barefoot on her deck, holding a rope, and another man waited on the quayside to catch it. 'Jack Duroll,' Gurdyman exclaimed with satisfaction. He turned and gave me a smug smile. 'He'll have exactly what we need. I shall—'

But his words were interrupted by a shout from the quayside, followed by a confusion of sounds: a lot of splashing, a babble of loud voices, a woman's high, thin scream. Gurdyman forged a way between the rapidly-gathering crowd of interested people, and soon we were standing on the edge of the stone quay looking out across the water.

Another boat had been following Jack Duroll's up the river, presumably heading for a berth a little further on. But something was wrong . . . I tried to see what had so alarmed the onlookers. The boat – a squat little tub of a thing, with weather-stained

boards and an unkempt look – seemed to be towing something
along behind, something attached by a line. From the conster-
nation among the boat's small crew, it was very apparent that
they had been unaware of whatever was accompanying them
until the people on the quay had drawn their attention to it.

What was it? I edged up beside two stout women who stood
muttering together, heads close, faces wearing expressions that
indicated both shock and curiosity. One of them turned to me
and, eyes alive with excitement, said, 'It's a body!'

She had to be wrong. Boats didn't tow their dead along
behind them, I was sure of it. I heard voices shouting out in
a foreign tongue: the boat's crew, busy claiming, no doubt,
that they knew nothing whatsoever about their unexpected
companion. I heard several local voices respond, with everyone
steadily growing more agitated. One man shouted, 'Bloody
foreigners! They'll have killed him and chucked him over the
side, you mark my words!'

Quite a lot of people did mark his words, if the mutterings
of agreement were anything to go by. I thought this theory
highly unlikely, for if the foreigners had killed someone
on-board and disposed of the body, surely they would have
made quite certain, before coming into the town, that they
weren't towing the evidence of the crime along behind them.

Then I heard a clear, authoritative voice that I recognized.
I didn't understand the words, for they appeared to be in
the same language that the foreign sailors spoke. But I knew
the tone: it was Gurdyman. He was addressing a tall, broad,
fair-haired and bare-chested giant of a man who appeared to
be the squat tub's captain.

I hurried to join them. Gurdyman posed a question, to which
the captain replied with a great gush of words, waving his
hands about and gesturing to his boat, his crew and the dead
body. Gurdyman waited until he paused for breath – which
was a long time, as the man apparently had huge lungs – and
then asked another question. The man nodded vigorously,
pointing back up river to the north-east.

I nudged Gurdyman. 'What's happened? What's he saying?'

Gurdyman turned to me, frowning. 'In a moment, Lassair.
First we must summon the sheriff.'

I was quite surprised. Gurdyman does not have a very great opinion of our town sheriff, suspecting him, as do many of the townspeople, of taking the common pasture and using it for himself. *Prowling wolf, filthy swine* and *dog without shame* are some of the more polite epithets applied to our sheriff. But I thought I knew why Gurdyman was even now sending a lad off to find him. There was a dead body in the water beneath the quay, and all business, commerce and trade would come to a halt until someone in authority did something about it.

Gurdyman took my hand and led me right up to the edge of the quay. Together we looked down at the body. It was floating, face upwards, just behind the boat, to which it seemed to be attacked by a length of rope. The eyes were shut and the jaws clamped together. The skin looked slightly tanned, a bit like leather, and from what I could see the body was naked.

'You don't really think the crew killed him and slung him over the side, do you?' I whispered.

Gurdyman shook his head. 'I am sure they did no such thing. The captain tells me they got lost in the fens last night – a fog sprang up, apparently, as so often it does at dusk – and they missed the main channel. They went too far over to the east and got caught up in a narrow channel in the peat workings. They had to turn round and the boat's stern was stuck in the bank. It took quite a lot of effort, apparently, to push them free.'

I would have thought that the blond-haired giant could have poled the boat along single-handed, but did not say so. 'Do you think the body became attached then, when they were stuck in the peat?'

Gurdyman did not speak for some moments. I had the sense that his thoughts were far away.

'Gurdyman?' I prompted. 'Was the body in the peat?' It would account for the tanned appearance of the skin. We have a lot of peat around us at Aelf Fen, and we know the effect that the brown water can have on anything immersed in it for any length of time.

He turned to me. 'Hmm?'

I was about to repeat the question, but we were interrupted

by a loud cry of 'Make way, there! Make way for the sheriff!'
And, with an advance guard of two armed soldiers and a
rearguard of three more, the puffed-up, gaudily-dressed figure
of Cambridge's sheriff made his way along the quay.

I melted away into the crowd and watched. The tall, blond
captain towered above the sheriff, but, even so, there was no
doubting who was in charge out there. A crafty fox our man
might be, but he had something about him. He seemed to
expect it as his right to have Gurdyman translate for him, and,
indeed, Gurdyman did not seem to mind. In fact, he appeared
quite determined to be included in whatever process of the
law was being enacted.

The body had, at last, been dragged out of the water. It was
indeed naked, and the general assumption that it was male
proved correct. I was used to male bodies by now, through
my work as a healer, and I looked with some interest and
without embarrassment at the dead man.

He had been in early middle age, I guessed; medium height,
spare build bordering on skinny, long limbs. His wet hair
trailed down on to his shoulders, swept back from the face.
Both the hair on his head and his body were dark, stained
slightly reddish by the peaty water. Long ropes hung down
from his wrists and ankles, and I thought I saw something
wound around his neck; perhaps it was one of those ropes that
had become caught on the boat and dragged him out of his
resting place. Had he been hanged, I wondered? Had they
bound him and strung him up, cutting him down once he was
dead and throwing him into the fen?

Gurdyman grabbed my hand. 'Come, child.' We fell into
step behind the small procession, which consisted of the sheriff
and his guards, now carrying the corpse between them, and
the captain of the squat tub.

'Where are we going?' I hissed.

'The sheriff wants to know how, when and where this man
died,' Gurdyman whispered back. 'If a crime has been
committed in his area of jurisdiction, he'll have to investigate
it.'

'How's he going to find out?'

He smiled. 'Well, I thought a couple of people who, in their different ways, know something about the human body might be able to help him, so I've just volunteered you and me.'

We were in a low-ceilinged, stone-walled room under the big building to which the sheriff had taken us. It was quite similar to Gurdyman's crypt, although neither as clean, tidy nor sweet-smelling. The body had been laid on a big oak table, and Gurdyman and I had been left alone with it.

Gurdyman rolled back his sleeves and nodded to me to join him at the table. I, too, pushed back my sleeves, glad that I'd braided my hair and covered it with a coif that morning, as I always did when I was working. There's nothing more disgusting than discovering your hair has been dipping in something smelly, whether it's a bowl of pungent oil or a pot of some sick patient's piss.

I stared at the dead man. Then I watched Gurdyman as, slowly and unhurriedly, he went over every inch of the body. 'A strong man,' he mused, 'perhaps a little on the thin side. His muscles are well developed; I'd say he was used to walking big distances.' He leaned over the corpse's head and deftly lifted an eyelid. 'Dark eyes. Aged perhaps in the mid-thirties; possibly a little younger. Uncircumcised.' He paused and raised the corpse's right shoulder a little way above the table, leaning across the body to repeat the process with the left shoulder. He leaned closer, studying the flesh. 'Look, Lassair,' he murmured.

I looked. I made out faint marks, almost like a pattern etched into the skin. 'Is it a tattoo?'

'No, I don't believe it is,' Gurdyman answered. 'I think he's had a whipping.'

A whipping. My mind filled with the sort of images I didn't really want to see. It was time to change the subject . . .

'How did he die?' I asked.

Gurdyman put gentle fingers to the rope around the neck. As he began carefully to remove it – there was an intricate knot beneath the left ear – he made a soft exclamation. 'Look,' he repeated.

He was indicating a cut, about the length of my little finger and quite deep.

'This incision would have severed the vessel that bears blood up to the head,' he said. 'Death would have followed swiftly.'

'But I thought he'd been hanged,' I protested.

Gurdyman was slowly unwinding the rope from around the throat. I saw now that it was not in fact rope, but a length of plaited leather. 'This is a garrotte,' he said. 'It is used to break the neck, like this.' He mimed throwing the rope around a neck and then rapidly pulling it tight, one end crossed over the other, with a sort of jerk. Then, horribly, he raised the head and wobbled it around. It was clear even to me that the neck was broken. 'The knot would serve simply to hold the rope in place,' he added vaguely. Again, I had the impression he was thinking about something else.

'In place round his neck?' I persisted.

'Hmm? Yes, that's right.'

I looked quickly at the dead man's neck. The indentations made by the garrotte were clearly visible – perhaps a little more deeply marked around the back of the neck than the front, although it was hard to be sure.

I looked up at Gurdyman. He had put down the leather braid and was now handling the ropes that were wound around the man's wrists and ankles, running his fingers delicately along them as he spoke, turning them over and over in his hands. 'That is very interesting,' he said softly.

'What's interesting?'

He looked up at me. 'The rope is made of fibres from the honeysuckle plant.'

I knew from his expression that this was significant, but I did not know why. I was about to ask when he put the ropes down and once more stepped up close to the body. He put one hand on the lower jaw and, holding the head steady with the other, forced the mouth open. He peered inside – the man, I saw, had had good teeth – and looked carefully at the tongue and around the gums. 'Hmm,' he said again. He had something on the end of his forefinger, and it looked a little like the small, pale, empty skin of a berry.

'What's that?' I demanded.

'I am not sure,' he admitted. Then, as if it were something we did together every day, he said matter-of-factly, 'I need to see what is in his stomach. We shall have to cut him open.'

My apprenticeship as a healer had not prepared me for anything like this. Hoping I would not disgrace myself by fainting or being sick, I steeled myself, took a deep breath and went to stand at my mentor's side. He told me to find a bowl of some sort, and I went to the shelves behind the table and selected a pottery dish. Gurdyman nodded his approval. 'I shall remove the stomach in its entirety,' he announced, 'and we shall open it on the workbench over there.' He indicated a bench beneath the shelves.

I watched as he cut a long slit from the corpse's breast to its navel. Then he reached inside and extracted the bag of the stomach. I had half expected blood, and Gurdyman must have seen my expression. 'He had a cut in his neck, and he has been in the water,' he said. 'The blood will have long ago left his body.'

That reminded me of something I had meant to ask. To take my mind off the fact that my companion was holding a human stomach in his hands and was just about to slice into it, I said, 'How long has he been dead?'

Gurdyman frowned. 'I cannot be sure, for peat is a natural preservative and sometimes bodies that look to have been only recently put into the ground were placed there hundreds of years ago.'

'*Hundreds* of years? Can a body last that long?'

'Yes, child.' He smiled at me. 'Your own ancestors, you say, lived in the fens long, long ago. They might have treated their dead in this way, slipping the corpse into the peat so that it would be preserved for ever.'

He seemed to be implying that the ancient people had deliberately buried their dead in order to preserve them, but I just couldn't believe it. 'Did they—' I began, but just then he pushed the point of his sharp knife into the stomach and cut it open, and I was so busy trying not to vomit that there was no room for anything else.

Edild told me once that the best way to overcome revulsion at some perfectly natural aspect of the human body is to concentrate hard on what it is teaching you. I did my best, making myself stare in wonder at what the inside of a stomach looked like, and after a few moments I felt I had won my private battle.

Gurdyman had poured the contents of the stomach into the pottery bowl. Using the end of his knife, he separated several tiny objects. Some looked like seeds, some like fruit of some sort. Those pale berries again.

'Fetch some water, please, Lassair,' Gurdyman said. I did as he asked and watched as, very carefully, he rinsed the seeds and the fruit fragments, washing off the tacky, viscous, smelly matter in which they were immersed. He placed them on the edge of the table on which the body lay. 'Hmm,' he said again. He beckoned me closer. 'Look,' he said. With the end of his knife he indicated a single seed. 'Rye, I think.'

'Yes.' I nodded my agreement. 'There are lots of them.' I pointed to a piece of berry skin. 'And the remains of lots of berries too.' I tried to think of an edible berry that was white in colour, and all I came up with was an unripe mulberry or strawberry, and the fragments in the stomach did not resemble either. 'What are they?'

Gurdyman looked up at me. 'Mistletoe berries.'

'But they are poisonous,' I protested. 'We use the plant, but only the young stems and the leaves, never the berries.'

'Interesting,' Gurdyman remarked. 'What do you use them for?'

'As a heart tonic and to treat water bloating. Oh, and as a sedative.' Briefly, I struggled with my pride. I won. 'Actually, it's only my aunt who administers mistletoe. She says it's too powerful a plant for me to use unsupervised.'

Gurdyman nodded. 'You learn by watching her, and soon she will trust you to work alone, even with potentially lethal plants,' he said.

That was just how Edild would have phrased it. For a wonderful moment she felt very close, and silently I sent her my love.

'And now to the rye seeds,' he went on, carefully picking one up on the tip of his knife. Then he selected another seed which, as I looked more closely, I could see was subtly different. It was darker in colour, and the shape of the seed was slightly distorted. I felt that I recognized it, and mentally I ran my eye along the top shelf in Edild's room, where she keeps the more dangerous items.

Then I knew what it was. Perhaps my aunt's spirit was still close by and she had prompted me. I sent her my thanks, just in case.

'It's ergot,' I said. 'It's a fungus that grows on rye and, like mistletoe, is potentially lethal.' Edild had warned me gravely about what ergot could do, and I thought the effects – hallucinations, agonizing, burning pains all over the body and, eventually, flesh rot in the extremities – sounded ghastly.

'You and your aunt use it?' Gurdyman asked.

'Yes. Edild prescribes it in tiny doses to help in childbirth, when the afterbirth is reluctant to detach and come cleanly away. Also, she sometimes puts it in headache remedies, although only for the terrible half-head afflictions that make people see dizzying visions and occasionally lose a part of their sight.'

Gurdyman's expression indicated his interest. 'You are lucky in your teacher,' he observed. 'Your aunt has a rare skill.'

Grateful on Edild's behalf, I gave him a beaming smile. Before I could thank him, he returned his attention to the tiny objects laid out before us. 'So, we have mistletoe berries and rye grains, many of which are affected with ergot,' he said, 'in a medium that looks like gruel or soup. What are your conclusions?'

I had been so busy congratulating myself on identifying the ergot that I'd lost sight of why it was important. Now my mind began to race, putting the picture together. Very soon I had the answer.

'Someone poisoned him,' I said. I thought of his wounds, the stab in the neck and the garrotte. Now we knew that he'd been made to consume a poisoned soup as well. 'Maybe his assailant gave him the gruel to make him unconscious, so that they could kill him at their leisure,' I suggested. 'If he did not suspect what was about to happen, then it would have been easier for the killer to invite him to share his gruel than to leap on him and stab him in the throat, or wind that garrotte round his neck.'

'Quite so,' Gurdyman agreed. 'In any case, we know the poisoned food came first, because a man cannot eat once he is dead.'

I felt myself flush. Why hadn't I thought of that? Gurdyman must have seen my embarrassment. He reached out and lightly touched my hand. 'Do not be hard on yourself,' he murmured. 'You think creatively, which is the first essential in work such as this.'

His remark comforted me. I watched him as, already immersed once more in the mysterious body, he bent down over it.

The silence extended for what felt like a very long time. I stood there beside Gurdyman, trying not to shuffle my feet; Edild complains if I fidget while she's trying to concentrate. When at long last he came back to himself – I knew from his face and his demeanour that he had been far away – I knew I had succeeded, because he gave a sort of a start and said, 'Lassair! I'd forgotten all about you, child.'

There was a new light in his eyes, and it seemed as if brightness was welling up out of him. Wherever he had been, whatever spirits he had been in communication with, his mind voyage had achieved the desired end. He grasped my hand and drew me back to the body.

He looked at the wound he had made in the belly, then glanced at the stomach, separate now from its shelter within the body. 'We must put him together and sew him up,' Gurdyman murmured. 'Can you do that, Lassair?'

'I—' If you did not try new things you did not learn. Besides, I had stitched the living, and surely it must be far easier to stitch the dead. 'Yes,' I said decisively. 'Er – if you will make sure I place the stomach correctly?'

'I will indeed,' he said with a smile. 'Then we must see about getting him buried,' he added, his face falling into sombre lines.

'We do not know who he is,' I pointed out.

'No,' Gurdyman agreed. 'Although we may be able to supply an identity and a name, in due course . . .' The absent look returned to his face, but quickly he came out of his reverie. His bright blue eyes firmly on mine, he said, 'This man was killed by a sorcerer. A man or a woman of considerable skill and power sacrificed him and gave his body to the fen.'

Too shocked to speak for a moment, I tried to absorb what he had just said. I swallowed and whispered, 'How do you know? And a *sacrifice*? People don't do that any more!' Still he watched me, his expression unreadable. 'Do they?'

'In answer to your first question, I surmise that he was a sacrificial victim because of the manner of his death: poison, the cut in the blood vessel that feeds the head and the garrotte round his throat that broke his neck.' I must have looked puzzled; I certainly felt it. 'Count,' he commanded.

One, the poison. Two, the cut. Three, the garrotte. From somewhere in my memory, I recalled my Granny Cordeilla speaking of something called the Threefold Death, used for ritual sacrifice when the victim went as a willing – or not so willing – offering to the gods, either to appease, to beg a request or in humble thanks for a prayer answered. But Granny had been speaking of a custom from generations past, long ago in the history of our people . . .

Something occurred to me. 'Is this – do you believe this man was killed hundreds of years ago?' I asked. 'The peat preserves, and—'

'No, child. It would be comforting to conclude that, wouldn't it? It would be easier to believe that this body has lain undisturbed since ancient times.' Gurdyman shook his head. 'But it is not so. He was, I believe, put into the fen within the last year, and probably more recently than that. See, these woven stems are still quite fresh, and certainly not more than a twelvemonth old.' He reached out and picked up a length of the fibrous rope that had been twisted around the man's wrists and ankles.

'Honeysuckle fibres,' I murmured.

He nodded absently. Then, looking closely at the rope around the man's right ankle, he carefully extracted a short length of wood that was trapped in the loop at the far end. 'And a hazel stake,' he said.

Honeysuckle and hazel. Two of the sacred plants; hazel is full of magic and is the diviner's and the dowser's wood of choice. It has a close affinity with water. Honeysuckle – which

we also call woodbine – is a friend both to the healer and, so
Granny used to say, to the magician. Edild and I use it a lot,
to ease constriction in breathing, for problems with urination
and for labouring women. It was honoured of old in binding
charms, and Granny told me that children used to wear brace-
lets made of woven honeysuckle to bind them to their homes
and keep them from straying into danger.

I tried to put the qualities of both woods together. Something
to bind, something to carry a message down into the water. If
Gurdyman was right, this man had been staked out in the fen
and given to the water. To appease, to ask for something, to
give thanks for something given.

I stared down at the dead man. His face was peaceful; I
found myself hoping that he had not suffered. He had been
. . . *used*, was the only word I could think of. Someone – a
sorcerer, Gurdyman believed – had needed to make a sacrifice,
and this man had been his chosen victim. Why? What had
been special about him?

I looked up from the dead man and found Gurdyman still
watching me. He made a small sound of assent, murmuring,
'I see that you agree with my conclusion.'

Did I? I wasn't sure. I realized I was very cold, and I had
a vivid sense that forces far too strong for me were whirling
and circling in the small room. Before they grew too powerful
and overcame me, I had to act.

'The first thing we must do is try to find out who he was,'
I said. To my amazement, two things happened simultaneously:
the spell, if that was what it was, broke. And Gurdyman burst
out laughing.

'Well done, Lassair,' he said when he had stopped. 'You were
quite right; the magic was growing too strong, and you and I
needed to be brought back.' Had I done that? I was both
surprised and secretly pleased. 'Now, we must find the sheriff,
and then I think we shall return home and decide what to do
next.'

NINE

Gurdyman summoned one of the sheriff's men and told him we were done, and the guard instantly hurried away to fetch his master. 'You need not stay, child,' Gurdyman said softly to me. 'Go on home and wait for me there. One of us will suffice to pass on our findings.'

'You're not going to tell him about the mistletoe and the Threefold Death, are you?' Something in me was rebelling furiously at the very thought.

Gurdyman chuckled. 'Of course not. I shall say as little as I can get away with. Our sheriff,' he added, lowering his voice, 'is not a man blessed with a lively imagination, so I think that a simple account of some unknown, unidentifiable victim who died by drowning, and just happened to get caught up in a rope trailing from a passing boat, will be sufficient.'

I hoped he was right. 'Won't he notice that the body's been cut open and sewed up again?' I whispered nervously. I was, I discovered, morbidly curious about that aspect of Gurdyman's inspection. How had he known what to do? Was he even allowed to do such a thing to a corpse? I wanted to find out, but now was not the moment.

'I shouldn't think so,' Gurdyman replied. 'If he does, I'll say we found several wounds on the dead man – that we conclude were caused by being dragged through the water – and dealt with the worst of them.'

'But—'

He put a hand on my shoulder, his touch firm. 'Enough,' he said. As if he knew full well what I was burning to ask, he added softly, 'We will speak later.' He smiled at me, and I saw the bright intelligence sparkling in his eyes. I wondered what on earth I had been worrying about, for I realized then that the sheriff was no match for Gurdyman. Whatever awkward questions might be posed, my teacher would answer them as easily as if he himself had put them in the sheriff's mind.

I did as Gurdyman bade me and set off for his house. As I strode along, it suddenly occurred to me that the way our man in the fen had died was uncannily similar to the way in which poor little Herleva had met her death: both had been poisoned, both had suffered a blow to the head, both had a cut to the throat. I was well on the way to deciding that our dead man and the chatty little nun had both been sacrificial victims when I made myself stop and think about it properly, and very quickly I realized I was wrong.

The dead man had been put in the water. He had been offered to the crossing place, that strange zone that is neither land nor water but some potent amalgam of the two. Such places hold their own magic. Like dawn and twilight, like a ford over a stream, they are where two different elements meet and part. Day and night; earth and water.

I knew that Herleva's body had been found in no such place. I thought hard and brought to mind my sister's words: *she was found behind the stables*. There was nothing remotely magical about the stable block of a place like Chatteris Abbey; quite the opposite, I imagined, for surely a stable was a place of animal sounds and smells, redolent with the stench of dung, horse sweat and hard human toil. No man intent on making an offering to the powers of the dark fen would leave his victim behind an abbey's stable block.

It must, I concluded as I hurried through the shadowy alleyways to Gurdyman's house, be after all no more than a gruesome coincidence that Herleva and the man in the fen had died in the same manner. There were only so many ways of killing a person. Slitting the throat and strangulation could hardly be uncommon, and I was left with the miserable, discouraging and decidedly worrying thought that not one but two killers were on the loose.

I had not been home for long when Gurdyman arrived. I thought this probably indicated that the sheriff had accepted the shortened version of Gurdyman's findings concerning the dead man, and so it proved to be.

'What will happen now?' I asked. 'Will they bury him?'

Gurdyman shook his head. 'No, not immediately. Enquiries will be pursued around the place where the boatmen think the body became caught up with their craft, to determine if anyone answering the dead man's description has been reported missing. Nobody likes burying a man with no name,' he added softly, 'and even our sheriff seems to be no exception.'

I gathered from Gurdyman's expression that this unexpectedly decent aspect of the sheriff's character came as quite a surprise. 'They'll keep the body somewhere cool in the meantime?' I said. The weather was mild for spring, and bodies quickly begin to decompose in all but the coldest seasons. The thought of that stomach I'd held in my hands, and its steadily rotting contents, brought on a wave of nausea, but I managed to control it.

Which was just as well, because with his next breath Gurdyman remarked in amazement that it was long past noon and high time I fetched us something to eat. We do not keep much in the way of supplies in the house – Gurdyman claims he has no idea how to cook, and, beyond a basic ability, it is not in truth among my skills either – but we have the good fortune to live close to a busy market square where people bustle about every day, not just on market days, many of them from out of town. Where there are hungry people, you always find food stalls eager to relieve them of their money, and not a hundred paces from Gurdyman's front door there is a stall whose proprietor sells the tastiest pies in Cambridge.

When I got back, the delicious smell of hot gravy making my mouth water and my stomach rumble so loudly that it embarrassed me, I found that Gurdyman had opened a stone jar of cool white wine and poured out generous mugfuls for both of us. We settled in the warm, still air of Gurdyman's little interior courtyard and began our meal.

When I had taken the edge off my hunger, I put down my knife and said, 'Gurdyman, how do you come to know so much?'

I realized straight away I had phrased my question wrongly, for if my teacher were to begin telling me how he came by

all his extraordinary knowledge, we would be there all night
and all the next day too. 'I mean, today I watched you remove
a man's stomach, open it up, inspect it, then neatly put it back
inside him in exactly the right place.' I shook my head in
wonder. 'You must have more skill in your hands, more wisdom
in your head, than all the doctors in Cambridge, if not in the
whole of England!' Any of whom, I reflected, would probably
have stood over the body, mumbling about death having been
caused by an imbalance of the humours, or Mars being in an
adverse conjunction with the Moon . . .

Gurdyman finished chewing a mouthful of pie and took a
considering sip of wine, nodding his approval. Then he wiped
his lips with a clean napkin and smiled. 'Thank you for the
compliment, Lassair.' He paused, his eyes gazing out, unfocused, over the little courtyard. I sensed his thoughts were far
away, and I hoped this meant I was about to get a full and
satisfying answer to my question.

So it proved to be.

'I was born a long time before the Conquest,' Gurdyman
began, 'in a little village on the coast road between London
and Hastings. My mother was quite advanced in years, as
indeed was my father, and my birth was treated as a miracle.
As I grew and thrived, my mother wished to give thanks, and
so the three of us set off on pilgrimage to Santiago.' His eyes
flashed to me. 'Do you know where that is, child?'

'No.'

'It is on the north coast of the land called Spain, right out
in the west where the land gives way to the great sea. We
reached the place safely, my elderly parents and I, but my
mother was exhausted by the long journey and we stopped on
our way home for her to regain her strength. We put up at a
simple hostel – there are many such places along the pilgrim
routes – and, since we were poor, my father found work to
pay for our keep.'

'What did he do?' I had never heard Gurdyman speak of
his past before; I was fascinated and quite happy to wait for
a while before getting the answer to my original question.

'My father brewed ale,' he said with some pride. 'There is
always work for a man who knows his beer. Soon he had more

orders than he could manage alone, and he took on an apprentice.'

'Was that you?'

Gurdyman laughed. 'No, oh, no. I was far too busy soaking up knowledge from a local man who had spotted my hunger for it. His name was Raymond –' I noticed that a look of great love and respect softened Gurdyman's features as he spoke of this man – 'and he it was who awakened my mind. But I digress. My parents found that they were happy living in Galicia – that is the name of the land – and my mother no longer suffered from the wracking coughs that had affected her every winter back in England, so they decided to stay. As for me – oh, Lassair, what an exciting place that was to grow up! The Moors held the land to the south, but Galicia was a Christian land, and the atmosphere around me was rich with the best of both cultures. My village teacher had travelled much in the Muslim lands, and, once he had taught me as much as he could, he suggested that I, too, go south, to continue my education. Accordingly, one bright spring morning when I was almost fifteen, I said a loving farewell to my mother and father, promised faithfully to send regular letters for Raymond to read aloud to them and set off for Al-Andalus.'

His eyes had gone unfocused again, and I sensed that his mind was far away in both place and time. Out of respect for his memories – what an amazingly long and interesting life he'd had! – I let him be for a moment. Then I said, very gently, 'And that is where you learned so much about the body? From the Arabs of the south?'

'Hmm?' His blue eyes opened widely again, and he looked at me. 'Yes, yes, that's right, from the great scientists and doctors of the Muslim world.' He leaned closer, adding in a whisper, 'In matters of learning, child, they are as far in advance of Christian men as Christian men are from the sheep in their fields.' He straightened up again. 'It was my honour and my privilege that one or two of them shared their wisdom with me.'

There was so much I wanted to ask him that I did not know where to start. I opened my mouth to begin, but he held up a hand. 'Enough for now, Lassair,' he said kindly. 'I do promise you, though, that what the teachers of my youth put into here –' he tapped his head – 'I will do my utmost to pass on to you. Now, eat your food.'

We had almost finished our pies when there was a rap on the door.

I went to get up – it is among the duties of the apprentice to answer the door, and that seems to apply whether your master is a physician, a priest, a scribe or a sorcerer – but Gurdyman pressed a hand to my shoulder and pushed me back down on to the bench. 'I'll go,' he announced. 'You eat the last of your food before it gets completely cold.'

I heard his footsteps hurry away along the passage, and there was a faint squeak from the hinges as he opened the door to the street. I wondered fleetingly if someone had come from the sheriff, perhaps with a further question or two, but then I heard Gurdyman and the newcomer talking together in low voices and I knew who it was.

Knew, and in the same instant was struck with fear to the depths of my very bones, for the man was Hrype, and there was something about the particular tone in which he was speaking to Gurdyman – so quietly and urgently – that told me without a doubt he brought bad news.

I flung my pie aside and leapt up, running out into the passage and colliding with Hrype as he approached. 'What's happened?' I demanded. 'You must tell me!'

I should have thought first about my parents and the rest of my family, for Hrype lived in the same village and it was most likely that the dread tidings he brought concerned one of my close kin. But I am ashamed to say that the only person in my mind at that moment was Rollo. How on earth it could have come about that Hrype was the one who first learned of his fate, I did not stop to think.

There were tears streaming down my cheeks, and the heaving of my chest as I sobbed made further speech impossible. Hrype took me in his arms and gently stroked my back, soothing me, steadying me, all the time crooning words in an unknown tongue which, of all things, made me want to go to sleep . . .

'That's better,' he said after a while. I had the strange sensation that quite a lot of time had passed, and I came back to myself to find that I was once more sitting on the bench and Gurdyman had topped up my cup of wine. I took a big sip, swallowed it and then made myself look up at Hrype.

The question I both longed and dreaded to ask must have been clearly visible in my face. He said without preamble, 'I bring news of your sister, Elfritha. She is very sick, and it is feared that she may die. The nuns at Chatteris have been caring for her to the best of their ability, but, knowing of the fine reputation of her healer aunt, they sent word to Aelf Fen, and Edild is now in charge.'

He paused, as if to let the news sink in. For a few moments I could not think at all. A part of my mind registered the fact that no harm had befallen Rollo – none that Hrype had heard of, in any case, which did not say a lot – but before I could even pause to be glad about it, the rest of my thoughts filled with grief for my beloved sister.

She is very sick, and they fear she may die. Oh, Elfritha! First we had feared she was a murderer's victim, and now this!

Out of nowhere came a tumble of happy memories, of a lifelong companion who, only a year and four months older than me, was as different as a sibling could be. Dreamy, gentle, impractical Elfritha, patient where I was impatient, kind when I wanted to hit out, and always, through everything that we shared in our childhood, full of love for me and my staunchest supporter. The beautiful shawl she made for me became, on the day she presented it, my most treasured possession, and it still is. I missed my sister from the moment she entered the abbey, and I think of her every day of my life.

Now she was sick. She was very possibly dying. I did not know how I was going to bear it.

Gurdyman, perhaps understanding that I could not speak, asked softly, 'What ails her?'

'I do not know,' Hrype admitted.

I wondered how long it was since word was sent to the village. Oh, *oh*, she might already be dead! I raised my head, trying to put this agonizing suspicion into words, but Hrype did not need words.

He knelt down in front of me and took hold of my hands. His felt very warm, or perhaps that was because mine were icy.

'She is still alive at this moment, Lassair,' he said. His voice was firm and cool, and his eyes did not leave mine. I believed him, although I would have liked to ask him how he knew. But he was Hrype, so I didn't.

Gurdyman was busy with some task, and at first I did not perceive what he was doing. I felt slightly affronted, I think, that he could calmly be getting on with his day when we had just had such dreadful news. Then I realized: he was packing up food and drink, setting it ready with my shawl.

He came over to me and patted my hand. 'If you set out straight away, you will be at Chatteris by nightfall.' He glanced at Hrype, who gave a faint nod. 'Hrype will look after you. He is a swift and canny traveller, experienced in the fastest ways of proceeding both by the track and over the water, and nobody could guide you better.'

I looked up at Hrype and mumbled my thanks. He gave another quick nod. Then, getting to my feet, I gave Gurdyman a low bow. He reached out and took hold of my hands, raising me up again. I wanted to say so much: to apologize for hurrying away and abandoning his teaching as if I did not value it at all; to thank him for being so considerate as to make it easy for me to go; to say even that I appreciated the pack he had so swiftly prepared. Like Hrype, he could read my thoughts as if they were words on a page. He smiled, gave my hands a squeeze and murmured, 'Good luck.' Then Hrype grabbed the pack, I swept my sister's beautiful shawl around my shoulders and we were off.

It was soon after noon when we left Cambridge. There was not much traffic on the road, even less going in our direction, so to begin with we walked. We were both fresh, however, and able to keep up a good pace. My mind reached out constantly for my sister, and once or twice I thought I sensed a response. It was feeble – more like a breath in my face than an actual voice speaking in my head – but nevertheless I made myself take it as a good sign.

It might help to take my conscious thoughts off my fear, I thought, to speak of something else. Breaking quite a long silence, I said to Hrype, 'Where did you go when you left me at Chatteris in the middle of the night four days ago?'

If he was surprised at such a question out of nowhere, he did not show it. 'It was in fact near dawn when I got up to go,' he said calmly. 'I would not have abandoned you during the night hours, Lassair.' He glanced at me, the suspicion of a smile on his face. 'I left you some food and drink, did I not?'

'You did,' I conceded. I decided to keep to myself my suspicion that he'd slipped a mild sedative into the herbal brew he'd given me. It does not do, I have discovered, to push Hrype too far.

'I wanted to try to discover more about the death of the nun, for which I needed to look at the place where she was found,' he said, after a pause that had lasted so long that I was quite sure he had forgotten the question, or decided not to answer, or possibly both. 'I recalled the nun who admitted us to the abbey saying that she was looking for the kinsfolk of the dead girl, if indeed they had made the journey to Chatteris, and I also made some careful enquiries to see if I could locate them.'

'Did you?'

'No. Nobody had gone to ask about Herleva.'

It struck me as very sad, and I was sure from Hrype's tone and his expression that he felt the same. 'Perhaps they haven't yet heard,' I said.

He shrugged. 'It is possible. Or perhaps she was alone in the world.'

I did not want to dwell on that.

'I, too, have been thinking about Herleva,' I said. 'In particular, how she died.'

Then I told him about the man in the fen, and how Gurdyman had taken me with him to assist as he inspected the body. I told him how the man had been killed, and what Gurdyman had concluded, and how I'd thought it was similar to how poor little Herleva had met her end. I confessed that, just for a moment, I'd wondered if she, too, had been a sacrificial victim. 'But she wasn't,' I finished, 'because if she was, she'd have been left somewhere in the marginal places between water and land.'

Hrype was deep in thought. I wondered if he'd heard a word I had said. Then, abruptly, he barked out, 'Where do you think Herleva was found?'

'I – er, Elfritha . . .' Oh, Elfritha! 'My sister said Herleva's body was found behind the stables.' A very worrying thought struck me. 'Hrype, you just said you needed to investigate the place where Herleva died, so you must have gone back inside the abbey walls!' I stopped dead and looked up at him. 'You did, even though it was so perilous, especially without me there pretending to be your daughter! Oh, what if they'd spotted you and recognized you?' I felt a chill round my heart. 'They didn't, did they?'

He waved an impatient hand. 'No, Lassair.'

'But how else—'

'*Enough*,' he said, quite sharply. Then, perhaps recalling where we were going and why, he said more kindly, 'Listen, and I shall tell you.'

I shut my mouth and hung my head.

'You misheard what your sister said,' he said after a moment. 'As, indeed, did I. We both understood her to have said that Herleva's body was found behind the stables, which we took to mean the big stable block within the abbey where the horses and mules of visitors are cared for. So when I realized that I had to know more concerning her death, I thought I would have to go back inside the abbey, and this was, as you rightly pointed out, quite risky.'

'I could have gone with you!' I protested. 'We could have disguised ourselves just like we did that first time! Why didn't you—'

Again, he silenced me, this time by raising his hand. 'It was not necessary for either of us to return inside the abbey,' he said, 'as I discovered when I asked the right questions. Lassair, we thought that Elfritha said Herleva was found behind the stables, but she didn't. She actually said *stable*, in the singular.'

Stables? Stable? What difference could it make?

But then I understood. 'The stable where she was found isn't within the abbey walls, is it?' I whispered. 'It's somewhere else entirely.'

'It is,' he agreed. 'In fact, it is more a shed than a stable: a crude and simple little construction set in the far corner of a field some distance from the main buildings. It's a shelter for the Chatteris donkey, on the rare occasions when the sisters aren't using him to help in any one of a hundred tasks.'

I knew without being told what sort of a location this shelter was in. I said – and it was a statement, not a question – 'It's down by the water, right at the edge of the land, and sometimes in bad weather that corner of the field floods, almost up to the door of the little shed.'

Hrype looked very closely at me for a moment. Then, sounding like someone trying just too hard to speak in their normal tone, he said, 'Yes, that describes it exactly.' His curiosity overcame him, and he added in an urgent hiss, 'Can you *see* it, Lassair?'

I nodded. He appeared to think about that for some moments. Then he said, 'Herleva's body was found half under water, right on the fen edge. But for her veil, still covering her head, she was naked. Her wrists and ankles were bound to hazel stakes with ropes made of honeysuckle.'

We had been walking for some time now, and the traffic travelling north out of Cambridge was building up as the day drew on and people made for home. Presently, Hrype flagged down a plump young woman driving a cart and persuaded her to give us a ride, on the pretext that his daughter (me) was lame and we still had many miles to go. I had the presence of mind to adopt a limp as the woman's eyes swept to me to verify Hrype's words. She didn't seem to mind helping us, however, and soon she and Hrype were chatting away like old friends. He continued to amaze me; there he was, sounding like some simple peasant whose mind never dwelt on anything deeper than whether his crops would grow or his ewes produce healthy lambs. I would never have guessed he knew so much about farming . . .

I sat in silence, thinking.

The plump woman dropped us close to where the boats for Chatteris tied up, and Hrype and I waited until one would turn up to ferry us across. The wait was long.

After quite some time, I said, 'If Herleva and the man in the fen were killed by the same person—'

Hrype snorted. 'I think, don't you, that we can omit the *if*.'

'If they were murdered by the same hands,' I repeated firmly, 'then we should think about what they might have had in common. Did they, for example, know each other? Were they the last remaining members of a wealthy family who had to be removed so that someone else could inherit?'

'Herleva wasn't a wealthy heiress,' Hrype pointed out. 'She was a novice nun.'

'Yes, I know that, but perhaps she was a rich woman before she became a nun,' I said, but I had to agree, it didn't seem very likely. 'Or . . .' I had run out of possibilities.

'You are, I imagine, just speculating on a possibility, which we are to treat as a hypothesis rather than an attempt at the truth,' Hrype said, his voice kind.

I wasn't sure if I was, but I nodded anyway. 'Or perhaps they were both involved in somebody else being killed,' I went on, my imagination coming to life again, 'and it became too dangerous to let them live.'

'Hmm,' said Hrype.

'Herleva was killed just a few days ago,' I went on, 'and Gurdyman thinks the man in the fen died within the last few months. It couldn't have been any longer because the honeysuckle used to bind him was still quite fresh.'

'Hmm,' Hrype repeated.

I was thinking very hard. There was something, some relevant fact, right on the edge of my mind, and I just couldn't pin it down. I ordered my thoughts, summarizing what I knew.

Who? I asked myself. Answer: a chatty little nun and a middle-aged man.

When? One within a week or so; one within a few months.

Where? One on the island of Chatteris, over on the western side of the fens; one over on the eastern side, in the maze of channels that wind through the marshes to the north of Aelf Fen and up towards Lynn and, eventually, the sea.

Then I knew what it was that had been niggling at me, trying to catch my attention.

'Hrype?' I said softly.

He turned to look down at me, his strange silvery eyes catching the gleam of the slowly falling sun. 'Yes?'

'I think there *is* a connection between them.' I was speaking too quickly, breathless in my excitement, and I made myself slow down. 'The dead man was found in the water over towards the fens' eastern margin, above where the two rivers flow down from the higher ground and below Lynn,' I said.

'What of it?' He spoke quite sharply, but there was a faint smile on his face. He knew already, I was sure, what I was going to say; it would not have surprised me if he did, for he is adept at reading other people's thoughts, and what was on my mind just then must have been shouting out at him.

'Herleva came from over that way,' I said, despite everything smiling back at him. 'I spoke to an old Chatteris woman who sells cheese to the nuns. She told me Herleva was from up beyond Lynn. She and the dead man might have known each other!'

'And they might not,' I thought I heard him mutter. He took my hand and patted it. 'That's a start, I suppose,' he said kindly. He could have added, *even if it's not much*, but he didn't.

We went on standing there. In time, we saw a boat approaching, and the ferryman agreed to take us across. I sat down in the stern, wrapping my shawl tightly round me against the chill air rising off the water.

My brief excitement had leaked out of me, and now I felt even lower than before. Hrype was right to be dismissive; so what if Herleva's home was roughly in the same area as the place where the man in the fen had died? It really didn't amount to very much and barely qualified for Hrype's *it's a start*.

And there was so much more I had to worry about. There we were, moving steadily across the misty water, and my poor sister lay deadly sick on the other side. Was she still alive? Again, I sent a tentative thought in her direction, and this time

I received no reply at all. I buried my face in my shawl; I did not want Hrype to see my tears.

There was Rollo, too. I no longer heard his summoning voice in my dreams, and in my waking mind I knew, with no room for doubt, that something had happened to him. He had called to me for help, and I had failed him. Now he was gone: out of my head, out of my life, out, perhaps, of this world.

The sky was darkening as the sun finally set. All around the little boat, the water was dark and sinister, no glimmer of light on its black depths. Despair took hold of me, and for a dreadful moment I was tempted to give up on the horrible struggle of my life and throw myself into the fen's cold embrace.

Then there was a gentle bump as the boat came alongside the little quay. The ferryman jumped out to make his craft secure, and Hrype climbed ashore after him. He turned back to me.

He said, so softly that I hardly heard him, 'Nobody is dead yet, Lassair.' And he held out his hand.

If he was telling me my dearest sister was still alive, that was, of course, something to rejoice over, although if she was as sick as we had been told, life could turn to death in the blink of an eye.

He could not be speaking of Rollo. He didn't know Rollo was in danger; nobody did except Gurdyman and me, and I was all but sure now that the danger, whatever it was, had overcome him.

I thought about it for a couple of heartbeats. Go on? Give up? Then I took Hrype's hand, jumped out of the boat and on to the Chatteris quay.

TEN

Rollo was attacked when he was in sight of the great sea that lies off the east coast of Britain. He had made his way steadily and swiftly, usually keeping the Wall in sight over to his left. As well as providing a clear aid to going in the right direction – due east towards the coast – he had discovered that what tracks and roads there were in that lonely and largely deserted country were better maintained near to the Wall.

They laid an ambush for him. The sun was setting in the west behind him, for he had been encouraged by the sea's proximity into travelling on later than usual. Darkness was rapidly descending. He was approaching a place where the road ran down into a shallow valley, on each side of which were stands of ancient trees. Up there in the north country, spring was late in coming and the trees were only just showing the first signs of leaf. Rollo would not have thought that the stark trunks and all but bare branches could have provided places of concealment for even one man, let alone four.

It was his horse who first sensed danger. Named as she was for an entity with supernatural powers, perhaps elements of a particularly keen awareness had rubbed off on the mare. As she bore Rollo down into the valley, she must have heard, seen or even smelt something which, wise horse that she was, she knew ought not to be there.

She had been going along at a smart trot, affected by her master's mood and as keen as he to reach the coast and turn south. Suddenly, she stopped, so abruptly that Rollo was almost unseated.

'Strega?' he said softly. 'What's the matter?'

The horse, of course, could not answer. She gave a soft whicker, and a shudder ran under the skin of her shoulder. A variety of possibilities ran like fire through Rollo's mind: was she exhausted? Had she picked up a stone in her foot? Was she throwing up lame?

He was about to dismount and check her over when at last, and far too late, he finally took in the topography of the place where Strega had so abruptly stopped. His heart pounding, he looked on down the road and saw the stands of skeletal trees on either side. Somebody made a small movement just as he was staring at the trees on his right.

He pressed his heels into the mare's sides and said to her urgently, 'On, Strega, on!' Still she hesitated. He leaned forward on to her neck and said, as close to her ear as he could, 'Yes, I know, I've seen them. Now *go!*'

She needed no further urging. Just as abruptly as she had stopped, she started to move again, her sturdy strength taking her from standing to a full gallop in moments. Her speed took the ambushers by surprise, and it was only when they had been flying down the track for some moments that Rollo heard the whoops and yells of the men who had lain in wait as they left their hiding places and raced after him.

He knew quite soon that two were no threat, for they were mounted on old, broken ponies whose laboured breathing was audible across the rapidly increasing distance between them and Rollo. Soon his swift glances over both shoulders told him that it was now between him and the two remaining men.

He knew what he would have done in their position. The track went on through the valley in a wide curve to the right, and the shortest distance to the far end was to cut across the curve. While the land inside the curve did not look secure enough for Rollo to risk it – what would happen if he floundered in a patch of boggy ground or if Strega failed to clear the fast-flowing stream that rushed through the valley? – he would, had he been one of the pursuing pair, have taken that chance and hastened to cut his quarry off as he hurried along the road.

He heard a shouted conversation between the two men, although they spoke in a language he did not understand. He was pretty sure what they were saying, however, and very shortly afterwards, he saw with dismay that his assumption was right. One man remained right behind him; his horse was perhaps not quite as swift as Strega, but it was close. The second man cracked his fist down hard on his horse's rump, yelled something in a high, wild voice and, with a fierce tug on the reins that had his horse jerking its head in pain, plunged down off the track and across the green grass of the valley.

Rollo's years of experience had taught him not to waste time worrying about things that might not happen. The second man was now some distance away, and Rollo would deal with him when the time came. For now, the man behind him was alone.

Rollo pulled Strega up, drew his sword and spun round. The man had less secure a control of his mount, and it seemed, in addition, that Rollo's unexpected move had taken him unawares. Leaning back in the saddle in what appeared to be a hopeless attempt to slow his horse's pace, he kept on riding, straight at Rollo, a long, wickedly pointed knife in one hand and a shorter stabbing knife between his teeth. His dark eyes blazed with blood lust; he was going in for the kill.

As the man drew level, Rollo nudged Strega with his knee to make her step aside. There was little need even to swing his sword – he could simply have held it out – but he swung it anyway.

The man's head was sliced from his shoulders, and it bounced away across the springy turf. The body remained upright in the saddle for some ten or twelve paces, and then the horse – perhaps aware of a sudden lack of control, perhaps simply alarmed at the smell of blood – abruptly swerved, gave a couple of bucks and threw the headless body to the ground. Then it gave a shrill whinny and, turning, galloped away, back along the track towards the last of the sunlight.

Rollo gathered Strega's reins, spoke some quiet words to her and then urged her on down the track. He could hear shouts and blood-curdling yells from the two men behind him – much closer now – and Strega needed no spurred heels to tell her she had to hurry. Rollo made himself concentrate on the ambusher who was attempting to head him off, realizing with a feeling of sick dread that the man was well over halfway across the valley and going fast.

It was going to be a race.

Rollo had the advantage of firm ground, but his pursuer had a lot less further to go. Rollo went through the options that would be open to him when the two of them came face to face. None was very attractive. None gave him better than fifty-fifty odds.

As he and Strega flew down the track, he was already calculating. He must get to the interception point first, for then, even if he did not have time to evade his pursuer, at least it would be he who selected the staging of the fight between them. He watched the other man, and it seemed to Rollo that his opponent's lead was slowly being eroded.

Had he hit wet ground? Was that bright green grass not as firm beneath his horse's hooves as he had hoped?

The man and his horse were approaching the stream that hurried through the valley. The track remained on higher ground and avoided it, but anyone cutting across the valley would have to ford it, wade through it or jump over it at some point. Rollo watched as the man looked frantically to his right and his left, trying to decide where best to cross.

From the vantage point of the higher ground, Rollo could have advised him. The obvious place was a stretch of water that looked shallow, for it was broken up by what appeared to be stones and boulders on the stream bed. To someone on the same level, it probably looked like a man-made ford.

Rollo could see that it was not; the obvious place was the one spot to avoid.

He couldn't be sure, but his guess was that it was deep water. What looked at first glance to be stones set in the shallows were the tips of rocks, perhaps the height of a man or more, for the water there was dark, deep and fast-running.

The man appeared to make up his mind. Expecting a firm-bottomed ford where the water would reach his horse's hocks at most, he spurred his mount on and raced for the stream. The horse tried to swerve, to slow down, to turn away from the danger it could see, but the man drove it on relentlessly, using spurred heels, whip and fists. The horse crashed into the deep water, gave a scream of fear and was swept over on its side and washed away downstream, taking the man with it.

Rollo heard more shouts and cries of dismay from behind

him. He risked a quick look and saw that one of the remaining pair was kneeling over the headless body – he appeared to be retching – while the other was setting off recklessly fast across the valley in pursuit of his drowning comrade. Rollo nudged Strega with his heels, and she took off.

It was not until much later that Rollo gave any real thought as to who his attackers had been. He and Strega had gone as hard and as fast as they could for the coast, only making the briefest of stops. The mare seemed as eager to press on as he was, and she pushed herself to the limits.

They rode down towards the great port at the mouth of the Tyne long after darkness had fallen. They were both exhausted, and Strega was soaked in sweat. Rollo knew it was no use trying to get into the town, for curfew would have sealed it long ago. He did not want to advertise his presence by banging on the town gates, alerting the watchman and demanding entry.

There was a sort of temporary camp beside the road leading into the port, where others who had also arrived after curfew huddled against the wooden walls waiting for dawn. There were rough shelters to keep off the wet, and a surly-looking man was doing brisk business selling hay and straw. Rollo found a place out of the keen wind that was blowing in off the sea and, dismounting, swung his packs off his horse's back and set about tending to her. She was still sweating, and he had to spend some time rubbing her down with handfuls of straw, speaking soothingly to her as he did so, before she would settle.

When he was satisfied that he had done the best he could for her, he tethered her, sat down close beside her and wrapped himself in his cloak and blanket. He took some food out of his pack, washing it down with water. He was almost at the end of his supplies.

Who were they? The question sprang at him as soon as he had swallowed his last mouthful. Were they opportunist thieves who habitually haunted that stretch of the track, waiting to pounce on solitary travellers and rob them? It was possible, even likely.

But Rollo didn't believe it. The men who had lain in wait

for him had been out to kill him. He knew it as well as he
knew his own name. The man he had beheaded had almost
succeeded, and he would have done so had Rollo not been
mounted on such an intelligent horse. He reached out a hand
and touched Strega's leg, and she gave a gentle whicker in
reply, stretching down her head and putting her soft lips to
his ear, blowing gently.

Why would a quartet of men lie in wait for him and try to
kill him? The answer was obvious. Rollo pictured the faces
of the four men slowly and carefully, one by one, and it seemed
to him that the features of at least one of them, if not two,
were familiar. He had seen both men – or he was almost sure
he had – at Hawksclaw's stronghold.

Weary, he lay down and turned on his side, trying to get
comfortable on the cold, hard ground. Maybe he was wrong
– it was quite possible, he thought with sudden bitterness, that
the wild men of the border lands were inbred and all resembled
one another. Nevertheless, there had been four of them waiting
for him, and, although one was definitely dead and a second
probably drowned, that left two. Two men, who clearly wanted
him dead. Whether or not they were out to avenge Hawksclaw
was not really relevant.

In the morning, he told himself as he gave in to his fatigue
and allowed himself to drop towards sleep, *my horse and I
will get away from here, as fast as we can.*

He was up and away as dawn broke. He did not venture within
the town's walls, for the fewer people who might see him and
remember his face, the better. He knew he must send word to
the king as soon as possible regarding the mission in Carlisle,
but he still felt threatened by his pursuers. He knew a good
man – very discreet, very efficient – who could normally be
found in a small port at the mouth of the Tees river. He would
seek him out and entrust the message to him.

He followed the track around the settlement, then at last,
with infinite relief, he hit the coast and turned south.

Something made him stop and turn around. Behind the town,
inland where the ground rose up towards the moor and the
desolate heathland, somebody was watching him. The figure

was some way away, and alone. As he watched, it raised an arm and pointed straight at him.

He knew who it was, and also that it was probably a woman. He had seen several of her kind in the border country. The locals called them witches and feared them deeply. They were nothing like the witches of Rollo's birth country; they were pure evil. He had come across a trio of them in a little dell close to the Wall. They were all grey-haired, wrinkled, dressed in ragged remnants and wild-looking; one of them had a huge wart on her cheek. They were huddled, muttering, around an ancient black cauldron set on a hearth, from which issued a steam so foul-smelling that, even at a distance of some twenty paces, the fumes made him retch and brought tears to his eyes. He had hurried away. He knew they had seen him, but he did not fear pursuit, since he was mounted and they were not. Unless, of course, the rumours were true and they could fly.

Those three had had no reason to wish him harm. They could not have known who he was, and he had done them no wrong. But that was before he had killed Hawksclaw and two of the brigand's men sent to ambush him. Now he had blood on his hands. Was either Hawksclaw or one of the other dead men under the protection of some powerful crone with malice in her heart? Was she even now standing up there where the hills ended, sending down her furious curse to land on him like some evil black crow, dogging his footsteps until finally he ran out of strength and succumbed?

He realized he was sitting stock-still on Strega's back, eyes fixed on the figure on the hillside. With a huge effort he made himself look away, and immediately the sense of dread diminished. It was as if he had been standing under a lowering, chilling cloud, which had suddenly moved away to allow the blessed heat of the sun to reach him.

He knew he should instantly ride on, as fast as he could, and put some distance between himself and that sinister figure. But the temptation was too strong. Turning to face her once more, he yelled as loudly as he could, 'I do not fear you! You have no power over me!'

It might have been his imagination, but as he hastened away

down the road, he thought he heard a scream of fury come flying after him.

Once the sun had fully risen and the bright daylight had banished the shadows, he stopped at a decent-looking inn beside the road. He dismounted and led Strega under a low arch into the yard, where he paid a lad handsomely to rub her down, feed and water her and then groom her. He also told the lad to do what he could with the saddle and bridle, which needed a good wash. Then he went inside the inn and ordered the largest breakfast the innkeeper could provide. While it was being prepared, he paid for hot water and towels and set about cleaning himself up.

He shaved, untangled his darkened hair, hacked most of it off with his knife and, liberally using the coarse lye soap, washed it several times, restoring its natural fair colour. He washed his body next, thoroughly ridding himself of lice, and he bundled up the old garments he had been wearing and gave them to the innkeeper to burn. He dressed in clean linen – and what a luxury it was – and a tunic of fine wool, from which he had managed to get out most of the creases by hanging it up in the steam from the lavish hot water in which he was bathing. His good cloak, unrolled from his pack, lay ready on the bench beside him. He had even cleaned the layers of mud from his boots, and the chestnut-coloured leather shone again.

When he sat down to his meal, he suspected he was barely recognizable from the filthy creature who had first walked in. The food was plain but abundant, and by the time he was ready to leave the inn, he felt like a new man.

As he rode the long route south, he tried not to dwell on those he had left behind who sought revenge. He did not allow himself to believe the danger was past: it was not and probably would never be. People had long memories, and, as he had once heard the king say, there was nothing else to do in the border country except pursue blood feuds and plan the next bout of rape, pillage and murder.

He told himself that he had increased his chances by

changing his appearance and by keeping off the best-known and most commonly used tracks. Sometimes he barely saw a soul all day. It was lonely – he longed for company, even that of some fellow traveller with whom he had nothing at all in common – but the loneliness kept him safe.

Or so he hoped.

At length he came to the wide estuary of the Humber river. He and the mare were both exhausted. They had travelled perhaps a hundred and fifty miles since turning south, and the cold winter they had left behind in the country around the Wall had turned into a mild spring. They had covered at least five miles every day, and sometimes, when the roads were flat and straight, as much as thirty. Now both of them needed a rest. Rollo, in addition, needed some time in which to think about the next phase of his mission. Its appeal had lessened with each day and every mile that had taken him closer to it, but he knew there was no avoiding it. In his heart he knew that he feared what he had to do. He did not like feeling afraid.

He had been born into a family of tough fighters: men who had gone to the hot southern lands to carve out a kingdom for themselves. His father was a Norman knight, and his mother was equally fierce and fiery. From a young age, Rollo had been taught that the way to deal with fear was to stare it in the eye and shame it into submission. He wondered, with a wry private smile, just how well that advice was going to stand up as he set about carrying out the alarming and strange task his king had entrusted to him.

He found a place to stay – an inn in a small village a few miles inland, on the northern shore of the estuary – and made his plans. He needed more information, and he needed to find the right people to ask. He knew what sort of people they would be and where to find them. He thought as far ahead as he could – as he dared – and then he gave in to his fatigue and went to bed, where in warmth, comfort and peace, he slept dreamlessly from mid-afternoon of one day to mid-morning of the next. Then he rose, bathed, ate, settled his account with the innkeeper and went to fetch Strega from the stables. She was as well rested and restored as he was, and together they set off on the last and most perilous leg of their long journey.

The rumour that had so concerned the king spoke of a specific location, although it had not been given a name. Its description, the king had hoped, would be enough to identify it, once Rollo was in the vicinity. The location was on the coast and, now that Rollo had reached the right area, he made the decision to proceed by water. He found a long quayside on the river's north shore, where ships of varying sizes were tied up. Others were arriving and departing and, as far as the eye could see, traders were busy. Rollo approached the captains of several vessels and eventually found one who was going in the direction Rollo wanted and was willing to take a paying passenger and his horse. The captain spat in his hand and the two of them shook on the deal, then coins changed hands and Rollo and his horse went aboard.

The ship sailed on the evening tide. She was a coastal vessel, not all that big, and usually plied along the east coast from the Humber to the Thames. Her crew were mainly old hands who had served with their captain for years. They knew their profession well and, to Rollo's relief, most of them seemed willing to enliven the monotony of their daily life by chatting to a stranger.

On the morning of the first day out, as the ship commenced her voyage around the wide bulge of Lincolnshire, Rollo got into conversation with the mate and the lad who, as his shadow, was learning his job. The two were uncle and nephew, alone in the world except for each other. The lad's parents – the mate's late sister and her husband – had died with the rest of her family and most of her village in the floods of the previous autumn. Rollo would not have pressed them to speak of such a recent tragedy, but both man and boy seemed willing, even eager, to do so. Perhaps, he mused, they were trying to get the grief out of their minds by talking about it.

'You've never seen seas like it,' said the mate, eyes full of horror as he thought back. 'The wind came howling down out of the north like some furious ice demon, and the waves rose up like – like – well, higher than the highest tree.'

Any man other than one from East Anglia, Rollo reflected, would have said *higher than a mountain*, but there weren't any mountains in the fenland.

'The tides were real high and all,' put in the lad, 'and what with the hurricane blowing and the sea pushing up with the swell of the tide, the water didn't have anywhere else to go, so it flooded over the low-lying land.'

'A storm surge,' Rollo remarked. He had heard tell of such phenomena, although he had never experienced one himself.

'We have funny old storms hereabouts,' the mate went on with the voice of long experience, 'and sometimes you'll think they're heading off out to sea and you can stop worrying about them, and then they have a change of heart and back they come and hit the land again.' He shook his head. 'There's no accounting for it,' he muttered, 'unless it's magic.' Both he and the lad made a surreptitious gesture with their right hands. Rollo thought he recognized the sign against the evil eye.

'You get fogs and all,' the lad piped up. 'Real strange, they are, floating up out of nowhere like great white phantoms and then vanishing as quick as they came.'

'Are there many shipwrecks?' Rollo asked. He was pushing his luck, he knew, for sailors were a superstitious bunch, and he thought he could well be castigated for asking such a question when actually at sea.

The mate and his nephew exchanged a glance. Then the mate leaned closer to Rollo and, dropping his voice, said, 'There's sandbanks, see, and they shift around like living things.' He gave a visible shudder. 'Round the edges of the Wash, you just never know from one trip to the next where you're going to find water deep enough for your boat's draft and where you're in for a nasty surprise because some stray wind, tide or current has piled up a mess of silt that wasn't there before.' He paused, nodding and slyly touching a forefinger to the side of his nose. 'There's captains I could mention who have come to grief because they didn't allow for a sudden change in depth,' he said softly. 'Add a stiff wind to the picture, and before you know it, you're blown on to a sandbank, your boat's tipping over, your cargo is ruined and you're like as not drowned, because out there –' he waved a vague hand – 'there's places where you think you're on firm ground and then you realize too late that you're sinking fast and you're trapped in the quicksand. Why, only last—'

'*Uncle!*' hissed the lad, making the sign against evil frantically with both hands. Even the mate seemed to realize he had gone too far.

With an attempt at a smile that convinced neither Rollo nor, apparently, his anxious nephew, the mate said, 'Course, nothing like that's going to happen on this ship!' Then he grabbed the lad by the collar, nodded a curt farewell to Rollo and hurried away towards the stern of the ship, where the two of them disappeared down a steep ladder to the quarters below.

What had the mate been about to say? Rollo wondered. He had an unpleasant suspicion that he knew. If so, it would mean that he had come to the right place . . .

He thought back to what the king had said. It had been sufficiently alarming back then, miles and miles away from the place where the terrible events were rumoured to have happened. Now, when Rollo was in the very vicinity, what the king's words suggested was utterly terrifying. If, that was, the rumours were true.

As he gazed out across the deceptively calm waters that he had just been told could so quickly and so devastatingly change, Rollo was all but sure that they were.

The little ship sailed on through the night and all of the next day. They put in at Skirbeck that evening. The weather was fine, warm and sunny with only a very light breeze blowing, and Rollo wondered why the captain had not opted to sail on across the mouth of the Wash. He did not ask – he did not want to draw undue attention to himself – and, as was his wont, he sat back in the shadows, made himself as unobtrusive as he could and listened to the sailors' talk. They were uneasy, that became immediately apparent; to a man, they seemed to fear the next day's voyage. They were muttering in low voices, as if they did not want to be overheard, and after a while one of them happened to glance up and notice Rollo, wrapped in his cloak and hunched up in the bows.

'Course, this time tomorrow we'll be well past the headland

and safely on our way,' the sailor said loudly, the forced cheerfulness evident in his tone. 'Where d'you reckon we'll be, master mate? Round the bump of Norfolk and heading south, do you think?'

The mate mumbled something in reply, and Rollo thought he was trying to hush the first speaker.

'Well, it's all the same to me,' the man said. 'Still, reckon we'll all be saying our prayers when we pass by, eh?'

Now several voices joined in to stop him saying any more. There was a brief scuffle and a sudden shout of pain, quickly suppressed. The mate turned to Rollo, and just for a moment, before he managed to control himself, Rollo saw stark fear in his face.

'Don't you worry,' the mate said. 'We'll see you right. Dropping you at Hunstanton, aren't we? Well, if we make a good, early start in the morning, you'll have your feet on dry land in good time for the midday meal.'

Rollo hoped that it was only in his imagination that the mate added under his breath, 'God willing.'

The next day, they set sail soon after dawn on a bright morning with clear skies and a warm breeze off the land which helped their speed as they crossed the mouth of the Wash.

By Rollo's guess, they were somewhere around halfway between the land behind them and the land ahead when the weather broke. He was in the boat's stern, looking out at the coastline far behind, when, with shocking suddenness, he couldn't see it any more. In only a few heartbeats he could make out nothing at all: they had sailed into a bank of fog so dense that it was like being inside a cloud. He heard the captain yelling commands and, unfamiliar with the nautical terms, Rollo watched anxiously to see what the crew would do. As far as he could tell, they did nothing except take in some sail to slow their speed, although in truth the little vessel had not been travelling all that fast. It made sense, he realized. If you couldn't see anything, the safest bet was to maintain exactly the same course and pray that any other vessels in the vicinity did the same. That way, if you hadn't been on a collision course before the fog, you would not have inadvertently moved on to one.

The little boat drifted on. The breeze had all but died, and above his head Rollo could hear the slap of slack canvas as the sails hung useless. Then suddenly he heard a horrible cacophony of noises: a crash, as if two immense sections of timber were forced together; the terrified whinnying of horses; an unearthly sound of vast, racing waters, as if all the seas of the world had gathered together and were sluicing down on them; the howl of a wind so fierce that he ought to have been blown off his feet and into the broiling sea; the screams of men about to die.

He shot out his hands to grasp the rail, desperate to steady himself, to cling on to something. Then he realized – and this was the greatest shock of all – that there was no wind blowing. No huge mass of water gathering up to fall on him. No screaming men and horses, no colliding ships.

He crouched there trembling with fear.

Around him the sailors also stood as still as if they had all been petrified. Then the captain called out, 'Clear air ahead!', the boat moved silently back out into the sunshine and the enchantment went away.

Rollo watched closely and saw several of the crew exchange nervous glances. Almost all of them held their right hands in the gesture against evil, and many fingered the crosses and other symbols they wore around their necks.

Nobody, however, said a word. Whatever it was out there that they all feared so much, they were not prepared to talk about it.

As the mate had predicted, Rollo was dropped off in Hunstanton around midday. He led Strega down the gangplank – mercifully short – and stood, far more relieved than he was prepared to admit, even to himself, on the firm stones of the little quay. He watched as the little boat set sail again, silently bidding her crew farewell and wishing them safe landfall. When the vessel was out of sight, he mounted and rode away.

The little port was busy, its narrow streets crowded with merchants and townspeople going about their daily rounds. Rollo found a tavern in the town centre, left Strega with a groom's lad and went inside to find something to eat. The tap room was humming, and, after a mug or two of ale, men were, as they always are, more than willing to talk to a stranger.

Rollo mentioned to a huge man with bare brawny arms and a scarred leather jerkin that he had recently made the crossing from Skirbeck and encountered a bank of fog.

The man looked at him with a smile. 'You're lucky to be here, then,' he remarked. 'Them's dangerous waters.'

'So I've been told,' Rollo agreed.

The big man leaned closer, and Rollo smelt beer on him. He'd obviously been in the tap room for some time. 'It's the old stamping ground of the sea witch, see,' he said in a low voice.

'The sea witch?'

'Aye,' the man said. 'She was there long before we were all born, and she'll be there long after we're dead. She's always been there, or so they say.' He frowned, took a long gulp of beer and belched quietly.

An ancient myth, Rollo thought, kept alive by the superstition of people who lived close to the sea and were dependent on it for their livelihoods. 'She's very powerful, this sea witch,' he observed. 'She blew up a fog so sudden that even our captain didn't see it coming.'

'Aye, the sea frets are a speciality of hers,' the big man concurred. 'They say she likes to hide herself inside them, so men can't see what she's up to. Me, I reckon she's no need of hiding places. She's far too powerful for that.'

'What else does she do?' Rollo asked.

'She lures ships on to the sandbanks, that's what she does,' the man whispered hoarsely. 'Or she sends a tempest down out of the north and blasts them on to the cliffs, hurling good men into the water so their drowned bodies wash on to our shores for the gulls to pick out their eyes and clean the flesh off their bones.' He was breathless, a sheen of sweat on his broad face, and Rollo could feel his deep dread.

I must keep him talking, Rollo thought. He sensed he had come to the right place, and he needed to know more. 'The crew of the boat I sailed on were very nervous,' he said tentatively. 'Has there – has the sea witch been particularly active of late?'

He had gone too far, and he realized it as soon as the words were out of his mouth. The big man slammed his mug down on the table and turned to glare at him. 'What do you want to know that for?' he demanded. 'What are you, some sort of ghoul come to gloat over the bodies of the dead?'

'No, of course not, I—' Rollo began.

The man did not let him finish. 'If you want a close encounter with her, you go and look for her,' he said in a vicious hiss. 'Go on up the coast to the north and call her.' Abruptly, he laughed, a cruel, harsh sound. 'You won't need to find her, my lad. *She'll* find *you!*'

Some of the other drinkers had glanced up at the big man's loud voice and were looking over in Rollo's direction. It was time to go. He shook out some coins to pay for his food and beer, then quietly made his exit.

Up the coast to the north, the big man had said. The day was sunny, and visibility was good, with no sign of any more fog. Rollo fetched Strega and, ignoring the fear and apprehension that growled deep inside him, set off along the coastal track.

Soon he had left all signs of human habitation far behind. The sea to his left glittered silver in the sunshine, and in the distance he could make out the sound of small waves flopping down on to the shore. He looked out over the land between him and the water, which, as he rode steadily north, changed from a line of low, honey-coloured cliffs into a steadily widening band of salt marsh. With a shudder, he remembered what the mate had said about quicksand.

After some time the path curved round to the right. Rollo realized that he had reached the northernmost tip of the land and was now going eastwards. He drew rein and looked around him. As far as he could see, there was not a soul about. The wide sands extended on ahead of him until, at a point he could barely make out, the land gave way to water and the sea began.

He did not like to admit it, but he was afraid.

He had come this far, he told himself. He had no choice but to go on. He was on a mission from the king, and he could not return to him until he had fulfilled it.

He turned Strega's head towards the sea and set out across the uncertain ground.

To begin with, the going was quite good. He appeared to be following a well-used track, which had a gravelled surface and was elevated slightly above the surrounding marsh. Strega was nervous – he could tell by the slight sheen of sweat on her coat and the occasional shudder in her flesh – but her head was up and her ears pricked forward. He was thankful all over again for her sturdy courage.

He peered ahead, trying to make out where the sea began. He was in a strange place, half land, half water. The light, too, was weird; sometimes the sun shone down clearly, and sometimes it was as if its light was reaching him through a fine mist, or a veil. He did not let himself dwell on that.

After some time he glanced over his shoulder. He was horrified to see how far he had come out across the endless shore. The line of the higher ground was far, far behind.

He turned back to face the sea. *Go on*, he commanded himself. *Go on, discover what lies out there, and then you can return to safety.*

He put his heels to Strega's sides, and she moved on reluctantly.

They went on for some time. The path had deteriorated, and now he had to think about every step the mare took. She, too, was worried; there was a tentative feel to her paces.

They came to a place where she stopped and would not go on. Rollo had been staring ahead, straining his eyes against the powerful light and trying to make out what was ahead. Now he looked down at the ground and was horrified at what he saw.

They were no longer on a path of any sort – at least, not one that he could make out. The horse's feet were embedded in the salty, sandy mud. As he watched, the mud crept a finger's breadth higher up her trembling legs.

He was suddenly aware of the sound of water. A slow, steady rushing filled his ears, and now he had noticed it, it was all he could hear.

Unless, carried on the gentle breeze, there was the sound of someone quietly laughing . . .

He raised his head and looked out at the water. He stared, blinked a couple of times and stared again.

There could be no doubt about it.

The tide was coming in.

ELEVEN

My heart sank lower and lower as Hrype and I climbed the gentle slope up from the quayside at Chatteris to the abbey. I felt like lying down and howling, but that would not have done anyone any good. There was, however, a chance that if I managed to pull myself together, I might, as an apprentice healer, be able to help in the care of my sister.

I pulled myself together.

Something occurred to me which, had I not been so self-pityingly miserable, I might have thought to ask before. 'Hrype?' I said.

He looked at me kindly. 'What is it, Lassair?'

'How did you know that Elfritha was ill? Did someone from the abbey come to the village?'

'Yes. They were directed to your parents' house, and your mother very sensibly sent them on to Edild. Your mother is praying, every minute she can spare,' he added gently, 'but she knew full well that if someone was to be spared by Lord Gilbert to come and care for your sister, it had far better be Edild.'

I nodded. I could picture my poor mother, torn between the sense of asking Edild to go, and the longing of her heart to run to her sick daughter there and then.

'And Edild told you, so you came here too,' I said.

There was a slight pause.

'She did,' Hrype said eventually, 'although not in quite the sense that you mean.'

'But—' I began, at first unable to understand in what other sense my words could be taken. I looked at him, and the expression in his strange eyes was enigmatic.

I understood. 'You weren't in Aelf Fen when the messenger came from the nuns, were you?' I whispered.

He shook his head, a faint, private smile hovering on his lips. 'No.'

'Where were you?'

'I was – a long way away.'

'Then how did you know?'

His eyes met mine. 'I heard her.' He pointed to his head. 'In here.' Now his hand moved to hover over his heart. 'And, more imperatively, in here.'

Yes. Hrype and my aunt loved each other, but probably only three people in the world were in on the secret, and I certainly wasn't going to tell anyone. As far as everyone else was aware, Hrype shared his home with his late brother's widow and her son. Only five people knew that Sibert was actually Hrype's son, the fourth and fifth being Edild and Sibert himself. He had only found out a year and a half ago, and, no matter how I hinted, he would never speak to me concerning his feelings about this devastating revelation.

Sibert's mother Froya would not survive without Hrype, and all the village understood that. She had never got over the traumatic events of her past, and she depended on her brother-in-law for just about everything. They had been lovers just once, when both were in despair, and Sibert had been the result.

All the time Froya was alive, Hrype was bound by everything he held sacred to honour his responsibilities towards her. He might dream of leaving her to go and live with Edild, where his heart undoubtedly had already preceded him, but he would never do so.

It had been my privilege to witness Edild and Hrype together on a few occasions when they were away from the ever-open eyes of the Aelf Fen villagers. It was both a joy and an ache to watch them.

Yes. It came as no surprise to me now to learn that some mystical communication between them had allowed Edild to summon him when her need for him was suddenly so great. When word had come from Chatteris that Elfritha was very sick and perhaps dying, the sudden pressure on Edild to hurry

away to the abbey and try to save her, bearing all the hopes
and anxieties of my parents and my siblings, must have been
vast. No wonder she had silently cried out for the man she
loved.

He was still watching me, a slightly quizzical look on his
handsome face that bore the dignity of ancient kings. He was,
I realized, checking to see if I had understood. I gave him a
quick smile and nodded – just at that moment, I could find
nothing to say – and he murmured, 'Good.' Then he braced
his shoulders and strode on up the long rise to the abbey.

When we were still some distance away and out of sight of
anyone watching from the settlement or the abbey, we paused,
stepped off the road into a small copse of willow trees and
resumed our old man and daughter guises. It was Hrype's
idea – I had, in truth, been far too preoccupied with thoughts
of my sister to think about the dangers that might or might
not be posed by a fanatical priest to a cunning man and an
apprentice healer, but Hrype was clearly taking no chances.
When we were ready, he looked me over with critical eyes
and then gave a curt nod.

We went on, at a much slower, more painful gait, Hrype
bowed over and shuffling as if every step hurt, to the abbey.
There were a few people moving around in the forecourt, and
I looked out for my cheese-seller woman. She did not seem
to be there. Hrype was at the gates and already knocking with
his staff.

After a few moments the small side gate opened an inch or
two, and a nun looked out. It was not the big, hatchet-faced
woman who had admitted us before. This one was thin and
pale and looked harassed. 'Yes?' she said impatiently.

Hrype nudged me. 'We're friends of the novice Elfritha,
who we're told is very sick,' I said, my voice shaking despite
my efforts to control it. Now that we were there at the abbey,
my anxiety was pressing on me so hard that it was all I could
do not to throw myself on the ground and start wailing.

On hearing my sister's name, a transformation came over
the sharp-featured face of the nun. Her eyes softened, and she
reached out and took my hand. 'Come in,' she said, opening

the gate more widely and ushering us through. 'I will take you to her straight away.'

'Is she – she's not—?' I could not get the question out.

The nun was still holding my hand, and now she gave it a squeeze. 'She still lives,' she said. 'We are praying for her every hour, and our infirmary nuns are doing what they can to help the healer who has come to tend her. She is from Elfritha's village, so you probably know her.'

I did not know whether or not to say that Edild was my aunt. I sent out a silent question to Hrype, but received no answer. I decided to keep silent. My instinct was to trust this kind nun, but, on the other hand, Hrype and I had just taken some precious time to disguise ourselves, and if we revealed our true identities, our efforts would have been for nothing.

The nun had been hurrying us along, and we had now reached a long, low building across the cloister from the big church. The nun opened the door and led us inside. It was clearly the infirmary, and rows of simple cots lined the walls on each side, about a third of them containing patients. The nun strode down the long room and, at the far end, turned down a little corridor that led off to the right. There was a door in the wall in front of us, which was partly open and led to the cloister. She strode on, coming after a few paces to another, smaller room. Its door was ajar, and the window set high in the wall was open. There was a faint scent of lavender mixed with the tang of rosemary, and I guessed that my aunt had been busy with her precious oils.

Neither open door and window nor sweet perfumes could do much against the stench. Even before I dared risk a glance at my sister, I knew from the smell that she was very, very ill. Anyone expelling that much from their body – from their suffering, heaving stomach and their constantly voiding bowels – must surely be in the last extremities of life.

I stepped inside the little room and looked down at the figure on the bed. Before I could prevent it, a gasp of horrified pity escaped me. My aunt, on her knees beside the low cot, turned round sharply and gave me a frown. One of Edild's maxims is: never to do or say anything to let a patient know how ill they are. Although my exclamation hardly counted as actually *saying* anything, she was quite right to admonish me.

I swept down beside her and knelt over Elfritha.

My sister had her eyes closed. They seemed to have sunk in her head, and the eyeballs stood out very round behind the pale, almost translucent lids. Her cheeks looked strangely flat, as if her face were falling in. Her skin was as white as the sheet on which she lay, and her short hair, swept back from her forehead, was soaked in sweat. She appeared to be wearing a thin shift, and that too was soaking, sticking to her body. A sheet was pulled up over her breasts, but I could see her neck, throat and shoulders. The bones stood out stark under the flesh; already, she looked more like a skeleton than a living woman.

I made myself take a few calming breaths. When I was sure I could trust my voice, I turned to my aunt and said, 'How is she?'

Edild shrugged. 'She is as you see her,' she said shortly. *You're a healer*, she seemed to be implying. *What do you think?*

Anyone who did not know my aunt might be forgiven for judging her as detached and unfeeling, considering it was her niece who lay dying on the bed. But I did know her, rather well. I was all too aware that it was her habit to adopt a chilly demeanour at the very times when her heart and her emotions threatened to force her sobbing to her knees.

I put out a hand and gently laid it on my sister's hot forehead. It might have been my imagination, but I thought she moved, just a tiny amount, as if in response. 'She is very hot,' I said. 'She has sweated a great deal, and her body must be desperate for water.'

'It is,' Edild agreed. 'Yet whenever she takes a decent mouthful, she vomits it up again almost instantly, thereby losing more than she has absorbed.'

That was even worse than I had thought. 'Oh, but then how—?'

'I am feeding her tiny amounts at a time,' Edild interrupted. 'Watch.'

I moved aside to let her take my place by the bed. Edild took a cup of cold water – I could see how cold it was, for it had formed beads of moisture on the outside of the cup, and I guessed that a concerned nun had just drawn it from some deep well that was their water supply – and dipped a small spoon into it. Very gently, she put the spoon against Elfritha's slightly open mouth and let one tiny drop fall on to the lower lip. After a moment, the tip of Elfritha's tongue emerged to lick it away. I wanted her to do it again immediately, over and over until my sister had taken in a decent amount, but Edild sensed my impatience and, turning to me, shook her head.

'We must not hurry,' she whispered. A very sweet smile swiftly crossed her face, there and gone again in the blink of an eye. 'I do know how you feel,' she added.

I watched as Edild put two more minuscule drops of water on Elfritha's lip. I fought my desire to grab the cup from her and do it faster, faster. Slowly, I felt the anxiety leave me, until I knelt at Edild's side, quite calm.

Then she handed me the cup and told me to carry on.

Intent as I was on my sister, I was aware of Edild's movements only on the edge of my attention. She went to stand beside Hrype, and he put his arms around her. She leaned against him – or, to be exact, she seemed to collapse into him – and for a little while he just held her, as if he were putting some of his formidable strength into her. Then, with a little smile just for him that went straight to my heart, she disengaged herself and stood away from him. I heard them muttering, and it appeared from what I picked up that she was describing the course of Elfritha's sickness.

'Is it some disease from which others too are suffering?' Hrype asked.

'No,' my aunt replied. 'It is possible that more of the nuns may succumb, but Elfritha has been sick for two days now, and I would have expected somebody else to be already unwell, were this something that is going to affect many.'

'I hope you're right,' Hrype muttered.

I was concentrating so hard on putting the smallest possible droplet of water on to my sister's lip that I missed what Edild said next. Hrype spoke, the low rumble of his deep voice a soft and sort of hypnotic sound. But then one word leapt put at me, and all at once I was fully alert.

Edild must have sensed my involuntary movement. She crouched down beside me, waiting as I administered another drop of water.

'How many has she taken?'

I knew she would ask and had been carefully counting. 'Seven.'

Edith nodded. 'Well done,' she whispered. 'That's enough. Now we wait.'

I did not need to ask what we'd be waiting for.

I stood up, putting the cup and the spoon down on the little table beside the bed. Straightening up, I was met with the disconcerting sight of two pairs of eyes, green and silvery-grey, watching me with the intensity of a hawk eyeing the mouse that will be its supper.

I collected my thoughts, for I knew what they were about to tell me.

'Someone tried to poison her, didn't they?' I said.

Instantly, they both shushed me, stepping closer so that the three of us stood in a tight triangle. 'We think so,' Hrype agreed.

I paused, again thinking rapidly. 'Have we a sample of the vomit?'

Edild's mouth turned down in a grimace. 'Not of what she brought up at the outset. Since I have been here, it has mainly been watery bile.'

The product of a stomach that had emptied itself, I reflected.

I had a sudden thought. 'What of her garments?' I asked eagerly. 'If the sickness came on her abruptly, might she not have been sick down herself?'

Edild glanced at Hrype, then back at me. 'Surely someone would have washed her clothes by now?' There was doubt in her tone.

I made the offer before either of them could ask me. 'I'll go and find out.'

I realized quite quickly that the nuns must be in their church, saying one of the daily offices, for the abbey was all but deserted. Two lay nuns sat at either end of the infirmary, and one nodded to me as I emerged from the short passage outside

Elfritha's room. Rather than go down the length of the long room, I used the door that opened directly on to the cloister. I paused to look around, gazing out over the abbey and listening. There was another stout lay sister on duty at the gate, and from somewhere close at hand I could hear voices, a man and a woman's.

I slipped back into the shadows of the cloister and wondered how I was going to find the laundry. It would have to be close to a water source, I reasoned, and I recalled having seen a little stream running along the western edge of the enclosing walls, where the abbey was closest to the surrounding fen. I turned in that direction and presently saw a small hut, its door propped open to reveal big tubs and a small hearth over which a large pot was suspended, presumably where water was heated. On a rough frame behind the hut, a load of washing was drying in the last rays of the setting sun.

I checked quickly, but there was nobody watching. I looked at the items on the frame, and most of them appeared to be bedlinen. I crept inside the hut.

There was a big pile of dirty clothes awaiting the laundress's attention. The pot above the hearth was full of cold water, and kindling had been set ready. The nun in charge must have been intending to do a wash when she returned after the office.

I fell on the bundle of clothing, searching for my sister's habit. I thought I was going to be disappointed, for almost all of the garments were light in colour – novices' white linen veils, several under-shifts – but then I saw something black rolled up tightly underneath them. I reached for it, my fingers finding the coarse cloth of a nun's habit. I drew it out from the pile, and even as I unrolled it I knew I had found what I was searching for: I could tell by the smell.

My beloved sister had been sick all over the front of her habit. Smoothing out the fabric so that I could inspect what was spread over it, I held it to the light coming in through the open door.

My heart seemed to lurch in my chest, and I smothered a gasp.

Among the sticky, smelly mess, I could clearly make out pale berries and those dark, distorted rye seeds.

I had seen enough – more than enough, for I was feeling pretty queasy myself, my fear and anxiety adding to the unpleasant atmosphere inside the little hut. I rolled up the habit again and pushed it back underneath the shifts and the veils, careful to make it look as much as possible as it had done before I disturbed it. I peered out through the doorway, checking to make sure there was still nobody watching, then I gathered up my skirts and hurried back to the infirmary.

Back in Elfritha's room, I found my aunt busy changing the soiled bedlinen, helped by two of the infirmary nuns. I did not at first see Hrype; looking round for him, I spotted him standing behind the door. I had already noticed what a master he was in the art of appearing invisible, and I doubted very much if either of the nuns, preoccupied as they were, had realized he was there.

Edild was too busy to stop and talk to me, so I met Hrype's eyes and inclined my head very slightly towards the doorway. He understood instantly. As I crept back outside, once more using the door that was closest to Elfritha's little room, I knew without looking that he was right behind me.

We found a place in the far corner of the cloister, where we sat down on a low wall. The cloister was deserted, and we positioned ourselves so that we could see anyone coming. It was evening now and beginning to grow dark. I checked that there were no doorways in which people could lurk and listen to our conversation.

I had a final quick look round, then I told him, as succinctly as I could, what Gurdyman had found in the stomach of the dead man in the fen. I was on the point of describing how Gurdyman and I had speculated that Herleva had also been given the same poison, but there was no need because, being Hrype, he had already worked it out.

'And the little nun – your sister's friend – she, too, had vomited,' he said.

'We've no way of knowing what it was that poisoned Herleva,' I went on. 'But I am pretty sure that Elfritha was given the same fatal gruel that the man in the fen ate.'

'Not fatal yet,' Hrype put in swiftly.

I ached for reassurance. Could he give it? I knew he had ways of seeing through the mist into the future. 'Will she live?' I asked in a small voice.

He turned to meet my eyes. 'I do not know, Lassair,' he said. 'Your aunt has not said, and she is the healer, not me.'

'Couldn't you—' I began. I dropped my head, unable to go on.

'Could I ask the runes?' he supplied. 'Is that what you would ask, child?' Mutely, I nodded.

There was quite a long pause. Then he said, 'I could, yes, and they would give an answer. But they do not lie, and they tell truths that often cause terrible pain, for sometimes to know of a dreadful event before it happens is to suffer it many times over rather than just once.'

'Then you do think she's going to die.'

'*No,*' he said very firmly. 'I said I do not know. Nobody does, Lassair. All we can do is look after her to the best of our ability.' His mouth creased up in a very small smile. 'By *we,* I mean, of course, you and your aunt.' He reached for my hand, clasping it for a moment and then letting it go. 'Nobody could have better care,' he added softly.

It was kind of him, but really undeserved. I would only be doing what Edild told me; if Elfritha survived, it would be thanks to my aunt.

We were quiet for some time. It was pleasantly warm in our corner out of the wind, and I thought fleetingly how lovely it would be to curl up in my shawl and go to sleep.

Hrype's voice broke the spell.

'Why should someone try to kill Elfritha?' he asked.

My eyelids had been drooping, and I had been sitting slumped against the warm stone of the wall behind me. Now I sat up, rubbed the drowsiness away and forced myself to think. I'd had a theory, hadn't I? Last time Hrype and I had visited the abbey, I'd worked it all out. I composed my thoughts and, when I was ready, began to speak.

'There *was* one thing that occurred to me,' I said. Hrype's sudden intent gaze told me I had his full attention. 'When we came here the first time, you insisted that we adopt the guises of an old man and his daughter, and I realized you wanted to hide our true identities from somebody. I wondered who it was, and why you didn't want them to recognize us.'

He went: 'Hrmph,' and I knew he was thinking. Then he said, 'What did you decide?'

'That you believed the abbey was dangerous to us. To me, especially, because the new fanatical priest you spoke about – Father Clement – might have learned that I'd spoken to Elfritha concerning . . . well, concerning my healing, which he probably would regard as pagan, sinful, the devil's work. Oh, *I* don't know,' I exclaimed in sudden frustration, 'I don't really understand.'

'You are quite right,' Hrype said, coming to my rescue. 'A man such as Father Clement believes there is but one true path to salvation. It is very straight, very narrow, the walls on either side are very high and there is no alternative way. He would view you as a sorcerer, a witch, and a practitioner of magic. And, worst of all, you're also a woman.' He gave me an ironic smile. 'Doubly damned, I'm afraid.'

I barely recognized myself from his description, other than the bit about being a woman. 'I don't do magic,' I whispered.

He raised an eyebrow. 'No? Then the stories I've heard about a certain young healer who can dowse for hidden paths and lost objects must be untrue.'

'That's different,' I began. 'That's just something I can do . . .' I stopped.

He grinned. 'There you are, then. It's magic, to someone as narrow-minded as Father Clement.'

There was a pause while I thought about that. Then I said, 'Do you think I'm right? Do you think Herleva and Elfritha were poisoned because they'd been whispering about forbidden things?' My words were hurting me, but I had to finish. 'Things I'd told Elfritha, that she'd passed on to her best friend?'

Oh, if that were true, if those two innocent young women had been harmed because of something I had done, then how was I going to live with myself? Nevertheless, I was convinced I was right. They'd sat in a corner somewhere, white-veiled heads close together, and Elfritha had told her friend all about the wonderful, thrilling, magical things her little sister got up to. Someone had overheard; somehow the conversation had reached the attention of a powerful figure in the abbey. And this person had killed Herleva, dressing her death up as a sacrifice to the spirits of the place, and then they had tried to poison my sister.

Although I shied away from the thought, I knew who I suspected, and there seemed no room in my mind for any other possibilities. But was I right? Could such evil have been perpetrated by the person I suspected?

I had to ask.

'Hrype?' I whispered. He turned to look at me, his face unreadable. 'Hrype, could Father Clement be so fanatical that he would murder two young nuns, simply because they had spoken of forbidden matters?' Even as I spoke the words, I found myself denying them. Surely no man of God could have done something so brutal, even a fanatic like Father Clement.

The instant denial that I'd been hoping for did not come. Instead, after a long pause, Hrype said, 'Father Clement is strict, blinkered and powerful. His own beliefs are so strong that he truly thinks his is the only path to certain redemption. He is, I feel, hard on others because he sincerely wants them to come to his god and, when they die, be permitted to spend eternity in paradise. Everything he does – and, as I told you before, he is as tough on himself as on his flock – is with that aim in mind.'

'But would he kill?' I persisted.

Hrype looked at me, smiling. 'No, Lassair.' He hesitated, then went on, 'He is the priest of the Chatteris nuns, responsible for their spiritual welfare, and, up to a point, he would be prepared to impose much hardship and even suffering, in the form of penance, if he thought he would thereby bring an errant soul to his god.' He leaned closer to me, the smile gone. 'But murder is a sin, a deadly sin, and a priest such as Father Clement would no more consider it than fly off over the fens. He is no killer, Lassair. Be assured of that.'

It was both a relief, because the thought of my sister and her friend being poisoned by a man they trusted was so dreadful, and a disappointment, because if Father Clement wasn't responsible, who was?

We sat there a little while longer, and then, without speaking a word, at the same moment we stood up and set off back to the infirmary.

It was dark in the little room where my sister lay, the only light coming from a tallow lamp set beside the bed. Edild sat beside her patient, watching her closely, from time to time letting another drop or two of cold water fall on the cracked lips. Hrype wrapped himself up in his cloak and lay down in the corner behind the door. Once more, if I hadn't known he was there, I'd never have guessed, so thoroughly did he seem to melt into the background.

There was no sound in the room. I felt my eyelids drooping and once or twice had to jerk myself awake from a light doze. I realized how tired I was; it had been such a long day . . . Then, as is the way when you're exhausted, all at once I was deeply asleep, lost in some worrying, muddled dream in which I had to find my way through shivering sands where one wrong footstep would drag me down to a horrible death. The thick, viscous mud was actually flowing into my mouth when once more I was kicked back into wakefulness.

The relief of finding it had only been a dream was short-lived. There were low voices in the infirmary: the soft, whispery tones of a nun, and a man's rumbling mutter.

There was, as far as I knew, only one man who could be in the abbey infirmary in the middle of the night.

Hrype had clearly realized the same thing. He was already on his feet, a deeper shade in the shadowy corner, and even as I watched, he slipped out through the partly-open door. There was a brief gust of cold night air, and I guessed he had gone out through the door that led on to the cloister.

My aunt sat for a moment staring at the place where he had apparently vanished. Then she turned to me, and I saw the relief in her eyes.

I heard footsteps: Father Clement was completing his rounds with a visit to the sick novice. There was just enough time to pull my shawl up over my head, concealing my face, and lie down with my eyes closed. I made myself take some deep, calming breaths. If I was going to be convincing in my pretence of being asleep, I would have to sound right. I tried out a small snore. It sounded authentic. I did another one, soon getting into a rhythm.

I sensed someone walk into the little room. I opened one eye and, through the fringe of my shawl, I looked at the man who stood not an arm's length in front of me.

It was the man I'd seen before, although at a greater distance. I studied his slim, broad-shouldered physique as he towered above me. In the dim light, it was hard to make out his features, but the light eyes seemed to glitter with intelligence. Again, I sensed his great power. Again, I feared him.

'How is she?' His voice was soft, very deep, and sent shivers through me.

'She is much the same,' Edild replied quietly. I noticed that she did not look up at him, but kept her eyes on her patient.

Father Clement murmured something – it could have been a prayer. I risked another quick glance and saw that he was staring down intently at Elfritha's still body.

After a few moments of silent contemplation, he slipped away as cat-footed as he had come.

Presently, Hrype came back. Edild looked up at him. 'Is it safe for you?' she asked anxiously.

'Yes. He has gone.'

Hrype came to crouch beside me. I struggled to sit up. 'You don't want Father Clement to see you, do you?' I whispered. 'That's why you've been insisting we disguise ourselves when we come to the abbey. It's not for my sake but yours.'

'It's for both our sakes, Lassair,' he whispered back. 'It's best that he doesn't know too much about you either.'

I thought about that. Then I asked, 'Why don't you want him to recognize you? What happened when you met him at Crowland?'

Hrype smiled thinly. 'He accused me of witchcraft. He saw me – well, never mind about that. Enough to say that I was careless enough to let him witness something he shouldn't have done. He was frightened, and his reaction was to accuse me of one of the worst crimes he could think of.'

I waited, but it became clear he wasn't going to tell me any more.

TWELVE

I slept for a while, but soon something woke me. I opened my eyes to see that Hrype had gone; perhaps it was his departure that had disturbed me. It's not that he would have made a noise as he got up and left – he wouldn't; despite being tall, he moves as silently as a shadow – it's more that he's such a vital person that his presence or absence in a room always makes itself felt. Well, it does to me, anyway.

I lay still for some time, warm in my cloak and shawl. I watched Edild, sitting close beside Elfritha. I noticed the slump of my aunt's shoulders; she was worn out.

I shook off my covers and crept across to her, crouching beside her for a while and joining in her close observation of her patient. Elfritha was breathing slowly and steadily and appeared to be deeply asleep. Was that a good sign? Or had I, in fact, mistaken for sleep the unconsciousness that precedes death?

'How is she?' I asked, when I could keep quiet no longer.

Edild reached out a gentle hand and stroked Elfritha's smooth forehead. 'She is sleeping,' she whispered.

'Is that good?'

Edild gave a faint shrug.

'But doesn't sleep heal people?' I persisted. 'That's what you always say.'

She made a faint sound of irritation. 'Lassair, I have never dealt with a case of acute poisoning from mistletoe berries and ergot-contaminated seeds before, so I really have no idea what is *good*, as you so blandly put it, and what isn't!'

I knew she was only being cross with me because she was desperately anxious and exhausted, but all the same, her sharp words hurt.

After a moment I felt her hand reach out and take mine. 'Sorry,' she said.

'It's all right,' I said quickly. 'I understand.'

We sat together, still holding hands, looking at my sister. I heard Edild give a huge yawn. 'Why don't you have a sleep?' I suggested. 'I'll watch for a while.'

She looked at me doubtfully. 'It is a very big responsibility,' she murmured.

'I'll wake you if she – if anything happens,' I assured her. 'I promise.'

My aunt looked at me for a while longer, then, abruptly making up her mind, nodded. 'Very well. Call me if she makes any move or sound.'

'I will.'

Edild got up, stretched – I could almost hear her cramped muscles creaking – and went over to the place where Hrype had lain. She settled herself, curling up in her cloak like a kitten in front of the hearth. Within moments she was asleep. I saw that one foot was uncovered, and I reached out to tuck it in.

Then I went back to sit beside my sister's cot.

They say that during the hours before dawn we are at our lowest ebb. It is the time, according to healers like my aunt, when the dying tend to slip away. It is the time, as I well know from my own experience, when your worries press most heavily on you, so that you wonder why on earth you are bothering to struggle on.

So it was with me just then. There was my much-loved Elfritha, my adored elder sister – kind, loving, much missed by us all since she became a nun, but still a part of the world, even behind her abbey walls. She was no better – in the privacy of my own thoughts, I did not try to fool myself – and it was very possible, even probable, that she would die. She had voided her poor suffering body, and now she lay, deathly pale, a mere skeleton covered with the thinnest layer of flesh. She had taken in nothing but a few drops of water for hours, days, and even now she was still occasionally bringing up some of the precious liquid. Unless something changed – unless we could get her body to take in the water she so desperately needed – she would not survive.

Just then I was far beyond trying to think who had tried to kill her: who had wanted her dead and out of the way and so had attempted to dispatch her, just as he – perhaps she – had done with the man in the fen and poor little Herleva. All I could think of was that she was my sister, and I loved her, and I might be about to lose her.

Had I had someone's loving arms around me to support and comfort me, it might not have been so bad. Full of self-pity now, I thought miserably that at least my aunt had had Hrype to hold her when she cried. I had nobody.

The man I loved had tried to reach me via my dreams. He had called out to me, several times, but now he called no more. My dreams of him had stopped. He had been in terrible danger, and whatever had threatened him had overcome him. He was dead; I was sure of it.

Grieving for Rollo, already dead, and for my dear Elfritha, about to join him, I crossed my arms on my sister's bed, dropped my head and wept.

I am dreaming . . .

It is twilight, or perhaps dawn. The light is unnatural; half-light. Magic light. I am close to water, for I hear it and smell it. My feet are on firm ground, but I know that the path is very narrow and that it twists and turns. It is up to me to find the safe way. Then I become aware that there are others with me, many of them, on the path behind me and depending on me to keep them from harm. The weight of responsibility sits heavily on my shoulders, pushing me down. With a great effort, I straighten my spine and stare anxiously ahead.

The safe way goes along the top of a spit of pebbly ground that snakes through the perilous sand, a spectral voice says in my head. *You know this. You have the gift of finding it, and you will not go astray.*

I do not know whose voice it is. I do not recognize it. But the words give me confidence, and I move on. I can feel the others, eager now, right behind me. I peer through the gloom. Where are we going? I look over my shoulder, and I see that, halfway down the long procession, there are big, broad-shouldered men who carry a heavy load. There are four of them, walking slowly, one at each corner of a sort of platform.

Proceed, says the voice.

I obey.

A cloud moves away from the moon, and now I can make out the landscape ahead. We are on the foreshore, a wide stretch of salt marsh that extends away to the distant sea. Between me and the water line there is a building of some sort. It is formed out of tall timbers, set in the damp, sandy ground in the shape of a circle. We go nearer, nearer. I begin to make out details, and I see that the timbers form an unbroken wall, in which there is one door that faces us. The voice intones, *Behold, the shrine of the crossing place.*

I glance up. I can tell from what I can see of the stars in the cloudy sky that the season is autumn, and that we are approaching from the west.

I can see through the open doorway into the interior of the wooden circle. Right in the middle there is the thick stump of a huge oak tree, the wide span of its roots up in the air and its short trunk bedded down deep in the sandy soil. The splayed roots look like open arms, ready to hold a precious offering up to the sky.

My dreaming self is puzzled, and for an instant my conscious mind breaks into the dream and whispers: *you know what that is!*

I am confused now. It feels weirdly as if there are two of me: one who walks through the dream and is unbelievably old, a figure from the ancient days of my own bloodline, and one who lies in a little room in Chatteris Abbey and wants so badly to communicate what she knows.

Then I feel my feet sink into the ground. I know in that instant that I have made a fatal mistake. I try to wrench myself free, but the shivering, sinking sands have me in a firm grip, and the more I struggle, the faster I sink. The wet sand reaches my ankles. My knees.

I look round desperately for help, but I am all alone. I try to cry out, but it is as if the deadly sand is already in my mouth and I can make no sound. Wildly, I wrestle with my silent enemy, twisting this way and that, as far as my imprisoned legs allow. There is no sign of the wooden circle. And the sea, inexplicably, is suddenly much, much closer.

The tide is coming in . . .

As the terror jerks violently through my whole body and soul, I hear a voice: *Lassair, LASSAIR! I need you!*

I woke in a sweat of horrified fear. In my dream I had been trying to scream, and it appeared that whatever had held me mute in my dream had also prevented any sound in my living body.

Had he really called me? Oh, and if he had, and it wasn't just some cruel element of my awful dream, then did it mean he was alive? I didn't *know*!

But I had other things to think about.

My aunt still slept, as did my sister. Trying to shake off the awful visions, I gave myself a stern reprimand for falling asleep when I was meant to be watching over my patient. I bent over Elfritha, putting the flat of my hand on her forehead and listening to her quiet breathing.

It might have been my imagination, but I thought she felt cooler. More relaxed. Very tentatively, I sent a gentle thought probing into her mind. *Elfritha? Are you there?*

There was no response. But then, as I knelt with my eyes fixed on her white face, I thought I saw a tiny smile stretch her lips, so brief that if I hadn't been watching so closely, I'd have missed it.

She had been lying on her back, corpse-still. Now I saw her give a little frown, then turn on to her right side. Her eyelids fluttered, and she muttered something – I could not make it out – then sank back into sleep.

Was this a hopeful sign? I had no idea. In my heart I felt that it was, but it could easily have been wishful thinking. Without taking my eyes off Elfritha, I reached out and took hold of Edild's foot, giving her big toe a firm squeeze. She made a sort of snort, mumbled something, and then sat up and glared at me.

'You told me to wake you if anything happened,' I said, trying to keep my tone neutral.

Instantly, she was at my side. She ran her hands over Elfritha – her face, her chest, her arms – and, opening one of Elfritha's eyelids, stared into her eye, repeating the action with the other one. I dared not speak, for I sensed how hard she was concentrating.

After an eternity, she said, very quietly, 'Lassair go and fetch some fresh water, and make sure it is not too cold.'

I did as she ordered. I filled a cup, put the spoon in it and held it out to her. She was supporting my sister's head with one hand, and with the other she put a little water on the spoon and held it to Elfritha's lips.

'You must drink, Elfritha,' she said softly. 'Your body needs water, and I have some here. Drink.'

This time, it was not just a question of a single drop. This time, my sister gulped down the entire spoonful.

She had barely stirred, and now, as Edild gently laid her head back down on the pillow, she went straight back to sleep. Quite soon she was making small snuffling noises, like a baby.

I met Edild's eyes. After a long moment, she permitted herself a small smile. 'We must not hope too much,' she said, 'but I believe that water may stay down.' She glanced back at Elfritha. 'We will just have to wait and see.'

I was burning to speak to Edild about my dream. I knew she could help; I knew it with absolute certainty. I pictured the strange wooden circle again, readily able to bring the vivid dream-vision back to mind.

I had once seen something similar; only, that one was off the east coast and it was a mere ruin, battered down by centuries – millennia – of wind, sand and sea. When I was first told of it, I had recalled, with a shiver of dread, that Edild had described another. Hers was up on the coast to the north of the fens, and it was one of the most sacred locations of our ancient ancestors, a people who had lived so long ago that even Edild, wise as she is, had not been able to tell me how many thousands of years stretched between them and us. Our memory of them was in our blood and our hearts rather than our minds; sometimes, my aunt had said, they could feel very, very close . . .

The wooden enclosure was one of our most profound mysteries and somehow connected with the ancestors who had died and gone before us into the next world. When I asked my beloved Granny Cordeilla about it, she told me that the place the ancestors now inhabited was beneath our world, a mirror image of it that stretched out below our feet. When first she told me this, I was troubled by the thought that my forebears would have to walk upside down, but Granny assured me that such things presented no problem whatsoever in the next life. She would know for herself now, I reflected with a smile. I had loved my Granny dearly, and I missed her all the time.

When Edild first mentioned the enclosure off the north coast, she had promised to take me there one day, once I was further advanced in my studies and old enough to understand its power and its strange pull. Did that – I hardly dared to hope – mean she knew where it was? And, even more crucially, would she deem that I was now ready to confront it?

I had to ask her.

I nerved myself, crept a little closer to her and said, 'Edild? I had a dream.'

She turned to me instantly, her full attention on me. She knew about dreams; she must also have known that I would not have mentioned it to her – especially under our present circumstances – unless it had been significant: what we call a power dream, in which, or so we believe, the spirits are trying to get an important message through to us.

She said simply, 'Tell me,' and I did.

I described the procession, the spectral voice and the salt-marsh location, and I told her in detail about the wooden circle and the quicksand. I did not, however, tell her that I thought I'd heard Rollo calling out to me. I could not bear to share the faint hope that he was still alive with anybody, not even my aunt.

When I had finished, she sat in thought for what seemed a long time. Then she said, 'You know, I believe, where this place is.'

'I think so, yes. You told me about the sacred place of our ancestors, off the north coast where the sands run into the sea. Is it – does it look like what I described?'

'It doesn't now,' she replied swiftly, 'for it vanished under the waves a very long time ago. Occasionally, a very strong tide or a particularly powerful storm will uncover it for a few days, but it always disappears again. Few who now live have ever seen it,' she added with a sigh, 'and the legends say it is changed beyond recognition. The high walls of strong timber have worn away, and the oak stump is breaking up.'

'It wasn't like that in my dream,' I whispered. 'It looked freshly built, and we were carrying something out to it.' I told her about the four big men and the bier they bore on their shoulders.

She looked down at her hands, folded in her lap. 'I should have loved to share your vision,' she said very quietly.

I wished I could have placed my dream inside her head. It was far beyond my powers. 'What were we doing out there?' I asked. 'What was being carried out to the circle?'

'We cannot know for sure,' she said. 'We can only guess. Those people lived so long ago, and all we can know of them comes to us through our ancient legends and our own blood.'

'Were they our ancestors?' I wondered how we could possibly tell.

Edild smiled, a small, private smile. 'We don't know that, either,' she said. 'They lived in the land where our ancestors lived, and our own stories go back a very long way. It's possible.'

A thought was slowly taking shape in my head, and I tried to put it into words. 'I really felt as if I were that person in the procession,' I said slowly. 'She could do what I could – find the hidden path, I mean – and I had the strong sense that she was me in an earlier time, that I was seeing through the eyes of one of my own forbears.'

Edild nodded. 'I have heard Hrype say much the same thing,' she said. 'He, too, believes that we share our skills with our ancestors; that such things come down through the generations in the same way that the colour of our hair does.'

I nodded, letting her words sink in. Then I murmured, 'You said we can only guess what they were doing. Will you tell me?'

'I will.' She composed herself, then said, 'The ancient people made a place of power, out there on the foreshore. It was a magical place, where the element of water meets the element of land and neither one nor the other truly prevails. One of our most obscure and incomprehensible legends tells of the upturned oak stump that you saw in your dream, its roots raised to the sky and its massive trunk thrust down through the crust of this world into the underworld.'

'Which mirrors this one,' I added. 'Granny Cordeilla told me.'

'Yes,' Edild murmured. 'Yes, she believed that to be true.'

'Do you?'

She shrugged. 'I do not know.'

'What did they use the oak stump for?' I had a feeling I already knew.

She sighed. 'The myth says it was where a very important member of the tribe was put after death. The body was borne in state across the sands, taken into the wood circle and laid out on the upturned oak stump's roots. It was – it is – a crossing place.'

'Where land meets sea,' I supplied. 'Yes.'

She gave me a strange look. 'Also,' she whispered, 'where souls cross over.'

I felt a shudder run down my back. Where souls cross over . . .

'The ceremonies went on for days,' Edild was saying dreamily. 'The people all wished to honour their dead leader, and they knew they would be bereft. The dead one had been a mighty sorcerer – perhaps the greatest that ever lived – and the people had no idea how they would survive without the protective magic they had taken for granted through all the long years.'

'Did they survive?' I whispered.

'Yes,' Edild answered, 'if the tales are to be believed.' She glanced at me, one eyebrow raised as if she were faintly mocking herself. 'For here we are.'

We sat in silence for what felt like a long time. Edild was watching Elfritha, and I was watching my aunt. I was trying to work out how to ask her the question that was all but bursting out of me in such a way that she would answer it in the way I wanted.

In the end, there was no need. She had just finished bathing Elfritha's face, chest and arms, and she put her washcloth down with a sigh, turning to me.

'It is inadvisable to ignore the summons of a power dream,' she said gravely.

My heart leapt. Did she mean what I thought she did? 'Er – it really takes two of us, to look after Elfritha,' I hedged.

Edild rinsed out the cloth. 'Elfritha does not need much nursing. I can manage alone.'

'Will Hrype be back soon?' I didn't like the thought of leaving her on her own.

She shrugged. 'Perhaps.'

I knew better than to ask where he'd gone. Knowing him and his secret ways, it was quite possible he hadn't told her, and I didn't want to put her in the awkward position of having to confess her ignorance to me.

She turned to look at me, her face intent. 'Do you know where to go?'

I shook my head, hardly daring to breathe.

'In that case,' she said – and I could hear her reluctance in her grave tone – 'I'd better tell you.'

THIRTEEN

Hrype was sitting under a low hazel hedge that meandered from the rear wall of the abbey down to where the water lapped against the shore of the little island. He had been there for a long time, so deep in thought that he had not noticed the chill night air. His mind was far away; he had been walking with the spirits.

He had been unable to remain in the little room where Edild and Lassair were fighting to save Elfritha's life. Neither of the two healers seemed very interested in discussing, or even thinking about, who had poisoned the young nun, and the question that so fascinated Hrype – was the same person responsible for the deaths of the man in the fen and Elfritha's friend? – did not appear to engage them in the least.

It did; of course it did, and he knew it. Had he been a healer, he was sure that he, too, would have been so preoccupied with caring for his patient that there would have been little room in his mind for anything else. But he was no healer.

He had forced himself to remain in the room at the end of the infirmary, his presence doing no good to anyone, for as long as he could stand it. He had even returned after the priest had made his brief visit. Hrype had sent a silent, fervent prayer of thanks to whichever of his guardian spirits had warned him that Father Clement was on his way. He was deeply thankful that the priest had not set eyes on him, for the business at Crowland had been far more serious than Hrype had revealed, and there was little doubt that, had Father Clement seen him, he would have recognized him. Hrype did not even want to think about what would probably have happened next . . .

He had sat in his corner of the room for some time, watching as Edild tended her patient and Lassair slept. He had sent out feelers to each woman and had understood that while the woman he carried always in his heart was simply exhausted, Lassair was deeply distressed, almost to the point of despair. He wondered why. Her sister, of course, lay before her, very sick, but Hrype knew by then that Elfritha was not going to die. If that were Lassair's sole concern, soon it would not distress her so deeply. There was, he felt, something more.

His thoughts had returned, over and over again, to the question of who had tried to kill Elfritha. From what Lassair had told him, it did indeed appear that the poison had been administered by the same hand that was responsible for the two deaths. But who was he, and why had these three people been his victims?

Restless, frustrated, impatient with himself and everyone else, eventually Hrype had got up, moved lightly across the little room and out through the open door. He had used the outer door that led to the cloister several times by now, and he knew it opened without a sound. Soon he had been out in the dark night, loping across the cloister, down the maze of passages that twined through the abbey and over the patch of rough ground inside the rear wall. He had climbed this effortlessly, then hurried over the damp grass to the hazel hedge, stopping at a point where a small stream flowed close by.

Now, deep in the shelter of the hazel bushes, he was lighting a fire. He controlled the leaping flames, keeping the fire small. It was not for heat that he had lit it; merely to give a little light and, crucially, to provide one of the four elements. Water was provided by the stream running beside the hedge; earth was beneath him, and air above.

When the fire was burning to his satisfaction, he sat down again, crossed his long legs and untied the thongs of a soft leather bag that hung from his belt. Opening it, he spread out a square of linen on the ground in front of him and then closed the bag, holding it in both hands.

For a long time, he sat motionless. His eyes were closed, and he was murmuring a long, involved incantation. He needed the help of his guardian spirits, and it took a huge effort to summon them. Some were his ancestors, fierce men and women whose roots were in the cold north lands and in whom had run a rich seam of magic and sorcery. Some of the guardians were animals; his own spirit animal was a great brown bear, whose protection and help were invaluable when he chose to bestow them.

When at last Hrype was ready, he loosened his tight hold on the leather bag and opened it, drawing out its cords so that it was wide open. Then, with a swift, neat movement, he turned the bag upside down, and his jade rune stones tumbled down on to the linen square.

He sat staring down at the stones. They were beautiful, the translucent green incised with the familiar rune marks, which had been filled in with gold. The gentle firelight caught the precious metal, sparkling off the runes and making them glitter and shine. Hrype looked from rune to rune, forming different combinations, seeing different versions of the same message. He frowned, shook his head to clear it and then looked again at the runes.

He did not understand what the runes were telling him. It was just not possible; he was as sure of that as he was that the moon would soon set and the sun come up. But the runes never lied. Their message might be obscure – in fact, it usually was – but they were incapable of an untruth.

Slowly, Hrype gathered up the stones, muttering a prayer of thanks and a blessing on each one as he put it back in the leather bag. Then he folded up the linen square and put it on top of the stones. Thoughtfully, he reattached the bag to his belt.

He stood up and trod out the small remnants of his fire, cutting a turf from beneath the hedge and neatly tucking it into the black space where the fire had been. After a few moments' work, nobody would have guessed what had happened there that night.

He set off back up the field towards the abbey, his agile mind trying all sorts of possibilities as he attempted to make sense of what the runes had told him. It was not until he was jumping down off the abbey wall that the solution hit him. He smiled briefly, wondering why on earth he hadn't thought of it before.

He was now desperate to get back to the room in the infirmary. He needed to speak urgently to Lassair; or even to Edild, he reflected. Nevertheless, he maintained his caution and stood for some time in the cloister, using all his senses to make sure nobody was about. Dawn would come soon, and the nuns would be going to their church for the office. But he thought he had enough time.

He opened the door into the infirmary just a crack, sliding through and closing it again. Then he tiptoed into the little room where Elfritha lay. Edild was beside her, spongeing the girl's face. She looked up and met his eyes.

'She is better,' he said. He knew it.

'Yes,' Edild whispered. 'Yes, I believe she is. She has now taken half a cup of water, and there is no indication that she will bring it up again.' She smiled, tentatively at first, then, as if she could not control her joy, her whole face lit up.

His heart leapt at the sight of her. He swiftly crossed the room and knelt beside her, taking her in his arms. Their kiss was brief, but he knew – and he hoped she did too – that soon there would be time for a full expression of their love. It had been such a long time since they had been alone . . .

He broke the embrace, holding her by her shoulders, his eyes on hers. Then the urgency returned. He looked round the room and, as the realization dawned, said disbelievingly, 'Where's Lassair?'

It might be that she had simply crept out to find the latrines, but he knew even before Edild spoke that it was not.

'She's gone,' Edild said.

He bit back a curse. He waited until he knew his voice would be calm, then said, 'Where?'

'She had a power dream,' Edild replied.

It was enough; she did not need to elaborate, especially not to him, of all people. You did not ignore a power dream. The spirits sent them for a reason, and if you did not act upon them, the spirits would decide you were not worthy and never send you another.

'Where did it summon her to?'

She told him. He nodded; he knew of the wooden circle, although he had never seen it. He wondered what the spirits wanted with Lassair. He was not at all surprised that she had received the call, for in the years that he had watched her mature, he had come to realize that she had a rare gift.

He made himself stop speculating. It was not his place to ask questions. What went on between the spirits and the mortals with whom they chose to communicate was private, and anyone else who tried to intervene – even someone far more experienced in sorcery than the recipient of the dreams – did so at their peril.

Lassair, then, was out of his reach. He would have to discover what he needed to know from Edild. He wondered how to phrase his question. After a moment, he said, 'What did the priest want?'

She was drowsy – he could tell by the way she was leaning into him – and apparently did not at first understand what he had said. He repeated the question.

'Oh, he came to see how Elfritha was,' she replied, yawning as she spoke.

Hrype thought carefully. 'Did he look as if he really cared?' he asked.

Elfritha shook her head. 'I don't know. I couldn't really see his face, for, as now, we had but the one small light, and it was on the floor beside me. The priest was in the shadows.'

Hrype frowned. That was a blow . . . He thought hard and soon understood that there was an alternative. He bent his head to give Edild one more kiss, then straightened up. Looking down at her, his heart overflowing, he wished that he could tell her of his suspicions. But sometimes knowledge could be dangerous, and that was without a doubt the case here. He said softly, 'I have to go, my love.'

She nodded. She was used to his comings and goings and did not ask questions. 'Very well.'

He hesitated. He had his own preoccupation, driving him now like a man whipping a tired horse, but he knew that she did too. 'Will you be all right, nursing Elfritha by yourself?'

'Yes. It is not demanding.'

That was not what he had meant. He was about to speak, but she forestalled him. 'I will have the assistance of another pair of watchful eyes to protect her,' she whispered. 'Sister Christiana is coming to join me as soon as the office has been said.'

'Sister Christiana?'

Edild smiled. 'You would recognize her if you saw her. She is the nun who admitted you yesterday.'

The thin-faced one whose severe expression had melted into kindness when Lassair told her they'd come to see Elfritha; yes, he remembered her. 'She has a good heart,' he murmured.

'Indeed she has,' Edild agreed. 'Moreover –' her voice dropped to the merest whisper, and he bent down to hear – 'she understands the danger and will stay with me by Elfritha's bedside until it has passed. Whenever that may be,' she added on a sigh.

He was reassured. He had not wanted to leave Edild alone, watching over someone who had just been poisoned and who might very well be attacked in some way again. Knowing she would have a companion – and one of such quality – was a great relief. 'I will not cease until the danger is no more,' he said. 'You have my word, and I do not break it.'

She looked up at him, her face full of love. 'I know,' she said.

There was nothing to be gained by staying. If he left now, there was little chance that anyone would see him go. He turned, drew up his hood and, with one last glance at her, he was gone.

I had not relished the idea of making my way on foot from Chatteris all round the west, south and east of the fens until I reached the far shore. But, of course, I did not have to, and fortunately I realized it before I had got very far. I had been standing on the quayside at the point where boats ferried passengers on the short trip across to the mainland to the south, and, reprimanding myself for my dimness, I walked right along the long curve of the waterfront until I was facing north-east. Then I waited.

I had imagined I would be there for some time, but I did not know much about boatmen. Before dawn had even begun to light the eastern sky, there were already people about, preparing their crafts and loading up crates and sacks. It proved a simple task to find someone willing to take me where I wanted to go. He was calling in at March and Lynn first, he told me, but with any luck he would be able to drop me off at my destination by mid-afternoon.

I was his sole passenger. I had no coins with me, but I carried my leather satchel of oils, herbs, potions and remedies, and in exchange for my passage over the fens I offered to provide any medicament, within reason, that he might be in need of. As it turned out, he was a very healthy man, but his old mother suffered terribly from the phlegm-producing cough that is so common in our damp, watery land. As soon as the sun had risen sufficiently to give me light to work by, I set about mixing a bottle of Edild's finest cough remedy. Once I'd handed over the medicine, I made myself comfortable, propped my back against a sack containing something soft – wool, probably – and snuggled up in my shawl. I had thought I was far too anxious to sleep, but I hadn't realized how tired I was. The gentle movement of the boat was like a mother rocking a baby in its cradle, and soon I was fast asleep.

I had never before been to the port of Hunstanton, nor, indeed, anywhere near it. I did not intend to change that now by actually going into the town. As far as the lord of my manor knew,

I was in Cambridge. I had been to Chatteris – twice – without his knowledge or his permission, and now I was embarking on another unauthorized trip. The fewer people who saw me, the better.

I set out on the track that led northwards out of the port, keeping as close as I could to the sea, over to my left. I had memorized Edild's directions, but so far I didn't really need them. I had merely to walk on until the land began to curve away to the east, then begin looking out for the land-marks she had described.

The afternoon slowly faded into evening. The sky was clear, and the light lasted for a long time. The weather was mild; it had been sunny all day, but now a cloud bank was building up out to sea. I was refreshed after my sleep on the boat. I stopped to eat some of my supplies – Edild had managed to scrounge a little food from one of the lay sisters on night duty in the infirmary, and I had filled my water bottle at Hunstanton quay – then walked on some more. I had probably walked eight or ten miles by the time I finally settled under the shelter of a dune to sleep away the rest of the night.

The onslaught began even while I slept.

It was so subtle, to begin with. I was dreaming: uneasy dreams, wherein I was threatened by a vague menace which, while I did not know what it was, I nevertheless knew to be threatening. Dangerous. Then, out of nowhere, the face of a drowned man was before me, empty sockets right above my eyes, gaping jaws open to expose a tongue eaten off by some sea creature. I screamed, and believed I had woken up, but somehow I could not escape from the dream vision. Was I still asleep? I did not know. The first spectre was followed by others, dozens of them, floating up to me and opening their mouths in silent howls of anguish and terror. Their garments were ripped and shredded, and they stank of the dead things that rot at the very bottom of the sea.

I lay and endured. I sensed the presence of many more of them, floating around me like a putrid, nightmare cloud. After a time, they were no longer there, or perhaps it was that they had ceased showing themselves to me. For the magic was still there; whatever malicious enchantment had shown me that vision was still at work. Its message was clear: *go away. It is perilous for you here.*

I wanted to gather up my satchel and run, back the way I had come. Aelf Fen was somewhere to the south, quite close, and I longed with all my heart and soul to fly to the comfort of my mother's large, soft bosom, my tall father's strong, protective arms.

But I had been summoned. The message in my power dream had been unmistakable.

I pulled my shawl up over my head and tried to go back to sleep.

It was the cold that woke me next. The light told me that dawn had broken, although it was a dim and miserable dawn. The cloud bank I had observed the previous evening had swept inshore, and it had thickened as it approached, so that now there was a thick, swirling mass of lowering dark grey above me. There was a wind blowing hard off the sea, bringing with it a fine salt spray which, I soon discovered, had the power to penetrate each and every one of my garments.

I ate a few mouthfuls of yesterday's food – dry bread, a hard piece of cheese, a small but sweet apple – and drank from my flask. Then I left the shelter of my dune and headed on.

I seemed to walk for a long time. The land around me would, I guessed, have been pretty featureless under even sunny conditions, consisting as it did of salt marsh giving way to a flat grey sea, with only a few scraps of bushes and the occasional stunted, twisted tree to break it up. Now the low cloud had ushered in pillows of mist that seemed to hover around me, before giving way to the steadily increasing wind and dispersing. The mist appeared to emerge from the ground beneath my feet. I stared down at the path. It was still quite well defined, and its surface was pebbly. I noticed, however, that on either side the sandy ground was becoming more and more waterlogged.

I told myself there was no need to be afraid of losing my way and sinking into the marsh. I knew how to find a safe way that was invisible to others. I stopped, waited till my anxious heartbeat slowed down a little, then began the steady deep breathing that normally allows me to enter the light trance state necessary for all dowsing work.

I needed help, for I was facing unknown danger and quite alone. I silently called out to Fox, and, as if he knew how much I wanted him and had been waiting for my summons, almost straight away I caught sight of him out of the corner of my eye. He looked eager and full of courage. His presence was immensely reassuring.

I closed my eyes and asked the spirits please to show me the safe way. You don't actually have to tell the spirits why you want their help, because they know far more than we do and will undoubtedly already have worked it out. Still, I always feel it's only polite to explain, and so as I stood there, eyes still shut, I reminded them about the dream and also about the summoning voice. I didn't ask if it really was Rollo's, and they didn't say.

Hesitantly, I stretched out my arms, palms down towards the ground, spreading my fingers widely. Nothing happened at first, but I was learning – very slowly, I admit – how to be patient. After a while, I had my reward. The familiar tingling began, in the very tips of my fingers and then centring in the middle of both palms. Confident now, I opened my eyes.

The clouds were still spread thickly right above me, heavy with the rain that was surely about to deluge down. The pockets and patches of mist were still swirling. Visibility should have been roughly the length of my outstretched arms, but through the obscuring fog I saw a shining, gleaming line snaking away across the salt marsh. It twisted and turned repeatedly; nobody who had not lived here all their lives and studied the land closely would have a chance of finding their way safely. I would have stepped off into the sinking sands within a very short time, for I had been heading straight for a boggy patch of wet ground that was without a doubt quicksand.

I sent up a song of gratitude to the spirits. I put down a hand to Fox – just occasionally, I feel the touch of his cool, wet nose on my fingers – and side by side we walked confidently on.

*   *   *

The rain replaced the light mist on the air and swiftly became a torrent. I was soaked through in moments, and I wrapped my shawl tightly around me: not to keep out the rain – which was impossible – but to try to preserve some body warmth. The wind had become a gale, howling and shrieking like the herdsman of the dead. And the drowned men were back, flying in low over my head like hawks attacking a helpless lamb.

I was not helpless, I told myself. The drowned men could frighten me – they did; they terrified me to my bones – but they could not harm me. Or so I hoped.

I pushed on.

The wood circle was off the northern shore. I realized I must be close now, although I could make out nothing but the blueish-silver of the safe path, glinting before me. Edild had said the circle was not as I had seen it in my dream vision. It was no more than a ruin, more likely as not obscured by the sands or the sea. Even if it had stood as tall and proud as I had seen it, I doubted whether I would have found it.

I pressed ahead on the safe path. The spirits had brought me here, and they must have had a good reason. I knew I would simply have to put myself in their hands and let them lead me.

We were close to the sea now, for I could hear the broiling waves crashing and tearing against the shingle. I kept a watchful eye on the sky, and all at once a minute break in the thick black clouds allowed me a glimpse of the sun. The silver path had changed direction; we were now going due north.

Straight towards the furious sea.

I was quaking with fear and so cold that my shivering was making my teeth clatter together. Without Fox, I think I might have turned back, but he would not let me. Coming from the spirit world as he does, no doubt he understood why I had been called and why it was imperative that I went on.

My steps were slower now. It felt as if I had to drag each foot out of sticky, tacky mud that only released me after a struggle. The muscles in my legs ached constantly with a fierce pain that felt like hot needles.

I was on the point of giving up. I was exhausted, and I was so close to the sea now that the spray from the biggest waves was catching me. I was wet to the thighs. Lonely, in pain and more afraid than I had ever been, I sobbed aloud.

There was an echo. The sob came right back to me.

Then it came again, a hoarse, deep cry that I could never have made . . .

I was racing down the shining path, my fears forgotten, my pain gone. The cry came again, and I shouted back, '*I'm here! I'm coming!*'

I flew on, my feet barely touching the ground, and Fox was a russet streak beside me. The fog still obscured everything but the safe path, but it did not matter, as it became clear the path was leading me in the right direction.

I came to a place where the path gave out. Just like that, with no warning at all. I jerked to a halt, staring down at the salt-crusted, sandy mud at my feet. No shining light shone out ahead; this was the end of the safe way, and to go on would mean death.

I did not know what to do.

I sensed movement, just over to my left. Spinning round, I saw the faint glimmer of a sort of loop that had formed, as if the safe path had curled round in a circle to mark its terminal.

There was someone there; I could make out a vague dark shape huddled on the wet ground.

I knew who it was. My heart recognized him even while my head was still thinking about it.

I ran down the short length of path that separated us. I flung myself down and took him in my arms. He was lying on his side on a thin patch of firm ground, as icy as death, soaked through and shaking with cold. For some time he simply clung to me. I was soaked too, but I had just been moving fast and my body was hot from the effort. He must have felt it, even through my wet clothes, and, desperate for warmth, he tried to absorb some of mine. I gave it gladly, putting my hands on his face, his neck, finding his own hands and squeezing life back into them.

After a while he raised his head from where he had burrowed it against my breasts. I looked down into his face, and my heart gave a lurch of pity. He looked terrible. He was thin, white-faced, he had several days' growth of beard and someone – perhaps he himself – had cut his hair, very badly. His clothes were torn and filthy with sandy mud, clots of which stuck all over his arms and shoulders.

He stared at me in silence for a moment. Then he said, 'I knew you would come.'

'I should have been with you before!' I cried. 'I heard you calling, but I didn't know where you were until it was too late, and when you stopped I thought you were dead!'

He gave a smile, very brief, no more than a stretching of his blue lips. 'You're here now,' he murmured.

Then, as I watched, his face fell. He was grieving; I knew it. There is no emotion that wrenches and stabs at you like grief, both your own and that of someone you love.

'What is it?' I asked softly.

He raised his dark, deeply troubled eyes to mine. 'My horse is gone,' he said, his voice breaking on the words. 'She went into the quicksand, and I couldn't get her out.'

Oh, *no*! I wanted to cry out aloud, send my protest shrieking up into the sky. I knew about death in the sands. I knew how the pressure builds up and makes the eyes and tongue stand out stark in the head. I knew how the mouth stretches open for the last desperate breath, how it fills not with life-giving air but with deadly, cloying, heavy, wet, muddy sand.

And this beloved man of mine had been forced to watch, powerless, as his horse had gone under.

He gave one sob, a harsh bark of sound that seemed to epitomize his loss, his longing and his pain. I closed my arms around him and pressed him against me. After a while I laid my cheek down on the top of his head. And there we stayed.

I don't know how long we would have remained like that. Although I was deeply affected by his grief for his horse, at the same time I was filled with joy because I had found him, he was alive, and now we were together.

Perhaps it was this potent mix of emotions that made me careless. Perhaps the force curled up ready to strike against me was too powerful and made sure I did not perceive its presence until it was too late. Either way, I did not sense the approaching danger.

There was a sudden sound, right above us, so startlingly

loud that my ears rang. It could have been thunder, but if it was, it cracked at the command of something other than the forces of nature. The lowering sky went totally black, and I could see nothing, not even the comforting glow of the safe path. Whatever was out there, it had power even over that. Rain lashed down, vicious as a whip, forming itself into icy droplets. I saw small cuts open up on Rollo's and my exposed flesh. The wind wound up to a screaming crescendo, in which I thought I could detect a terrible voice.

I tried to raise my head to look up, but I could not move.

What was assailing us out on that lonely shore was the most powerful force I had ever felt.

And it did not like us at all . . .

FOURTEEN

Hrype, too, had managed to find an early-rising boatman, in his case to ferry him over the short stretch of water between Chatteris island and the mainland to the south. The ferryman was inclined to talk, but Hrype was deep inside his own thoughts and did not respond. With a shrug, the boatman bent to his oars, muttering under his breath about miserable sods who wouldn't brighten up a cold, dark morning with a bit of a chat.

Once on the far side, Hrype drew up his hood against the moist morning air and trudged on as fast as he could. There were few other people about. Presently, the path met the major road that swept round to the south-west of the fens. The traffic increased, and quite soon Hrype got a ride with a man heading into Cambridge with a load of mushrooms. The final ten miles of his journey passed swiftly, for the farmer's horse was fresh and kept up a lively pace.

It was late in the morning when Hrype hurried along the maze of passages leading off the market square. He mounted the steps up to the familiar wooden door and rapped his knuckles against it. For quite a long time nothing happened, so he knocked harder. Finally, the door creaked open, and Gurdyman's bright-blue eyes looked out at him.

'Come in, Hrype.' He stood aside to usher his guest inside. Neither his voice nor his manner displayed the least surprise. 'I am sorry to have kept you waiting,' he added as he led the way along the passage. 'I was in the crypt and could not leave my workbench until a critical stage in my experiment was complete.'

'I hope I did not disturb you,' Hrype said politely.

'No, no.' Gurdyman waved a hand, indicating the little courtyard, sheltered from the cool breeze and warm from the sunshine spilling in and reflecting off the stone walls. 'I was expecting you. Will you have some refreshment?'

Hrype realized he was ravenous. 'I will, thank you.'

He watched as the sage fetched a tray of bread and cold, spiced meats, accompanied by mugs of ale, wondering how Gurdyman had known he was coming.

As if the wizard read the thought – he probably did – he chuckled and said, 'There was nothing magical about it, my friend. Lassair's sister is sick – how is she, by the way? I am sorry, I should have asked you that straight away. Only, I would guess by your demeanour that she is better?'

'She is, thank you. Still very ill, but no longer on the point of death.'

'I am very glad to hear it. As I was saying, I know that Lassair's sister is sick, and Lassair had told me that her sister's best friend was dead and had been poisoned. Given that in addition we have the case of the man in the fen, who was also poisoned, it was not particularly clever or astute to work out that, sooner or later, you would come to me.' He paused, eyeing Hrype closely. 'Once you had established the question, Lassair was not, I presume, available to provide the answer?'

Despite everything, Hrype began to laugh. 'She has gone on a mission of her own,' he said. He explained about the dream.

'What can have taken her there?' Gurdyman mused. 'Have you any idea?'

'There is a place of power off the north coast,' Hrype replied. 'It could be that the spirits have a quest for her. The summons was urgent, I understand.'

Gurdyman nodded. 'Then she had, of course, no option but to obey it,' he murmured. He met Hrype's eyes. 'We shall just have to manage without her.' There was only light irony in his tone; he too, Hrype realized, had recognized Lassair's worth.

'She has a long way to go,' Hrype said, 'for she is still too subject to the influence of her emotions. Until she can govern her heart, she will always be unreliable.'

'You are too hard on her, Hrype,' Gurdyman countered. 'She is yet young, and the power in her is strong.'

'You are satisfied with her as a pupil?' Hrype had first introduced Lassair to her mentor, and he hoped Gurdyman did not feel he was wasting his time.

'Entirely,' Gurdyman said firmly. 'Now, have some more of this ale.'

'I guessed,' Gurdyman said as they finished the food, 'that, having seen Lassair's sister and learned what you could there, and in the absence of any opportunity to view the body of the dead nun, you would wish to hear all that you could concerning the body of the man found in the fen. Lassair has gone off on a purpose of her own, and so here you are, talking to me. Am I right?'

Hrype smiled. 'You are,' he agreed. 'Please, tell me all that you can of the dead man.'

'He was tethered on the fen margins,' Gurdyman began, 'somewhere over on the eastern edge of the wet lands, south of Lynn. The boatmen could not be more specific. They lost their way in the fog and had to make a turn in a narrow channel, and their guess is that it was there they picked up their extra cargo. The ropes that had bound the man became entangled somehow in the boat; perhaps in the steer board. Anyway, they unwittingly towed the corpse behind them all the way to the quay here at Cambridge, where someone spotted it bobbing along in their wake and raised the alarm.'

The eastern edge of the fen, south of Lynn. Hrype recalled how Lassair had seen such significance in that, believing it must be relevant because the little nun who had died was also from that region. He was not so sure; it could be no more than coincidence. 'He had suffered the Threefold Death, I believe?' he asked.

'He had,' Gurdyman confirmed.

'A sacrifice,' Hrype murmured.

'You think so?'

'I do. The signs are unmistakable. Who else would go to all that trouble? It was clear the murderer was easily able to overcome his victim, so why not simply hit him a bit harder on the head, or hold him under the water till he drowned? No; the details of the involved method of killing must surely point to a sacrificial death.'

'So we are dealing,' Gurdyman said slowly, 'with a magician of the Old Ways.' It was not a question; he knew it as well as Hrype did.

For a moment the sunny little courtyard felt cold, as if a cloud had covered the sun.

'Why did he need to make a sacrifice?' Gurdyman said after quite a long silence. 'What is happening now, to make such a measure necessary? It's not as if the Normans are a new phenomenon and, although many of us still resent their heavy-footed presence in our land, the time is surely not ripe for another revolt?'

'I agree,' Hrype said. 'There is always dissent, and there always will be as long as people are alive who remember how life used to be. We may be more secure from the lawless ways of thieves and brigands under the new rule, and they tell us our shores have never been safer from attack than they are now, but this is still our land and they are still the invaders. I do not, however, sense that there is a major move at present to rise against them.'

'So, if the sacrifice was not to appease the gods, and seek their aid and support in an attempt to throw off the new ways and return to the old, then what *was* it for?' Gurdyman seemed to be thinking aloud, his voice soft and almost dreamy.

'Sacrifices are made also in thanks for help already given,' Hrype pointed out. 'What if the killer had been required to carry out a mission fraught with danger and, having achieved his purpose, dispatched his victim in the old way in gratitude for his success?'

Gurdyman gave him a sharp look. 'That is possible,' he acknowledged. 'I think, my friend,' he added perceptively, 'that you do not merely speculate.'

'No,' Hrype agreed. 'As you surmise, I speak of events that have in fact happened. Or so I believe.'

Gurdyman settled back more comfortably in his chair, his refilled mug in his hand. 'Tell me,' he invited.

Hrype paused to gather his thoughts. Was he right? Had the runes led him to the correct conclusion? Or had he allowed emotion to creep in and influence him? Was he guilty of the same weakness that he had just accused Lassair of? Gurdyman was watching him intently; he had no choice but to go on.

'We have two deaths, both carried out in the same distinctive manner, which, we surmise, makes the man and the young woman the victims of sacrifice,' he began. 'We also have the case of Lassair's sister Elfritha, who was given exactly the same poison, possibly – probably – as a first step in a similar Threefold Death.'

'How was the poison administered?' Gurdyman asked. 'And why did the killer not proceed with the next phases of the death?'

'We do not yet know,' Hrype replied. 'The girl is too weak to speak, and I would guess that it will be some time before Edild risks asking such distressing questions.'

'And dangerous ones,' Gurdyman said softly. 'If the poisoner is still at large and has access to Elfritha, he will not wish her to expose him. He may well try to prevent that by attacking her again.'

Hrype nodded. 'Yes, yes, I worked that out too,' he said. 'Edild has been offered the help of one of the infirmary nuns. If the two of them are always present in the sick room, I do not see how the murderer will be able to do anything to harm their patient.'

Gurdyman looked at him doubtfully. 'I hope you are right. It appears to me that we have a very clever, devious killer here.' He waved a hand. 'Carry on with what you were saying.'

'We can, I think, safely conclude that all three poison victims were meant to die,' Hrype said, 'although it is impossible to say what the killer had in mind for Elfritha, nor why, indeed,

he was unable to carry out his scheme. It may be that the girl
has some natural resistance to the particular substances that
she consumed, and that she was thus able to remain conscious
long enough to seek help. Once she was in the infirmary, the
murderer had lost his opportunity, and any further plans would
have to be abandoned.'

'Or postponed,' Gurdyman added darkly.

Hrype frowned. 'I do not wish to—'

'Acknowledge the danger, Hrype,' Gurdyman interrupted
quietly. 'It exists, and you must surely recognize that.'

Hrype bowed his head. 'I do.' He straightened up again.
'We should ask ourselves what the three victims have in
common. Lassair found out that Herleva – that's the name of
the dead nun – came from the Lynn area, which is roughly
where the boat picked up the corpse of the man in the fen.
Whether or not we should view this as significant remains to
be seen.'

'Elfritha has no connections with Lynn,' Gurdyman said.
'Or does she?'

'Not that I know of. Lassair would have mentioned it if it
were so.' He leaned towards Gurdyman. 'But what if Herleva
revealed some secret to Elfritha? Supposing she knew some
fact that was dangerous to the murderer, so that he had to kill
her before she spread it about? She might not even have shared
it with her friend – perhaps she did not appreciate the significance of what she knew – but the murderer had no way of
knowing that. He could not take the risk, and so he killed
Herleva, taking the opportunity of turning her death into
another sacrifice, and then attempted to do the same to Elfritha.'

Gurdyman sat silent for some time, and Hrype guessed he
was thinking hard. 'And the man in the fen? Did he possess
this dangerous knowledge as well?'

'It's possible,' Hrype agreed. He paused, taking a few steadying
breaths. This was where sound logic stopped and speculation
began.

'Come on, you may as well tell me,' Gurdyman said mildly.

Hrype smiled briefly. 'The death of the man in the fen is
no great mystery,' he said, 'for he was presumably attacked
out in the open. But I have been trying to think who had access

to the two young nuns. The abbey at Chatteris is secure behind its walls, although the gates frequently stand open to admit visitors and those in need of the nuns' help, and it is quite a simple matter to climb over the walls, as I know from my own experience. But the two young nuns were – are – both novices, whose comings and goings are strictly monitored. It is difficult to imagine a situation where their attacker would have access to them.'

'He is, we agreed, a clever and devious man.'

'Yes.' Hrype hesitated. Then he said, 'Lassair had a theory. She wondered if she herself were the cause of the attacks on her sister and Herleva. I told her that Father Clement, the abbey's priest, is a fanatic who will not tolerate the smallest deviation from his religion. She feared that her conversations with her sister had been overheard and reported to the priest, who would undoubtedly have seen their content as heretical.'

'Lassair having been unable to resist the temptation of bragging a little, impressing her sister with the extraordinary things that I have been teaching her,' Gurdyman said. 'It is understandable, Hrype.'

'She should keep such matters to herself,' Hrype grumbled. 'They are not for the entertainment of outsiders.'

Gurdyman watched him. 'You are a stern man, my friend,' he murmured. 'So,' he went on before Hrype could comment, 'Lassair is berating herself because she thinks this fanatical priest learned that an apprentice healer, who also receives tuition from a wizard, had been whispering her secrets to her sister, who probably shared them with her best friend, leading him to the conclusion that both young nuns had to die. And why, then, kill them by the method of the Threefold Death?'

'This is Lassair's theory,' Hrype pointed out, 'not mine. But, to answer your question, I imagine he thought that by dressing the deaths up as sacrifices, he would avert suspicion from himself, being the last man to use such methods.'

'She reasons thoroughly, if not very convincingly,' Gurdyman remarked. 'But you think differently, Hrype. Let me hear how you see it.'

'I consulted the runes,' Hrype said, his voice dropping to a whisper. 'I asked them who had poisoned Elfritha, and who had killed Herleva and the man in the fen. As I had expected, they gave the same answer: one person was responsible for all three attacks.'

'Did they reveal who it was?' Gurdyman, too, spoke very quietly.

'I thought not, at first, for the figure they went on showing to me could not have been the killer, and I was left with the conclusion that I had not asked the right question.' He looked up, meeting Gurdyman's eyes. 'They showed me a priest; a shadowy figure dressed in the unmistakable robes of a minister of the church. They indicated that he belonged to the place I was then in; to the abbey. Odal, the rune for home and hearth, was in conjunction with Thorn, the rune of warning and magical power, and in prominence was Beorc, the symbol of growth and new beginnings; a new broom, as they say. There were other indicators, too; the pattern was extremely complex.' Again he leaned closer to Gurdyman. 'Father Clement has been at Chatteris only since last autumn. They refer to him as a new broom.'

Gurdyman nodded slowly. 'The runes told you Father Clement is the killer. Yet you could not accept this?'

'No, I could not; I cannot,' Hrype agreed. 'I have met him, you see. I was very near to Crowland once, the abbey where Father Clement was before he went to Chatteris. Crowland burned down last year, and most of the monks have dispersed while it is rebuilt.'

'Was your presence there anything to do with the fire?' Gurdyman asked.

'No. It was some months before the fire that I was there. But I was careless, Gurdyman. I was preoccupied with another matter – I will not explain, if you don't mind – and I allowed Father Clement to witness something that no man should have seen, especially a fanatic like him. He accused me of the usual list of crimes: witchcraft, being in league with the devil, raising evil spirits. You know the rest.'

'Only too well,' Gurdyman said with a sigh.

'But he only threatened me,' Hrype repeated. 'He had all the evidence he needed to have me tried and put to death, believe me. Yet he did not. Instead he commanded me to leave

aside my sinful ways and turn to his Lord. I sensed then that
he was a good man: hard and tough, unrelenting in his battle
to save souls in the way that he thinks is right, yet fundamen-
tally merciful. I managed to speak to others who knew him
well, and my first impression was verified. I learned in addition that he was as hard on himself as on those for whom he
was responsible. He fasted frequently and was rumoured to
administer the whip on his own back.'

Gurdyman's eyes narrowed. 'I see,' he murmured.

'Father Clement was not a man to kill,' Hrype stated flatly.
'It is inconceivable that he murdered two people and tried to
poison a third.'

'And so you conclude what?' Gurdyman prompted. There
was a new light in his blue eyes, and Hrype had the strong
suspicion that he already knew what was coming.

'The man at Chatteris Abbey who claims to be Father
Clement is an impostor,' Hrype said. 'For some reason he
needed to gain access to the abbey, and so he murdered the
real Father Clement, made the death a sacrifice and gave him
to the waters of the fen.'

'But you have been at the abbey,' Gurdyman protested
suddenly. 'Surely you would have noticed if the man calling
himself Father Clement was not the man you knew?'

'I made sure he did not see me,' Hrype said grimly, 'and
so, naturally, I did not see him either. Both Lassair and Edild
did, but by the time I had worked it all out, Lassair had already
gone and so could not describe him to me. And when I asked
Edild if she knew what this Father Clement looked like – she
only met him once – she said it had been too dark to make
out his face.'

'With Lassair gone, you could not ask her about the appearance of the dead man in the fen either,' Gurdyman added.
'And so you came to me.'

'Yes. Will you describe him to me?'

'I will. He was a man of medium height and build, with dark
hair and dark eyes. He was thin, almost emaciated, with long,
skinny arms and legs. He had a mark around his neck, which
at first I believed to have been left by the garrotte that broke
his neck, although I came to think subsequently that it was

more likely caused by the habitual wearing of something heavy around his neck, for the indentation looked old, and the result of long practice.' His eyes on Hrype blazed. 'And he had the marks of a whip across both shoulders.' He raised his right hand, miming the flicking of a whip over his shoulders. Left, right. 'Had someone else beaten him, the marks would have been quite different. I have seen the back of a man who has been whipped,' he added, his face grave.

'The description fits the man I encountered at Crowland,' Hrype said quietly. 'It all fits: the colouring, the physique, the emaciation that resulted from rigorous fasting. The marks of the flagellum, I suggest, make it all but certain.'

Gurdyman nodded. 'Yes, I agree. So, my old friend, if Father Clement's body is now in the custody of the sheriff, awaiting burial, who is the man at Chatteris?'

'He is a killer,' Hrype said. 'Three people were somehow in his way, or perhaps represented a danger to him. He did not hesitate to murder two of them, and he tried to kill the third.' He met Gurdyman's eyes. 'The question is, why?'

FIFTEEN

We clung to each other, crouching down as close to the ground as we could, pressing our bodies against the cold, wet sand. There was no shelter. All we could do was suffer the furious onslaught and hope that in time it would lessen.

It didn't.

The wind was screaming and howling; the rain was like handfuls of small stones flung hard at us from close at hand; the temperature seemed to have dropped so far and so fast that it was as if midwinter had broken out in the middle of spring. Rollo was shivering so violently that I could hear the chattering of his teeth, and I was scarcely any less cold.

Whatever force was out there, it did not want us anywhere near.

It was magic: fierce, angry magic.

The swift succession of events had shocked me deeply. I felt assaulted by the dark power opposing me, shaken to my core at the way it had robbed me of my ability to see the safe path. It was, I am ashamed to say, some time before my mind woke up and began to organize a response. *You are not help-less*, a stern voice seemed to say inside my head. *You have weapons of your own. Use them!*

I sent out a thought to Fox, hoping and praying he was still close. I caught a flicker of russet brown as he flicked his tail. Then, still clutching Rollo, deliberately I put him out of my mind; to do what I was about to attempt, you have to clear your thoughts of everything else, and that was going to be difficult when the most vital part of *everything else* was holding the man I loved in my arms again. It would have been better to let go of him and move a short distance away, but I knew I wasn't going to be able to be that strong.

It was a new skill. Hrype had told me about it some time ago, but as a teacher he doesn't have Gurdyman's patience, and it was my present mentor who had slowly and steadily increased my confidence. Believing you can do something, he always says, is three-quarters of the way to doing it.

I might be helpless, and Rollo all but unconscious, but there was another with me who surely was not: I was attempting to put my own awareness, my own consciousness, into Fox; or, I suppose, make myself become him. It amounts to pretty much the same thing. Under Gurdyman's tuition, I had become much closer to my animal guide, discovering, to my intense delight, that once I was in the light trance state, I was gaining the ability to see through Fox's eyes, scent with his acute sense of smell – this could at times be quite alarming and sometimes downright nauseating – and, perhaps most crucially, share his vivid perception of approaching danger.

As yet I was not very good at it, but I was going to try. I made myself relax, deepened and slowed my breathing, and closed my eyes. I sent my thoughts out to Fox, and he, friend that he is, accepted me. After a time – I have no idea how long it takes – I slid quietly into him.

With the part of me that still crouched on the ground

clutching Rollo, I was aware that Fox was trotting away, nosing back along the safe path that he could see as well as I once could. I felt a sort of wrench as he disappeared into the fog. But, in some unfathomable way that I did not begin to understand, part of me was going with him. And through his bright brown eyes with their golden lights, I saw what I had hoped and prayed to see: the storm, if that was what it was, only pounded down on the place where Rollo and I lay, at the end of the safe path.

I called Fox back to me and withdrew myself from him, thanking him, thanking the wise guardian spirits that had made our link possible. He stayed close, or at least I thought so. There was no need now for me actually to see him, for his job was done. I now knew that I would only be walking blind for a short distance, just until we came out from beneath the storm, and Fox had shown me where to put my feet. Once we were free of the malignant power beating down on us from out of those deadly black clouds, I would be able to guide us again.

'We must get away from here!' I shouted to Rollo. Even though I yelled right by his ear, he barely heard me, for the wind and the hard rain had reached a cacophonous climax.

'It's not safe!' he yelled back once I'd made him understand. 'One slip and we'll be in it!'

'No we won't because *I'll be able to see the path*!' I screeched.

There was a moment – a precious moment that I knew would live with me for ever – when he looked right into my eyes and gave a small nod. It was as if he was saying: *I remember your uncanny ability, and I will put myself in your hands.*

Without letting myself think about the awesome responsibility, I struggled to my feet, pulling him with me. He was very weak, and when he picked up his heavy pack and slung it over his shoulder, he staggered. I tried to take it from him, but he would not let me. My heart sank a little as I realized how tough it was going to be to get all the way back along the path.

But there were other dangers to overcome first. I pushed

him behind me, pulling his arms round my waist and holding them there with mine; I wanted him to follow me so closely that he would be putting his feet exactly where mine had been. Then I slipped back into my trance state and set off along the exact route that Fox had shown me.

One step, two, three, then Rollo and I got into a rhythm and we were moving swiftly back along the path. I counted almost fifty paces, and then quite suddenly the pulverizing rain stopped, the temperature shot up and the fog rolled itself up and disappeared.

I stopped. Ahead of us was the salt marsh, and I begged the spirits to show me the safe way back. Some benign ancestor must have been with me, for straight away the snaky line of the path lit up as if it had been set on fire. It was so brilliant that I was quite sure Rollo could see it too, and I turned my head and cried, 'Look! That's the way we must go!'

His blank stare told me he could see nothing at all.

I did not let that affect me. I felt jubilant, invincible. With my eyes fixed on the shining track, I stepped forward. We were walking under a clear blue sky, and the welcome, blessed sun was beating down on our backs.

I spun round.

Not even one little puff of fog remained, and there was no sign of the storm.

I wondered what would happen if we set off back towards the end of the path and the sea that had lapped up so close. I had little doubt that the malevolent power out there would instantly beat down on us again.

I was not going to put it to the test.

We were still too close to danger. Taking Rollo's hand – warmer now, I was relieved to find – I urged him on.

I had long lost count of the time, but as we neared the line of dunes that marked the end of the salt marsh, the light suggested that it was around noon. Rollo was almost done for. I knew he must rest, and hopefully eat and drink a little, for his strength was all used up. I raised my eyes and looked along the ridge of higher ground, searching for some sort of shelter. The weather was warm and sunny, but I had just had an eloquent demonstration of how quickly conditions could change, and I did not want our period of restoration to be interrupted by having to leap up and find somewhere out of the rain.

Eventually, I spotted something that I thought might do. It would mean a trudge through the dunes, which would be hard work on legs already aching with fatigue, but I thought it would be worth it. A few hundred paces back from the dunes, I could make out a row of sea-buckthorn bushes, and behind them the dark form of a stand of pine trees. It was, I decided, the best we were going to find.

The journey across the dunes almost finished us. I don't know how Rollo kept moving. He was so far gone that he did not even notice when I took his pack from him and slung it on my back. With that heavy load and my leather satchel, it was all I could do to put one foot in front of the other.

Finally, we reached the pine trees. There were eight or ten of them, and I saw that further inland there were more. But this first little stand was enough. The ground was slippery with a bed of pine needles, which would insulate us if the temperature dropped. I found a sort of cave beneath the lowest branches of two trees, standing so close together that their limbs intertwined. I wriggled my way in, finding that it was just about big enough for two.

Rollo had slumped down against a tree trunk the moment I had removed my arm from around his waist. Without even asking, I opened his pack and delved down through the first few layers. I found he was well supplied for the outdoors. I also discovered why his pack was so heavy, for in addition to a cloak and a thick blanket, he had a rolled-up animal skin that had been cured so as to make it waterproof.

I wished I'd looked in his pack when we'd been out there beneath that furious storm. Then – and the thought was an unwelcome one – I wondered why Rollo hadn't remembered about the contents of his pack himself. Was that malign power so strong, then, that it could even affect a man's mind, making him unable to help himself?

I put that thought from me. We were safe now, I assured myself.

I spread out the animal skin and smoothed Rollo's blanket on top. Then I got out my own blanket, for, although it was warm enough then, it would grow cold as the day wore on towards evening. Backing out of the pine tree cave, I unwound my shawl and spread it on the ground to dry, in a patch of sunshine that filtered down through the trees to the floor of the glade. My gown was soaked, too, and after a moment's reflection, I took it off and laid it down beside my shawl.

Then I turned to Rollo. He was almost asleep, or perhaps lapsing into unconsciousness; I did not know. I felt the urge to hurry, so without giving myself time to think about it, I unfastened his belt and then took off his tunic and hose, spreading them beside my clothes. His undershirt, too, was wringing wet, so I took that off as well. There was a cut on his upper chest, quite new. It ought to have been stitched, for it had healed ragged and bumpy.

I had to keep telling myself that at that moment he was my patient and I was honour bound to do my best for him. The fact that I was taking such thrilled delight from the sight of his beautiful, naked body must be put right to the back of my mind . . .

I half-led, half-dragged him inside the shelter. I made him lie down on his blanket, then covered him as far as the waist with mine. I watched as he turned on his side, curling up his legs. His breathing deepened, and I knew he was asleep.

I stood thinking. My shift was uncomfortably clammy, and once I was lying beside Rollo, it would make him cold. That was my excuse.

I took it off, put it with the rest of our clothes and, mother-naked, slipped under the blanket beside him.

Rollo had endured a living nightmare. Physically and mentally exhausted, he slept, motionless and dreamless, for a long time. When at last he began to struggle up towards wakefulness, he found himself, in a mixture of dream vision and memory, going back to the events of the last hours. The path that led nowhere. The terrible quicksand. Strega, dying while he stood helplessly watching. The storm that had driven him to the ground like a feeble blade of grass.

Kneeling there, collapsing over on his side, believing he was about to die.

Then, a miracle: Lassair, appearing out of the mist like a beautiful angel . . .

He was awake.

He opened his eyes and looked up into the branches of a tree. There was a strong smell of pine resin, reminding him of the wine the Greeks made, sealing their bottles with resin so that the wine was subtly scented with the essence of the tree. He stared down across the blanket that covered him, peering out into the glade beyond. It must be night, for the space between the trees was full of moonlight.

He realized he was naked. Moving first an arm, then a leg, and feeling warm flesh beside him, he realized that she was lying next to him. She was on her back, and she, too, was naked.

He could remember only vaguely how they had ended up here beneath the trees. She had virtually carried him for the last few yards, his heavy pack slung over her back, bowing under the combined load. They had both been drenched to the skin. She must have put their clothes out to dry.

He felt something under his head: a bundle of some sort. Exploring it with one hand, he discovered that it was his tunic and hose. She must have got up at nightfall to fetch them, because if she'd left them out in the glade, they would by now be damp again, from the dew. He reached out and touched a similar bundle under Lassair's head. He smiled. She could easily have dressed once her gown was dry, and he was both touched and excited by the fact that she had chosen to stay as bare as he was.

The moonlight was strong, and, looking down at her, he could make out her features quite well. Her face was thinner, he thought, but still beautiful in his eyes. The high cheekbones stood out more clearly now, and he could see the fine white scar on her left cheek, shaped like the crescent moon. He had been with her when she had acquired it. She had fought like a tiger that night, throwing her whole self into the struggle, just as she had in the interminable journey from the end of the path back to safety.

Her body next to him was filling his senses, and he was responding to her powerfully. He very much wanted to touch her, to run his fingers over her smooth flesh until she woke up, and then to bend down and kiss her: her mouth, her neck, her throat, her small, firm breasts, her flat stomach . . .

He clenched his hand into a fist and firmly drew it back. She was naked, yes, and she had stripped him too, but he knew full well why. They had both been worn out, and had they slumped down and slept as they were, soaked through, they would have woken cold and shivering. As it was, both of them were warm and dry, and their clothes were neatly folded, ready to be put on when they rose. He did not believe she would repulse him if he reached out for her, but somehow he felt that it would have been taking advantage. She meant far too much to him to risk taking a wrong step, especially now, at the beginning of it all.

He knew without even having to think about it that this was indeed the beginning.

He lay down again. She sensed his movement and turned on to her side, facing away from him. Her breathing settled down again, rhythmic and deep, and he realized she hadn't woken up.

He curled his long body round behind hers, arm around her slim waist, legs drawn up and pressed to hers. For a while, her nearness aroused him, but he told himself that now was not the time. Besides, he was still very weary. Soon he fell asleep again.

It was daylight when I woke up. I lay looking out at the thin sunshine in the glade beyond our shelter, and I knew from the quality of the light that it wasn't long after dawn. I was blissfully comfortable, for Rollo's blanket beneath us was thick and soft, and the animal skin had kept the ground chill from penetrating. I was warm, too, for not only were we covered by my own blanket, but also his arms were around me and his body was pressed against my back. I sighed with pleasure, relaxing against him.

As I grew more fully awake, the reality of my situation dawned on me. I was lying naked with a man I barely knew!

Yes, I loved him, and I was fairly sure he loved me. The fact that I'd heard him when he called out to me, even though he was far away, told me that, in some great pattern that humans are not meant to understand, he and I were bound together.

Nevertheless, we were virtually strangers to each other, and the fact of our sharing a bed without a stitch on was out of necessity, not desire. Well, I desired him then, without a doubt, and I could tell it was the same for him, for all that he was still asleep.

It would happen, and I knew it. One day, probably quite soon, we would fulfil our destiny and become lovers. The day was not that day, however; every instinct told me so. Carefully removing his arms – not without several pangs of regret – I crept out of our lair and, gathering up the bundle of my folded clothes, stepped out into the glade and got dressed.

I had just finished brushing and braiding my hair – quite dry now – and was putting on my coif when I felt eyes on me. Bending down to look back inside the shelter, I saw he was propped up on one elbow, watching me with a smile on his face.

His eyes ran over me, from my head to my feet and back again, taking in the fact that I was dressed. I thought he murmured, 'Shame.' Then he unfolded his own clothes, and I turned my back to give him privacy.

I felt him come and stand behind me. He put his arms round me – already they felt familiar – and he said, right in my ear, 'You came to find me, and you saved my life. I am now bound to you, by ties of indebtedness and also by ties of love.' Then he turned me to face him and, as if putting a seal on his words, gently kissed me on the lips.

It was the first time he had spoken to me of love; the first time any man had done so. Glad, so very glad, that it was Rollo, I lifted my chin so that I was looking into his eyes. 'As I am to you,' I whispered.

We stood for some moments, not speaking, not moving, simply absorbing each other. It felt as if we were enchanted, as if that little glade among the pine trees was a place of magic that had bestowed its gift on us.

With a sigh, he broke the spell.

'We should get going,' he said, and the obvious regret in his tone made me want to sing. 'There is much I have to tell you, my love, and a task that I must complete.'

'Let me help,' I said, without even a pause to think. I didn't care what his task was. It would be dangerous – of course it would, for yesterday the forces ranged against him had had him at their mercy, on the point of death. I wanted to share the danger. Just at that moment, I was so exhilarated, so full of joy, that I'd have died with him if he'd asked me to.

He was watching me, his dark eyes intent. 'I am reluctant to ask you,' he muttered, 'but I have the feeling that I'm not going to be able to fulfil my mission without your help.'

'I will do anything,' I said softly.

He made a sound in his throat, half anguish, half a moan of happiness. 'I know,' he said. 'That is why I don't want to involve you.'

'I can take care of myself,' I said gently. 'Remember who it was who got us away from the storm at the end of the path?'

He smiled grimly. 'I'm not likely to forget.'

We studied each other for some moments. I was pretty sure I knew what he was thinking. It must have come hard, for a man such as he to face the fact that a skinny village healer could do something he couldn't do, and that, in truth, he still had need of her assistance.

In the end he gave a sigh, but he didn't seem to be able to stop the grin spreading over his face. 'Are you hungry?' he asked.

It was not what I was expecting, but I was, very. 'Starving,' I said.

'Me too.' He reached down for my hand, gave it a squeeze and released it. 'Let's pack up and head off for some place where they'll serve us breakfast. I'll treat you to anything and everything you fancy –' he patted a purse at his waist and I heard the chink of coins – 'and when we've eaten all we want, I'll tell you why I'm here and what I have to do. What do you say?'

'Yes,' I said.

SIXTEEN

Gurdyman leaned back in his chair, kneading the flesh of his brow as if his head hurt. Watching him, Hrype would not have been surprised if it did. The intense concentration he had brought to bear on the matter, and the awful, underlying sense of urgency spurring them both on, were enough to give anyone a headache.

'If the man at Chatteris isn't Father Clement,' Gurdyman said heavily, removing his hand, 'then who is he? And if we are right in our conclusion that the dead man *is* Father Clement, then what was he doing over in the eastern fens? Was he killed at the spot where he became entangled with the boat, or did the murderer take the body there because it was a fitting place for his sacrifice?'

Hrype gave a brief sound of frustrated irritation. 'Too many questions, Gurdyman,' he said shortly. 'I can give no answers other than useless speculation.'

Gurdyman smiled. 'Your speculation is never useless, old friend,' he murmured.

Hrype barely heard. 'It would be quite possible for anyone with a boat to have done the killing in one place and then transported the body to the spot where it was found,' he said slowly, 'but my heart tells me it was not done like that.' He hesitated, trying to catch the nebulous impression that so convinced him and put it into words. 'From what you have told me, I have a picture in my mind of a body, naked and suffering the marks of the Threefold Death: the stab to the neck, the garrotte, the drowning. In his stomach are the remains of his last meal; the powerful substances that rendered him unconscious have done their work all too well. The killer forces hazel stakes into the soft ground at the fen edge, lashing his victim to them with honeysuckle ropes. This was not so much a killing, Gurdyman, as a performance, done for the benefit of the only witnesses.'

'The spirits. The gods of the place,' Gurdyman said softly.

'Yes. Our killer was making an offering to them because he wished something from them; perhaps because, having already been granted whatever he had asked for, he was giving thanks. Either way, this performance would have been enacted in its entirety in the place where the body was found.' He added, with quiet conviction, 'I am quite certain of it.'

Gurdyman nodded slowly. 'Yes. I, too, see it that way,' he agreed.

'So, let us ask the question again,' Hrype said. 'Why was Father Clement over on the east side of the fens?' Abruptly, he stood up, moving to the side of the sunny courtyard so that he could look up into the sky. 'Not long past midday,' he murmured. 'If I leave now, I should be there by noon tomorrow.'

Gurdyman got to his feet. Stiff after sitting still for so long, he pressed a hand to the small of his back. 'It is a long way,' he said. 'I will pack some provisions for you.'

He did not need to ask where Hrype was going; if they were to find out what reason Father Clement had had for journeying to the area where his body was left, then one of them must go and ask at the last place where he was known to have been: Crowland Abbey.

Hrype had lived for much of his adult life in the fen country, and he would have said that he was immune to the fears and the superstitions of outsiders. He had visited the Crowland area twice before, but the first time had been before the latest fire, when the abbey was bustling with life, and on the second occasion, he had been intent on a specific mission – to find out more about Father Clement from locals in the vicinity – and he had not taken much notice of his surroundings. Now, however, when in the early afternoon of the following day he finally reached Crowland, he discovered he was wrong. He was as susceptible to irrational fears as anyone.

He was entirely alone. He was exhausted, for yesterday he had walked for almost twenty-five miles before giving in to his hunger and fatigue and finding a place to sleep for what remained of the night. Today he had travelled sometimes on foot and occasionally by boat, in the places where the waters were too wide to jump over or ford. Since mid-morning, when a boatman had dropped him off after ferrying him over a meandering river, he had not seen a living soul. The sky was cloudy and lowering, heavy with the threat of rain. Spirals and twirls of white mist rose up from the damp fen, coalescing into a sort of pale layer lying just above the ground. Looking down, Hrype had the impression that he had no feet. Or, perhaps, was walking on cloud . . .

He shivered, wrapping his cloak more tightly around him. From somewhere quite close there was a sudden booming sound, like someone blowing across the top of a large jar. The reed beds and the swampy conditions were perfect for bitterns, but such was Hrype's state of mind that it took him several moments of heart-pounding fear to remember that. He stood quite still, and presently the sound came again. It was spring, Hrype mused. The bird was seeking a mate.

He trudged on. Peering ahead, he could make out a hump of higher ground ahead. The intervening terrain was sodden but not actually under water, or so he thought. But then, still some hundred or so paces from the island, he realized that it was, in fact, surrounded by water. Not very deep, and clogged with reed banks, but nevertheless he was going to have to get his feet wet. Reaching the water's edge, he stopped and looked around. Now he could make out the fire-blackened ruins of the abbey, but they appeared to be deserted. If there was anyone in residence – there had to be, he told himself firmly, refusing to believe he'd come all this way for nothing – then they were not keeping a lookout for visitors and preparing to send out a boat.

He noticed that there was a line of stakes sticking out of the water. Hoping that these had been placed to mark the shallow way across to the island, he sat down, removed his boots, rolled up his hose and stepped into the water.

He was too busy watching where he put his feet and trying to avoid the deeper water to look up, so when a voice hailed him from the far shore, it took him by surprise. It was only then, when he had evidence that there was someone there other than himself and the spirits whom he sensed crowding around him from all sides, that he let himself acknowledge how the atmosphere of the place had unnerved him.

'Halloa!' the voice cried. Hrype saw a tall, spare man in his middle years standing on the shore just above the water line. 'Go over to your left –' the man waved the appropriate arm vigorously in case his visitor did not know his right from his left – 'and you'll find the ground slopes up more gently.'

Hrype did as he was bid, soon finding himself climbing up out of the water on to the soil of Crowland island. His feet were filthy with black, slimy, clinging mud. They were also so cold that he could not feel them. He appeared to have cut his right heel; he saw a line of blood snaking out through the foul mud.

The man hurried to meet him. 'That looks nasty,' he observed, studying Hrype's foot. 'Come along with me to what is left of our infirmary, and I'll see if I can find something to bathe it with.'

Hrype followed him up the shore. He looked around, noticing the remains of the church and the buildings that had formed the sides of the cloister beside it. Judging by one that had survived the flames, they appeared to have been made of timber, with wattle infill and reed-thatched roofs. No wonder the abbey had burned so thoroughly.

The thin man led him to a makeshift hut that stood within the outlines of what had been a bigger building, rectangular in shape. 'We've put everything we salvaged in here,' he said, ducking his head and leading the way inside the little hut, which was crowded with sacks and crates and had a small fire burning in a central hearth. 'It's not much, but at least it keeps the rain off. Now—' He stared around, his eyes alighting on a small three-legged stool. 'Sit there, and I'll wash and tend your foot.'

Hrype sank down on to the stool, watching as the man moved around him, fetching a bowl, filling it from the iron vessel suspended over the hearth and adding some drops from a small bottle made of green glass. Then he rolled up his sleeves, hitched up his robe and knelt before Hrype.

'Our infirmarer is not here,' he said as he bathed Hrype's wounded heel, 'since, like most of my monks, he has been

sent to be useful in another abbey until this one is up and running again.' The *my monks* was a clue, and Hrype was prepared for what the man said next. 'I am Ingulphus,' he said, looking up and smiling, 'and I am abbot here.'

'I heard about the fire,' Hrype remarked. If he began with some general comments, he thought, then it might be easier to pose the question he'd come to ask without raising suspicion.

Ingulphus made a sound of despair. 'I am not surprised. We lost so much. All our buildings burned, including our library, with its precious manuscripts and the experimental model Brother Luke had been working on, with which he hoped to demonstrate the movements of the planets in their spheres.'

'How did the fire start?' Hrype asked. 'Was it a raid?'

'No, no, it wasn't,' the abbot replied. 'In a way, that would have been easier to bear, since it would have been outside our control. No; a plumber was working in the church tower. A moment's carelessness, and you see the result all around you.' He sighed, returning to Hrype's foot and rinsing it carefully, then applying some drops of whatever it was in the little green bottle.

For a few moments Hrype felt as if someone had set fire to his foot. He cried out, and Ingulphus grinned.

'Sorry,' he said. 'I should have warned you, I suppose, but I always feel that if I'm going to experience pain, I'd rather not be warned, since then you suffer twice, once from the anticipation, once from the pain itself.'

He put another couple of drops into the cut, and this time the pain was less acute. 'What is that?' Hrype asked.

The abbot looked up. 'I have no idea. Our herbalist makes it, and it is his sovereign remedy for cleaning cuts. Now, a dressing, to keep the wound clean –' he worked as he spoke, his busy, capable hands wrapping and tying the strip of clean linen – 'and you can put your boot back on.' He looked at Hrype's other foot and, after only a brief hesitation, washed that as well.

'Thank you,' Hrype said gravely when he had finished.

The abbot grinned. 'That's all right. It seemed a shame for you to have one nice clean foot and one filthy one. Now, why

not tell me who you are and why you are here? I thought, when I first spied you coming across the water, that you were one of my monks returning, but I soon saw my mistake.'

'Are you here alone, then?' Hrype asked.

'No, four of the brethren are with me.' He grimaced. 'The four strongest, for our work just now consists mainly of tearing down the ruins and clearing the ground so that the new build can begin.'

The four strongest, Hrype reflected. They would not necessarily be the four brightest, and he thought he understood the abbot's rueful expression. 'Is there not work elsewhere for you too, My Lord Abbot, more suited to your abilities?'

Ingulphus smiled. 'This is my abbey,' he said simply. 'It is up to me to rebuild it.' His smile widened. 'It is often acknowledged among us here that we have a very comfortable life compared with our founder, for our blessed Guthlac clad himself in crude skins, his daily fare was no more than a morsel of barley bread and a cup of muddy water, and he bore his ague and marsh fever without complaint. Men say the island was the haunt of terrifying creatures, demons and vengeful spirits, yet Guthlac prevailed. Perhaps it is no bad thing for we who dwell here two hundred years later to experience the hardships our founder encountered and to celebrate his stout courage, which has enabled his successors to begin again each time our settlement has been destroyed. We shall not fail him now.'

He had finished tidying away the bowl and the wash cloths, and now, straightening up and turning to face Hrype, he said mildly, 'You still haven't told me why you are here.'

The mildness was, Hrype decided, deceptive. The abbot was an astute, brave man and, with such as he, the best thing – perhaps the only thing – was to tell the truth.

'You had a priest here by the name of Father Clement,' he said.

If the abbot was surprised at the remark, he did not show it. 'Yes, indeed. He was our confessor until the fire and, like my monks, he was sent elsewhere afterwards. The five of us here go over to Thorney for confession,' he added, 'for it would be a waste of Father Clement's talents to have him tend

to the spiritual welfare of so small a group.' He studied Hrype intently. 'Did you hope to find Father Clement here? If so –' he answered the question before Hrype had a chance to – 'then I am afraid you have had a wasted journey, for he now minis-ters to the nuns at Chatteris, although we hope very much that he will be permitted to return to us soon, once we are a proper community again, because he—'

'My Lord Abbot,' Hrype interrupted, as gently as he could, 'I am very sorry to tell you this, but I fear that Father Clement is dead.'

The abbot's lean face paled. '*Dead*?' he said in a whisper. 'But how? He was not an old man, and I would have said he was fit, and he—'

'If the body has been correctly identified, and I fear that it has, then Father Clement was murdered,' Hrype said.

The abbot's eyes closed, and his lips moved in silent prayer. Then he stopped, his eyes flew open and he glared at Hrype. 'This cannot be true,' he said angrily, 'for I have had word that Father Clement is safe at Chatteris!'

'The man there is not Father Clement,' Hrype said. 'My guess is that this impostor took his place, although why he should do so, I cannot say. Yet,' he added softly to himself.

The abbot studied him intently. Then, apparently detecting something in his visitor that inclined him to trust him, he said, 'You wish to ask, I dare say, when I last saw Father Clement, and where he was bound when he left here.'

'I do,' Hrype agreed.

'He did not, in truth, wish to leave us,' Ingulphus said, his voice breaking on the words. 'He had requested an audience with the bishop – this was back in the final months of last year, October perhaps, or early November – where he intended to plead his case for remaining here at Crowland. Not that he held out much hope,' he added with a rueful smile. 'He promised to let us know, as indeed he did: not very long after he had gone, we learned he was bound for Chatteris. Then later, as I said, we had word that he was settling into his new life ministering to the nuns.' He shook his head in bemused misery. 'But now you are telling me that was a falsehood, sent by this impostor, and that in truth poor Father Clement never got there . . .'

Hrype was torn between respecting the abbot's raw new grief and pressing on to find out what he had to know. He waited a short while, then said, 'My Lord Abbot, where does your bishop reside?'

He realized as soon as the words were spoken that he should have said *the* bishop; the implication that he might be Ingulphus's man but he certainly wasn't Hrype's was rather obvious.

The abbot, fortunately, had other concerns. His mind clearly still on his late colleague, he said vaguely, 'He's one of the new men brought in from Normandy by our King William. His name's Herbert of Losinga, and originally he came over here to be bishop of Ramsey. Then Thetford fell vacant, and he came here to us.' As if only then recalling the question, he added, 'He is building a fine new church and a dwelling for himself at Lynn, which men are taking to calling Bishop's Lynn in his honour.'

Hrype felt a moment's violent exaltation. The trail was becoming clear . . .

He became aware of Ingulphus's eyes on him, their expression hard. 'I am thinking about this man at Chatteris who pretends to be Father Clement,' Ingulphus said, and Hrype could sense the abbot's anger, although it was tightly controlled. 'The fact that he has taken my friend's place suggests strongly to me that he may also have taken his life.'

'I am inclined to agree,' Hrype murmured.

Ingulphus studied him for some time, and Hrype had the definite impression that he was being sized up. 'I believe I trust you,' the abbot said. 'I dare say you have reasons of your own for pursuing the business of this murder,' he went on shrewdly, 'but the fact remains that, whatever they are, your present desire coincides with mine. You wish to see the killer brought to justice and Father Clement's death thereby avenged.'

'I do,' Hrype agreed. He hesitated, then said, 'Your priest was not the only victim. The killer also murdered a young novice at Chatteris and poisoned another.'

Ingulphus gasped, muttering a swift prayer for the dead girl. 'But the second one is still alive?' he asked anxiously.

'When last I saw her, she seemed to be a little improved.'

'I shall pray for her,' Ingulphus announced. 'As I shall for the souls of my friend and the young nun.'

There was a short silence. Then Ingulphus said, 'Will you stay the night here? The day wears on, and you would not, I am sure, wish to be caught in the marshes once the light fails.'

'I would gladly accept your hospitality, but—' Hrype began.

'Such as it is,' the abbot put in.

'—but I am filled with urgency, and I sense that there is not a moment to lose,' he finished.

Ingulphus watched him, compassion in his face. 'There is so much that you do not tell me,' he mused. 'You are a man of deep secrets, my friend, and I sense something very alien in you.'

The words sounded like the prelude to an attack, yet, even with his highly efficient defences fully alert, Hrype felt no threat. On the contrary, he had rarely sensed such well-being flowing towards him out of a man who had been until very recently a stranger.

'I am many things,' Hrype said carefully. 'By my own lights, I am not evil.'

'*Evil*?' The abbot gave an incredulous laugh. 'Indeed you are not. But come, if you are resolved upon going, I will take you across the water in our little boat.'

They walked together away from the ruins of the abbey and down across the foreshore. Leading the way off to the left, the abbot pointed to a small rowing boat. The two of them dragged the craft down to the water and got in, Ingulphus taking up the oars. In a short time, they were gently bumping up against the bank on the far side.

Hrype got out, turning to say farewell.

Ingulphus was studying him again, a puzzled expression on his face. 'May I ask you something?' he said, and the tentative quality of the question was surprising in a man of his status.

'Of course.'

'Would it offend you if I said I will pray for you?'

Several answers flashed through Hrype's mind. He had formed an opinion of men of the church – soundly based, in his view, and uncompromising. Yet there was something about this Ingulphus . . . From out of nowhere came a quiet voice, echoing in Hrype's head: *all gods are one god, and behind them is the truth.*

And it had been a long time since he had met a man quite like Ingulphus of Crowland.

He bowed his head. 'I would be honoured.'

Then he shouldered his pack, swirled his cloak around him and strode away.

SEVENTEEN

R ollo and I had drifted eastwards to find our shelter under the pine trees, and now we set off back towards the fens. We seemed to be on a different track from the one I'd come out on, although it was difficult to tell, for there were many barely-visible animal trails leading along the ridges that had built up like frozen waves behind the foreshore. We veered slightly inland, and presently emerged on to a proper road, simultaneously dragged out of our magical solitude and back into the world of living men and women.

The road was busy with traffic of every kind, from single pedestrians, most of them carrying loads of varying weights and sizes, to huge, overloaded ox carts lumbering along right on the crown of the road and holding everyone up. After only perhaps a quarter of a mile, we came to a crossroads, where another track ran roughly north-south and intersected with the one we were on, going east-west.

As soon as I set foot on the track that came up out of the south, I knew it for what it was. Involuntarily, I stopped, quite unable to go on.

Rollo, beside me, spun round to look at me, his face full of concern. 'What is it?' His voice was so low that nobody but I could have heard.

I shook my head, incapable of putting into words the huge emotions that were coursing through me. He took hold of my arm and led me to the side of the road; by pure chance, the place where we sat down on the grassy bank beside the crossroads happened to be on the east-west stretch rather than the north-south. Immediately, the fierce sensations abated and I was able to speak.

'The road coming up from the south is a greenway,' I said, my voice rather shaky. I knew he would not know what that meant, so I made myself go on. 'It's difficult to explain, but there are certain tracks which have always been used: some for reasons of practicality, perhaps because they run along higher ground and so keep relatively dry; some because they are power paths which link places where the forces in the earth are particularly strong. I can—' No: that would be too boastful. 'The paths emit a sort of vibration –' it was the best word I could think of, yet it did not begin to describe the extraordinary feeling that had so recently fizzed and sparkled up through me – 'and some people can sense it.'

He nodded. 'And you are one of these people.'

'I'm only—'

'No time to be coy, Lassair,' he said with a grin. 'Don't forget, I've already seen what you can do with a concealed path across a bog.' I knew what he meant, although I could have argued with his description. 'These greenways,' he went on, 'link particular places, you said?'

'Yes.' It seemed that he would not be content with the brief explanation, so I thought quickly for a way to elaborate that would not involve being there all day. 'Our ancestors have always lived in these lands,' I began, 'or so we are led to believe. Our bards trace the lineage back to the days of the gods, and legends tell of a time long, long ago when men were given the gift of fire and taught how to use metals. In those days the spirits still walked the earth, teaching mankind and encouraging them always to question, always to explore, to push back the boundaries of darkness and superstition so that they could see the pure light. In return, mankind honoured the spirits, making sacred spaces where they were worshipped and where sacrifices were made. These holy sites are long gone, but their power was so strong that they have left an echo.'

'Which people like you can sense,' he said softly.

'I – yes.' It was not really a time for false modesty. I was about to go on, but a glance at his expression suggested he had something very important on his mind: his dark eyes were full of light, and he looked as if his entire being had suddenly been lifted up.

'That place at the end of the path,' he said, 'where I was about to die and where you found me. Is there one of these sacred places anywhere near it?'

'There is,' I whispered, although there was nobody anywhere near enough to have overheard, and those who were passing by were far too intent on their own troubles. 'There once was an ancient wooden circle, in the centre of which stood an upturned oak stump, its splayed roots open to the sky.'

And I went on to tell him, as briefly as I could, about the dream I'd had which had led me to him.

When I had finished there was a long silence. After a while he reached out and took my hand. I had no idea what he felt about magic; on the one hand he was a Norman, and the Normans were not renowned for being sympathetic to the old ways. On the other hand, the strange abilities with which I'd been bestowed had saved his life.

When at long last he spoke, it was not at all what I was expecting.

'Before we go any further,' he said – in itself a lovely remark because it suggested we would go on together – 'I should tell you that, while my father was born into a powerful Norman family, he refused to marry the suitable but dull daughter of his father's best friend who had been selected for him. Instead he chose my mother – they never bothered to get married – and she is a dark-haired, black-eyed woman of the south, fiery and fierce, and the peasants of Sicily fear her because they say she is a *strega*.' A shadow passed over his face, and for a moment he looked grief-stricken. 'Strega means witch,' he said huskily. 'My mare was called Strega.'

Then I understood the sorrow. Before we left our shelter in the pine trees, we had said a blessing for his lost horse. I had seen his face wet with tears, and loved him the more.

I felt the sharp edge of his grief retreat a little, and the respite allowed me to reflect on what he had just told me. So his mother was a witch, was she? That answered quite a lot of questions I'd been storing up about him . . .

One of us had to reassert the impatient present, and it was him. 'So this old road led up to the wooden circle?' he said.

'They do say so,' I agreed. 'It's claimed that it was built by the southern invaders when they needed to be able to move their armies around quickly – after the Great Revolt – but we know there was a greenway there long before that. There's nowhere else it could lead to except the shrine of the crossing place.'

'The crossing place,' he repeated, almost to himself. I knew there was no need to explain; he already understood. Then, so abruptly that it took me by surprise, he stood up, pulled me up after him and said, 'This is a crossroads, and where you find them you usually also find an inn, so let's go and seek it out.'

He kept his promise and treated me to the biggest meal I'd ever eaten. It was probably breakfast, because although we seemed to have been awake for ages, it was still early. There was another promise he had made – to explain what he was doing – and he had not yet honoured that one. I was prepared to wait, for a while at least.

We were sitting at a long table, sharing it with other hungry travellers. One of them mentioned the weather – in a group of strangers flung together, someone usually does – and after a few grumbles about it being too wet, too cold, too hot and not hot enough, an old man next to Rollo leaned closer into the group and said, 'No more storms like that one back at Michaelmas,' and a sudden silence fell.

It was Rollo who broke it. 'I heard tell of that storm,' he said, an awed note in his voice. 'Many men died, or so it was said.'

'Many men is right,' another man agreed. Wide-eyed, he added, 'Bodies washed up all along the shore, there were! Made you scared to venture out of your door, for fear of what you'd find waiting for you.'

'That weren't no normal storm,' another old man put in. I saw the sudden sharp attention in Rollo's eyes, as if this were somehow of crucial interest. 'I've lived on this coast all my life,' the old man went on, 'and I've never seen a force like that. Straight out of the north it came, like a snow spirit whipping up a vast team of wolves and driving them ahead of it. Water built up like a wall, and down it fell on everything and everyone in its way. And *cold*!' He paused, rheumy old blue eyes wide for dramatic effect. 'There's never been cold like that, I'm telling you; it bit clear through to the bone. Those poor bastards in the sea didn't stand a chance. They'd have frozen to death even before the waters rushed in and drowned them.'

Poor bastards. I wondered why he had called them that. He seemed sympathetic for the terrible way they had died, and I concluded that the disparaging term was just his usual habit.

'There was wreckage and all!' a new, excited voice put in. 'All sorts of goods washed up on the shore, and we – *ouch*!'

The abrupt cessation of his remark suggested strongly that somebody had kicked him, very hard, to stop him blabbing to a couple of outsiders how the locals had helped themselves to the bounty that the storm had so kindly provided.

'What happened to the bodies?' Rollo asked after an awkward few moments.

'They were taken away and buried up at Frythe,' the first speaker said.

'Where's that?'

'Up on the coast road.' The man waved an arm roughly towards the north and the sea.

'They came from the water,' the very old man said in a wavering voice. 'Seemed only right to lay them to rest close as possible to the place they were lost.'

Frythe. I committed to name to memory. Glancing at Rollo, I knew he had done too.

We stayed chatting to our fellow diners for a while longer, talking about everything except the storm. Then Rollo got up, saying we had to be on our way. It might have been just my imagination, but I don't think the men were sorry to see us go.

* * *

Frythe turned out to be a small village set to the west of the road as it drove on towards the sea. There was an open space with a pond, a row of mean-looking dwellings, one or two bigger houses and some hovels. There was also a dilapidated inn and a church, beside which was a graveyard enclosed within a stone wall set with flints. Rollo and I went to look, and straight away we saw several lines of raw new graves. Not one had any flower or token to indicate there was someone who cared about the dead body lying down there in the earth.

The sacristan was over by the church, busy sweeping the path leading up to the iron-studded wooden door. He had a barrow beside him on which lay a heavy spade; perhaps his next job was to dig another grave. It was clear that he had seen us, and presently he put down his broom and came to pass the time of day.

'There are a lot of fresh graves,' Rollo remarked once we had exchanged greetings and the sacristan had observed that it was warm for the time of year. 'Are they all casualties of the September storm?'

'Every one,' the sacristan said heavily. 'Most of them pulled dead out of the sea and strangers to us, but there's quite a few of our own too, caught up in the floods and drowned or struck by lightning. Three of them struck, there were!' His eyes were round with amazement. 'Three! And I've only heard tell of one other, and I've always doubted that tale because it was my cousin's husband that told me, and he's famous for exaggerating a story when it suits him.'

I was getting a clearer picture of this storm. To the image of huge seas and an icy north wind, I now added thunder and lightning. Which was very strange, as the weather lore I had learned ever since I was a child suggested you did not normally have thunderstorms with a very cold northerly wind.

'There were drowned horses, too,' the sacristan was saying. 'They disappeared very quickly, I can tell you.' He put a finger to the side of his nose. 'People are hungry, and there's good meat on a freshly-dead horse.' He fell silent, clearly thinking back. 'Some of the creatures made it to shore, mind,' he went on. 'Seems horses swim better than men.'

'What else came ashore?' Rollo asked. I was not deceived

by the light tone; this question was, for some reason, important.

'Oooh, let me see, now.' The sacristan frowned. 'Sacks of supplies – good food and drink it had been, before it was all spoiled by the salt water, although much of the bacon and preserved meat found good homes, it being salty already, as it were.' He chuckled at his own small wit. 'There were crates of fighting gear, too. Arrows, bows, flints and steels, stuff like that.' He shrugged. 'Being a man of God, I don't know about those things,' he added piously.

Rollo was staring down at the long lines of graves, but I did not think he was seeing them. His attention was far away.

The time was ripe, I decided, for him to tell me what this was all about. I said a courteous farewell to the sacristan, wished him good luck with his day's toil and, taking Rollo firmly by the arm, led the way out of the graveyard and back to the road. When we were safely away from the village and sufficiently out in the open to be able to spot anyone approaching, I stopped, selected a low, grassy bank beside the track and sat down, pulling Rollo down beside me. I dug in my leather satchel for my flask of Edild's special restorative for travellers, offering him a sip and taking one myself. I think he already knew why we had stopped, for there was a wry smile on his face.

I looked at him and said, 'Now, if you please, explain to me what we're doing here.'

Rollo had already gone through it in his mind and had a fair idea of how he would tell her all that she so richly deserved to know. Consequently, he was able to start speaking almost immediately.

'I had no idea, when this whole business started, where it would lead,' he said. 'It began, I suppose, at the beginning of last year. The king was off in Normandy, and it was feared that the Scots in the north would take advantage of his absence and organize an invasion into English lands.'

He studied her face. She was clearly listening intently, but he could not read her expression; it was almost as if she had deliberately arranged her features so as to give nothing away.

She knew of his involvement with the Norman ruling power; he had told her of his allegiances when they first met. He had remarked lightly then that he would pass on a comment of hers to the king, and she had laughed, thinking he was joking. One day – one day quite soon – he would have to enlighten her. He was fearful, though. She had told him that her family were Saxon, and that the Norman rule was inimical to them – and that was putting it mildly. He was afraid that, once she knew how close he was to the king, she might discover she could not – no. He would not let himself even think it.

'The king needed people up on the border country to keep watch for signs of any advance by the Scots,' he ploughed on. 'If anything should happen, William needed to know about it as soon as possible, and word would be sent to him via the chain of messengers that he has set up all over the land. It's amazing,' he added, 'how fast a message can travel, for each man covers only a short distance and so his horse is fresh and fast.' But he was digressing. 'The king was right to be apprehensive, for in early summer last year, King Malcolm led his forces into England, pushing down south of the Forth river and penetrating deep into English-held territory. As soon as the Scots king's intention became clear, the message to the king was initiated and sent on its journey over all the long miles from England's northern border to Normandy.'

'So King William came rushing back to defend his territory.' Her tone was neutral; he had no idea what she was thinking.

'Yes. He crossed back to England in August, bringing his army with him, and immediately set about organizing his forces for the expedition into the north. He was, they say, quietly furious at the thought of King Malcolm and his men encamped on English soil, apparently doing nothing but waiting for him to get up there and face them.' He paused, gathering his words. 'King William elected to send his great force north in two different ways: one army going overland; one sent by sea, up the east coast to the Scottish border.'

Watching her closely, he saw a sudden flare of excitement in her eyes. *She understands*, he thought.

'The king was riding at the head of his land-army, and in due course he met King Malcolm, and peace, of a sort, was negotiated between them. King Malcolm agreed to swear allegiance to King William, and in return William undertook to restore to Malcolm the towns he had held under the rule of William's father, the Conqueror, and in addition pay him twelve marks every year.'

'A far more advantageous arrangement for King William than for King Malcolm,' she remarked, 'for William not only achieved his purpose of getting the Scots king out of England, but he also gained him as a vassal. King Malcolm left the confrontation only with a couple of promises.'

Astute of her, he reflected, to have instantly seen to the heart of the matter. 'King William returned south,' he went on, 'but not without first making some further arrangements regarding the border.' He paused, for what he was about to tell her was confidential. Should he go on? His head said no, but his heart and all his senses were full of her. She had just saved his life; did that not give her the right to share some of his secrets?

'King William is very aware that last year's treaty with the Scottish king was an insubstantial thing,' he went on, speaking fast before he could change his mind. 'In the long term, the solution is to fortify the border lands, and before he can set about doing that, he needs to know the number and the quality of those forces that may be ranged against him. He therefore placed eyes and ears—'

'Spies,' she put in coolly.

'Very well. He put spies, then, in the border lands which he plans to take later this year.' The king would have long since received Rollo's information concerning Carlisle, and doubtless he was already sending his conquering forces up to the north-west, if not riding with them himself. But there was no need to say so.

He paused, seeing again the body of Hawksclaw lying across the bed of animal furs, efficiently dispatched even while he slept. He glanced at Lassair. He had killed Hawksclaw; he had killed other men. Did she know these deep things about him? Did her remarkable powers enable her to see into his heart and understand who and what he was?

But that, too, was something from which he shied away.

He made himself go on.

'The king had a second task for me,' he began. He was reluctant to speak, and the words had to be forced out. Even back when William had first issued the orders, Rollo had been wary. Now that he knew so much more, wariness had given way to dread.

'I said just now that, in order to counter King Malcolm's advance, King William sent half of his army by sea. They perished, almost to the last man, their ships hit by a storm of unbelievable violence that struck somewhere off the east coast.'

She gave a soft gasp. He waited, but she did not speak.

So he went on: 'William has ears and eyes throughout his land. He is a man who always needs to know what is happening, even in the far, forgotten corners of his realm, and he has organized a highly efficient network of men and women who are well paid to keep him informed.' She nodded; perhaps she had heard tell of such people. 'Someone came to him with a whisper overheard, a rumour, the merest suspicion, yet for some reason its effect on the king was powerfully strong.' He fell silent, recalling vividly how the king had looked and sounded as he conveyed to Rollo what he had learned. He felt again the shiver of dread that the king's words had caused.

'What did the whisper say?' Lassair asked quietly.

He met her eyes. *You know, don't you?* he said silently. She made no response.

He took a deep breath that sounded more like a sigh. 'The rumour said that the storm which wiped out the ship-army was no natural storm, but a magical one, raised by a tempestarius.'

He sensed a sudden tension in her, and for a moment she did not speak. Then she repeated the word. 'A tempestarius?'

'It means a storm-raiser.' He lifted an eyebrow, half expecting her to say: *oh, yes, I know all about them.* She didn't. 'There are many ancient tales about such people, or so the king's informant assured him. Some tell of a magical land of clouds called Magonia, where the inhabitants sail the skies in ships made of storm clouds. They are in league with the tempestarii – the storm-raisers – and when the violence of the weather reaches its peak, the Magonians fly down to earth and raid the farms of anything they can carry away.'

Her expression suggested she thought the story a little far-fetched. 'I've never heard of anyone – even the greatest magicians – being able to carry off a herd of cows inside a cloud,' she said. 'It doesn't sound very likely.'

'That's just what the king said,' he murmured.

'But there are certainly shamans and sorcerers who can control the weather, or it's said that there are,' she went on, frowning as she thought. 'The men who teach me have told me of such people.' Her eyes met his, and he saw that she was deeply troubled. 'But this is high magic,' she said, 'and far beyond anything I have ever encountered.' She gave a sudden violent shiver, so strong that it set her entire body shuddering.

'What's the matter?' he asked.

'I was remembering the place where I found you,' she said, so quietly that he had to strain to hear. 'It was a place under an evil spell; there was no doubting it. Someone had put a powerful enchantment on it, and usually that's done to keep people away from something that has to be kept secret.' Now she turned to face him, eyes blazing. 'Supposing the rumour was right and a storm-raiser *did* create the tempest that drowned the ship-army. They perished just off the coast, right here. Out where the shore gives way to the sea there was once a place of power, built by the people who in ancient times held sway in this land. Its power will still be there, and someone capable of raising such a storm would know that.' She paused, fear and excitement competing in her expression. 'He stood out there, right on the site of the circle at the crossing place, and invoked all the force of its long existence to help him. He cast his spell, and the ships and the men were lost. Then, because he did not want anyone to know what he had done, he set an enchantment on the place to stop the curious venturing out on to the salt marsh to investigate.'

There was a light in her face, and he sensed she was being inspired by some power outside herself. 'He knew you would come,' she said, and her voice sounded dreamy, distant; unlike her normal one. 'He's been aware of you, questing after him,

and he set the trap for you and your horse, meaning to draw you on and on, out across the shaking ground, until you both succumbed.' Tears were streaming down her face. 'You lost your poor mare, whom you loved. He got her, but – but . . .'

He opened his arms to her, and she fell against him. He cradled her against his chest, dropping kisses on her soft hair. He wanted to weep with her, for the loss of Strega was raw and pained him constantly.

After a while, he felt able to finish what she had tried to say. 'But he did not get me,' he whispered.

He took her face between his hands, gently turning her that she looked up at him. Then he bent his head and k her lips.

'Thanks to you, my sweeting, he did not get me,' he

She drew away from him a little, eyes fixed on as if the talk of narrowly-avoided death had ma vitally alive, she in her turn took hold of his f him back.

His kiss had been tentative, gentle.

Hers, however, was neither.

EIGHTE

Some time after we had r him and realized just h much I would give to followed seamlessly on th fearsome place was so and my knowledge th

But I had to con not leave alone.

He was on hi looking north to all that we could no was neither good nor evil. elemental power – and it sca

fier
he d
'I
dread
far bey
who wi
making
did some
just now
the other o
wager that'
I had Rol
almost hurt.
I smiled. '
He shoulder
a grin, I hurrie

Hrype was on th
He was half a day
a few miles away.

I said, having thought carefully, 'I am not equal to what the storm-raiser has imprinted on this place. I cannot fight his magic and find a way out to the place of power within the old wood circle.'

He spun round to me. 'I would not ask you to,' he said. 'But I—'

'You are even less well equipped to fight what is out there than I am,' I said, trying to keep my voice steady and sound authoritative. 'You—' I had been about to remind him what happened the first time he made the attempt, but it was too cruel.

He knew, though. His face had clouded again into grief. He hung his head.

I hurried over to him. 'There is nothing more that either of us can do here,' I said urgently. 'You have done what you were commanded to do; you have found out that the rumour s true, and that the storm was raised by human agency.' uman? I wondered about that. The being who possessed such gic was more than human . . .

e raised his head and stared up into the sky. He looked e, full of energy that could not be released in the direction sired.

ave a suggestion,' I said, moving closer to him. 'The deed whose echoes still haunt the very air here may be nd my experience, but I know of not one but two men l be able to help.' I was not quite as certain as I was ut, but I was desperate to get him away before he hing rash. 'I'm not sure where one of these men is ' Hrype could have been almost anywhere – 'but e does not venture far from his home, so I would where we'll find him.'

o's attention now, so fully focused on me that it Where does this man live?' he demanded.

a twisty-turny house in Cambridge.'

d his pack and set off down the road. Hiding to catch him up.

road too, heading for the same destination. ahead, although recently he had been only

He had covered the journey from Crowland to Lynn in a very short time, driving himself on and only giving in and taking a short rest when he was all but exhausted, and he conserved his strength wherever possible by waiting for ferries and lone boatmen to take him by water and give his aching legs a respite.

Nevertheless, it was mid-afternoon of the next day when he finally reached the port. He was intending to request an audience with a bishop, so he found a quiet back street where nobody would notice him and spent some time amending his appearance. When he was satisfied, he stepped out from his alley and mingled seamlessly with the crowd pushing and shoving along the quay.

He had not known what to expect of Lynn. He understood it to be little more than a trading settlement which had grown up because of its location, on the south-east corner of the Wash at a spot where several river and land routes converged. Yet the port he entered that day was virtually growing before his eyes, with building work on many sites and a general sense of stimulating activity. Hrype bought himself a pie and a mug of ale from a stall by an impromptu fish market and engaged the man standing beside him in conversation.

In response to Hrype's mild remark that the town seemed much busier than he recalled, the man drowned him in a flood of chatty, gossipy comments. 'It's all thanks to our Bishop Herbert,' he said brightly. 'That's Herbert de Losigna, him that the king brought here, but we've got over minding about him being a Norman in view of what he's doing for the town.' He ran a hand down the cloth of what was very plainly a new tunic, and Hrype guessed that he was benefiting in no small measure from Lynn's new prosperity. Leaning so close that Hrype could smell the onion and garlic taint of his breath, the man added, 'They say he paid the king handsomely for Thetford, but we're prepared to forgive him that as well, being as how he's all set to build us a fine new church!'

'Really?' Hrype responded, slipping into the role of wide-eyed innocent visitor. 'I heard tell of maybe a priory as well'

The man gave him a sly look. 'That's only talk as yet,'

said reprovingly. 'But the church, why, they're already pegging out the site, and it's going to be a fine building, my friend!'

'Has the bishop constructed a fine building for himself, too?' Hrype asked.

'He has, and you can go and see it for yourself if you head out across the square and take the road over there!' The man waved his beer mug in demonstration, and, thanking him, Hrype slipped away.

The bishop's residence was clearly still in the process of construction but already very fine. Hrype got as far as a big hall just off the courtyard, where he was informed by a black-robed cleric with a permanent sneer on his thin face that Bishop de Losigna was very busy and could not be expected to make time for importunate strangers demanding to see him without an appointment. Hrype adopted a humble pose and said would it be all right if he waited, just in case? The cleric gave a sniff, a swirl of his generously-cut robe and turned away, as if to say: *if you want to waste the rest of the day, it's up to you.*

The bishop appeared shortly afterwards, and Hrype leapt up and went to stand in his path. One of the two men flanking the bishop tried to brush him aside, but Hrype would not be moved. He leaned close to the bishop and said softly, 'My Lord Bishop, it is imperative I speak to you concerning Father Clement, late of Crowland Abbey, who I understand came to see you some months ago and who, I regret to tell you, is dead.'

The swift words achieved the right effect: the bishop grabbed Hrype's arm and hustled him aside, down a short passage and into a beautiful room furnished with plain oak, the very simplicity of which spoke of fine craftsmanship.

'How and when did he die?' The bishop, it seemed, was not one to waste words.

'He was found on the fen margins a little to the south-west of here,' Hrype replied. 'He had been poisoned, stabbed and garrotted, and his body was tethered to stakes. It would appear that he was killed soon after he came to see you, probably as he set out for Chatteris, where another man impersonates him.'

The bishop assimilated all this information without comment. There was a brief silence, and then he said, 'There is no doubt of this?'

'Very little, if any,' Hrype replied. 'The description of the dead man appears to be that of Father Clement.'

That seemed to satisfy Bishop Herbert. 'What do you want from me?' he demanded.

'I need to know when he came to see you, and when he set out for Chatteris.'

The bishop thought briefly, located the relevant information and said, 'November last year. Crowland had burned; the few monks who remain there could go to the Thorney priest for confession, and there was no need for a man of Father Clement's abilities to stay. He came to ask me to reconsider, but I had already decided to send him to Chatteris. We spoke briefly; he accepted my orders and left.'

It accorded with what Abbot Ingulphus had said. 'This was early in the month?'

'No. It was the last week of November. I remember it because we were almost in Advent.'

So Father Clement's body had been in the fen for five months or more. And there it would have stayed, Hrype reflected, but for a boat captain losing his way.

'Thank you, My Lord,' Hrype said. 'I will take my leave.'

'Wait.' The word was spoken mildly, but carried great authority. Hrype, who had already turned towards the door, stopped. 'I wish to see the man who killed my priest brought to justice,' the bishop said softly.

Hrype turned back to him. 'I do not know who that man is, nor where to find him.'

'You have some ideas, though. In here.' The bishop tapped his head. 'You are a resourceful man.' He paused. 'Do you wish me to provide you with men to help you in your quest?'

Trying not to show how much he didn't, Hrype shook his head. 'No. If the killer can indeed be sought out, it will be by subtlety and not by force.'

The bishop regarded him steadily for some time. Then he said, 'Please make sure that I am kept informed.'

Hrype returned the look. This was, he realized, a man have on your side. 'I will,' he said. And meant it.

*   *   *

Rollo and I made good time to Cambridge, taking advantage of where we were and where we were bound by going by sea to Wisbech and then down the river to Cambridge. It made such a difference to travelling when you didn't have to worry about not having any money; Rollo's coin purse seemed inexhaustible. To a man like him, though, no doubt our expenditure seemed modest in the extreme.

I realized, as we progressed smoothly over the dark water, that at some point we must have begun to follow the boat that had unwittingly towed the body of the man in the fen to Cambridge . . .

We tied up at the quayside late the following day. I led the way down the road towards the centre of the town, crossing the market square and diving off into the maze of alleyways that led to Gurdyman's house. I knocked on the door, and it opened almost instantly; he probably knew I was on my way.

I saw a big, beaming smile spread across his face. He turned to speak over his shoulder: 'She's here!'

Another figure materialized out of the shadows, and Hrype strode down the passage and briefly took hold of me by my shoulders, looking intently into my eyes. 'You are unharmed,' he said. It was not a question; he knew I was.

Then he saw who I had brought with me, and his entire body went very still. He glared at Rollo, a fierceness in his eyes that I had rarely seen before. I turned to say something to Rollo and observed that he was glaring right back.

Gurdyman intervened. He pushed Hrype unceremoniously away from the doorway – only Gurdyman, I reflected, would have dared shove Hrype so firmly – and ushered Rollo and me inside. 'Go on into the courtyard,' he murmured to me. 'Take your friend and help yourselves to food and wine. It's all set out ready.'

He *had* known I was coming. It was both a thrilling and a rather scary thought.

I very much wanted to stay and listen to what Gurdyman was saying so urgently to Hrype, but I did not dare. I took Rollo's hand and led him down the passage and through the chway into the courtyard. It was still warm from the day's shine and lit with the soft golden light of evening. Wine, goblets and a platter of bread, cheese and dried meat had been set out, but neither Rollo nor I were hungry. We did, however, both pour out wine, and Rollo raised his goblet to me in a silent toast.

Then Gurdyman came out into the courtyard, Hrype close behind. Gurdyman gave me a quick glance of apology, then said, 'You are welcome, both of you.' There was a definite emphasis on *both*. 'There are grave matters for us to discuss,' he went on, 'but before we can do so, Hrype wishes to speak.' He shot an irritated glance at Hrype. 'Go on, then,' he said tersely.

Hrype stared at Rollo. 'You are a Norman,' he said baldly. He narrowed his eyes. 'There is something else in your blood that I do not recognize, but your allegiance is to the king.'

'It is,' Rollo said coldly. 'Not because he is a Norman, but because I have seen strife tear a land apart, and I believe peace is better. A strong ruler on the throne brings peace.'

'We were used to life under our own kings!' Hrype replied. 'We had no need of the brute force of William and his son to bestow their *peace* on us!' He all but spat the word.

Rollo made no reply but for an ironically raised eyebrow. I thought for a moment that Hrype was going to hit him, but, with a very obvious effort, he held back.

I could not have stood it if they had fought. I stepped between then and said, 'Hrype, Rollo is my choice. Do not judge him by what you believe him to be; wait and discover for yourself what he truly is.'

I intercepted a look between Hrype and Gurdyman. There was a message in it, for I could tell that Gurdyman was urgently putting a thought into Hrype's head, although I could not tell what it was. Hrype made himself relax, and the tension went out of the air.

'We shall sit down and have some wine,' Gurdyman said, in the sort of tone that does not allow dissent, 'and then we shall all reveal what we have discovered and what we think we should do next.'

Rollo and I sat down on a bench; Hrype subsided, with very obvious reluctance, on to a stool; and Gurdyman walked round and poured more of the lovely, cool white wine into each of our goblets. Then he sat down in his own chair, took a slow and appreciative sip and said, 'Hrype informs me that the real Father Clement left Crowland back in November, visited his bishop over in Lynn at the end of that month and then, it seems, was murdered soon after he left Lynn for Chatteris. Another man now poses as Father Clement at Chatteris, and we surmise that this man probably murdered the real Father Clement, although we do not know why. This impostor also killed a young nun at Chatteris and attempted to poison another, who is sister to Lassair here. Again, we suggest no motive. Now, Lassair –' he glanced at me with a smile, which he then turned on Rollo – 'what have you and your friend to tell us?'

I nudged Rollo. 'You'd better go first,' I muttered. I did not know how much of his secret mission he would be prepared to reveal to two men he'd only just met, one of them distinctly hostile, and, as it turned out, the answer was not very much.

'There was a violent storm off the east coast last September,' Rollo said. 'There's a rumour that it was raised deliberately, to destroy the king's ship-army, which was on its way to the north of England.'

'Raised deliberately?' Hrype's sudden interest seemed to be overcoming his antipathy. 'You speak of a tempestarius?'

'I do,' Rollo said shortly. He glanced at me. 'Lassair tells me such people are not unheard of among your kind, and I do not speak of the strange legends and tall tales of the Magonians.'

Gurdyman went straight to the point. 'This storm, you think, was raised by someone who supported the king's enemies in the north? Who wished to hamper the king in his retaliatory measures by removing half his army?'

'Yes.'

Gurdyman thought about that. 'Scotland is by no means entirely under the rule of King Malcolm,' he said. 'The northern and the western reaches of the land are Norse and Gaelic, and neither people look kindly on King Malcolm and his queen, for Margaret is a forcibly Christian woman and wishes her entire country to be as devout as she is herself.' He paused. 'And the ability to raise storms was said to be a particular talent of the Norsemen who lived in the lands now ruled by Malcolm and his rigid wife.'

That was all very well, but in my opinion we were drifting away from the main point. 'We should look at what connects the activities of the storm-raiser and the killing of Father Clement,' I said decisively. Three pairs of male eyes turned to stare at me, with varying amounts of warmth in them, but I pressed on. 'Rollo and I have fairly convincing proof that the storm-raiser carried out his magic up on the northern tip of the land, where the ancient wood circle once stood at the crossing place.' Briefly, I described what we had learned and what we had experienced up there. Neither Hrype nor Gurdyman argued with our conclusion. 'The nearest settlement of any size to the spot where the storm hit is Lynn, which is where Father Clement was last seen and near to where his body was left. In addition, the little nun who was killed at Chatteris came from up beyond Lynn.' I echoed the exact words of the cheese-selling woman who had told me this. 'She arrived at Chatteris last September.'

I knew the month was significant, and I was just working out why when Rollo opened his mouth to speak.

But Hrype got there first. 'Supposing she saw the storm-raiser,' he said slowly. 'Supposing she was making her way around the favourite places she had known all her short life, saying goodbye before she went off to her new existence at Chatteris.'

'He realized she'd seen him,' Rollo went on, picking up the story, 'and he knew he had to prevent her telling anyone what she saw. He and his fellow conspirators discovered where she had gone, and they learned that, by sheer good fortune, a new priest was on his way to the abbey where the girl had gone.'

'Her name was Herleva,' I said. It was bad enough that she had lost her life, and I did not see why she should also lose her identity.

'Where Herleva had gone,' Rollo amended. He gave me a quick look, and I saw from his eyes that he understood. 'I am sorry,' he muttered, for my ears only.

'He consulted with the others,' he continued, 'and they selected the most suitable of them for the task of removing Father Clement and replacing him.' He frowned. 'How would one of them have managed to impersonate a priest so well that a whole abbey was convinced?'

I'd been wondering the same thing. I had seen how someone like Hrype could change his appearance so thoroughly that even his nearest and dearest wouldn't recognize him, but we were speaking here of a man pretending to be a priest, which would surely be incredibly risky, full of potential pitfalls at almost every moment of the day . . .

'Perhaps he had once been a priest,' Hrype mused.

'Or else had been put in a monastery school and thus able to observe the habits and the manners of a priest at close and constant quarters,' Gurdyman added.

'Are all priests exactly the same?' I asked of no one in particular.

Gurdyman glanced at the others, then replied. 'They are all taught the same things, and of course the entire cannon of dogma is common to all, but no doubt there are small variations in their behaviour.'

'Nobody at Chatteris knew Father Clement before he arrived,' I went on, developing the thought as I spoke, 'and anyway, they are nuns, used to obedience and accepting what their priest said and did without question.'

'So no one would have remarked on it,' Rollo finished, 'if this false Father Clement had not performed every single act in precisely the same way his predecessor had done.'

'Exactly.' I gave him a smile.

'This man, then, killed Father Clement in order to get into Chatteris and silence the nun – Herleva – who saw his colleague raise the storm,' Hrype said. 'He also tried to poison Herleva's best friend, Elfritha, because he suspected that Herleva had revealed the secret to her. Is that what you are saying?'

'Yes,' Rollo and I said together.

Hrype looked at Gurdyman, and I could see that neither was convinced.

'Have you a better suggestion?' I demanded.

Gurdyman smiled. 'For my part, no. Hrype?'

With obvious reluctance, slowly Hrype shook his head.

*   *   *

It was too late to set out there and then, for twilight was coming on and Hrype, Rollo and I were all very tired. Gurdyman busied himself preparing more food, and we drank quite a lot more wine. Then Gurdyman set out paillasses and warm woollen blankets in the courtyard for Hrype and Rollo – I wondered, not without amusement, how the two men would manage to sleep just a few feet from each other with the antagonism crackling between them like lightning – and I climbed the ladder to the peace and comfort of my little room up in the attic. I had not realized how worn out I was, and I started to drift into sleep as soon as I had lain down.

The last thing I was aware of was Gurdyman's voice. I do not think he was actually speaking to me; I think I heard him only in my mind, for I knew he had gone down into his crypt to sleep.

His words suggested he was giving me a warning.

Very early the next morning, when the eastern sky was just beginning to suffuse with the pink of dawn, Hrype, Rollo and I set out for Chatteris. Gurdyman had woken us and fed us, providing food and drink for the journey. As he bade us farewell, I wondered why he wasn't coming with us. He read the thought and gave me a totally unexpected hug. 'I am too old for travelling and would slow you down,' he murmured, adding, 'but it's nice to be wanted.'

I looked back at him as he stood in the open doorway, his lips moving silently. I guessed he was putting his own brand of protection on us.

When we reached the island, I was so full of the need to see my sister that I kept forgetting that was not why we were there. Hrype had assured me again and again that when last he saw her she had been starting to improve, but even he had to admit that virtually anything could have happened in the meantime. Rollo, understanding my anxiety and my fear, kept close beside me, and I took strength from him. I hadn't needed to tell him how much I loved Elfritha, since he seemed already to know.

As we approached the abbey, he stared intently at its walls

and the surrounding terrain. Then, with a brief nod, he called softly to Hrype, who stopped and turned to face him.

'I will keep watch from up there.' He indicated a low rise about twenty or thirty paces to the left of the abbey gates, where a stand of trees grew close to the wall. 'I'll climb the tree closest to the wall.' He glanced at me, then turned to Hrype. 'Lassair told me how the two of you disguised yourselves on the previous occasions you were here, and it'll cause fewer interested glances if the same pair visit again.'

Hrype nodded curtly. Even he, it seemed, could see nothing to argue with there. Then he and I went through the process of turning ourselves into an old man and his waddling daughter, and we set off for the abbey.

Again, I had the definite impression that our arrival was expected. The nun who had met us the last time we were there was standing in the doorway of the infirmary, her thin, angular face tense with anxiety.

My heart began to thud painfully in my chest. Had she come to forewarn us of what we would find inside? Oh, Elfritha!

Hrype had stepped forward and was speaking urgently to her. 'Sister Christiana, what has happened?'

But she was smiling now, her face transformed, and as she reached out to take each of our hands, I saw tears in her eyes. 'Elfritha is much better!' she said, her expression radiant. 'Edild has just been feeding her soup, and she has taken a whole cup! Come in, come in, and see for yourselves!'

We hurried in her wake down the length of the infirmary. I had the impression of several pairs of eyes watching us with interest, but I barely noticed. Then we were hurrying up the dark passage and through the open door into the little room, and there was my beloved sister, propped up on pillows, pale and feeble-looking, but smiling so widely that I could not help but respond. 'Elfritha, you're – you're—!'

It was no time for words. I leapt forward and, sinking to my knees, took my sister in my arms and held her so close that I could feel her heartbeat. We stayed like that for some moments – not speaking, not moving – then I felt a light touch on my shoulder and Edild's quiet voice said, 'Let her go now, Lassair. She is still very weak.'

I turned to look at her. Sister Christiana had disappeared – presumably out of tact, to give us some quiet time together – and Edild stood within Hrype's arms. I stared up at my aunt.

Oh, I had so much to tell her . . . She had predicted that Rollo would come back into my life. How right she had been. I was about to tell her so when Hrype spoke.

'Lassair's got her Norman with her,' he said. 'It appears he, too, has an involvement in this business.'

Edild flinched at the harsh emphasis he put on the word *Norman*. She turned to look at Hrype. 'I imagine that Lassair's life has become entwined with his for reasons and purposes far above political allegiance,' she replied. Then, her expression softening, she added quietly, 'Do not judge, Hrype. Lassair is too wise to fall in love with someone unworthy of her.'

I didn't think I was supposed to have heard that, so I pretended to be busy smoothing over Elfritha's bedding. She was, however, fizzing with interest. 'Who is he, Lassair?' she hissed, her eyes huge. 'Is he handsome? Are you very much in love?'

I took her sweet, too thin face in my hands and gently kissed her cheek. 'Wait and see,' I whispered back.

Edild disengaged herself from Hrype and, taking his hand, drew him forward to kneel beside Elfritha and me, crouching down at his side. She said, very quietly. 'Elfritha has something to tell you.' She took my sister's hand. 'Are you strong enough to talk?' she asked.

Elfritha nodded. Her expression grave, she composed herself, then said, 'Not long before Herleva died, she told me something. I didn't think any more about it at the time, because she – well, she loved to tell tales, and she often entertained us at night with her ghost stories. She was always getting into trouble for it and—' She broke off, but quickly recovered. 'Anyway, I only realized it could be relevant when I started to feel a bit better and Edild told me what had happened: how she thought I'd been poisoned, and that someone had tried to kill me.' She paused again, and her eyes were full of horror.

'You're safe now,' Hrype said firmly. 'We shall not allow anything more to happen.'

She nodded, accepting the assurance. 'Well, I did as Edild suggested and tried to think why anyone should want me dead. At first I could think of no reason at all. You don't really make enemies here, and it always feels as if the abbey is full of good emotions, like kindness and love. But then I thought about Herleva, and how someone had killed *her*, and then I remembered her story about the wild man and the storm.'

I sensed Hrype's sudden, fierce attention, shooting out at Elfritha like a spear. I wanted to protect her. Even more, I wanted to hear what she would say.

'The wild man?' Hrype said. I was amazed – and also full of admiration – at how cool he sounded, as if we were discussing nothing more important than what was for supper.

'She'd been up on the coast north of Lynn,' Elfritha said. 'That's where she used to live, and, although she didn't say much, you could tell her life had been dreadful. She was an orphan, and she'd been sent to live with some distant relative who treated her like the lowliest of labourers.'

I remembered how, when news had got out that a Chatteris nun was dead, no one had come rushing to see if it was Herleva. If word had reached them, her kin hadn't cared enough to find out.

'She loved the countryside around Lynn,' Elfritha was saying, 'and she'd set off to say goodbye to some of her favourite spots. She was up on the coast, looking out across the salt marsh to the distant sea, when a storm blew up, and she realized that it was going to be a bad one. She hurried inland to get to higher ground and the shelter of a thick hedge, and she was so scared that she tried to press herself right in among the branches. She hardly dared look, but something compelled her to. There was a howling wind, a deluge of rain and sleet, and the seas rose up in a great surge that swept right across the marshes and roared off inland.' She paused, then whispered, 'There were ships, many ships, and they foundered. There were men, sailors—' But she could not bring herself to speak of that horror. 'Herleva was almost borne away,' she said after a moment, 'and survived only because she'd tied herself to a tree trunk.

'Then she saw him. He was dressed in a long, swirling

cloak that was the colour of the mist and the sea spray, he had a staff in his hand, his eyes were light and his wild hair and beard were deep auburn. She was so frightened that she couldn't move, and she had to watch as, slowly and surely, he turned round towards her and saw her, crouched under the bushes, still fastened to the tree.'

'Why did he not kill her there and then?' Hrype whispered.

'She had the sense to turn her eyes from his,' Elfritha said, 'and the spell broke. He was some distance away, and she managed to scramble up, untie herself and run. She knew the area, and she guessed that he did not, for she managed to evade him. She spent that night hiding behind a woodshed, then next day she set out for Chatteris.' Elfritha's eyes were full of tears. 'She thought she was safe here,' she said softly. 'But she wasn't.'

I took her hands in mine.

'We believe the storm-raiser had an accomplice,' Hrype said gently, 'and that this man was able to gain access to the abbey.'

'How?' Elfritha looked round wildly, as if expecting to see some alien creature slide in through the doorway.

I glanced at Hrype. Was it wise to voice our suspicions? Someone might overhear, and word might reach the very person we did not want to alert . . .

Hrype smiled. 'I will tell you, Elfritha, I promise. We will explain everything to you, in time.' He got up. 'But for now, we have to—'

Footsteps sounded in the passage outside. Hrype, Edild and I stared at each other. They looked as horrified as I felt. It was him, it had to be – he had seen us come in, he had rallied his forces, perhaps even sending for the storm-raiser himself, and now they were about to surprise us, take us outside and—

Rollo appeared in the doorway.

Even in that moment of desperate urgency, I had an instant to notice my sister's appraising look at him. And the quick, mischievous smile she shot at me.

'He's here,' Rollo said, his voice low. 'He's just left the church and is on his way out. We must go after him. Come quickly.'

Hrype and I leapt up and followed him. Edild made to join us, but then stepped back. Looking at Hrype with yearning eyes, she said, 'I will stay here with Elfritha. Don't worry, Sister Christiana will come back as soon as you've gone.' Then she added something else; it sounded like: *take care*.

We hurried after Rollo, ran down the long infirmary and out of the door.

The false Father Clement was striding out through the abbey gates. He appeared to be alone. If we were going to confront him, it would be best to do so now, when he was without the support of the storm-raiser or any other of his companions. Hrype and Rollo obviously thought so too; the three of us set off in pursuit.

He did not appear to realize we were following him. It became clear quite soon where he was bound. Although I had not been to the spot myself, I had heard it described. He strode swiftly round the abbey walls and left the settlement behind. He crossed several fields, always heading straight for the places where the hedges were low enough to climb over and the streams and winding little waterways fordable or narrow enough to leap over. He had obviously come this way many times before.

Hrype and Rollo both seemed to know how you followed someone without letting them become aware of your presence, and I just did as they indicated. We trailed the black-clad figure for some time, and he never even suspected we were there.

Or so we thought.

He led us to the far corner of the last field before land gave way to water. There was a rough wooden shelter, very dilapidated, and the pile of dung on the dirty straw suggested the abbey donkey had been there not long ago. He was not there now.

The false priest went right to the edge of the field and stood above the brownish water that lapped at his feet. Then, without turning round, he said mildly, 'I know you are there. At least one of you is armed.'

Slowly, he spun round to face us, his hands in the air. 'I have no weapon,' he added. He smiled, a warm, friendly expression, and I was filled with the dreadful certainty that we were wrong, totally wrong, and this man was exactly what he claimed to be. I reached out to grab Hrype, intent on telling him, on warning him, but Hrype could see with clearer eyes than I.

As, it seemed, could Rollo, for he was drawing a short sword out of the scabbard he wore across his back, concealed beneath his over-tunic.

I had not even realized he bore a weapon. He certainly hadn't carried it when I stripped his wet clothes from him up on the foreshore. It must have been tucked right down inside his pack, and he had quietly strapped it on before we left Gurdyman's house.

Father Clement stood watching us, his expression benign and warm. His eyes were watchful, and, as they met mine, I felt a jolt as if someone had nudged me hard in the ribs.

And I began to think we might have been right all the time.

It was as if he had cast a spell on the three of us, and for a while nobody spoke. Then Hrype gave himself a violent shake, like a dog emerging from water, and raised his right arm. I felt a brief crackling force in the air, and the priest stepped back, flashing a sudden grimace at Hrype.

It appeared that whatever Hrype had just done had also released Rollo from the enchantment. He leaned towards Hrype and said quietly, 'We should be quick. He will not remain alone for long.'

Hrype nodded. Then, drawing himself up so that he stood tall and strong, he said, 'We do not know your name, but we know you are not Father Clement, whose body lies at Cambridge. You sacrificed him as a victim to the Threefold Death, giving his body to the water and securing it in the old way, with honeysuckle ropes and hazel stakes. You took his identity, and you came here to the abbey, where you killed the young novice, Herleva, because she had witnessed your accomplice raising the storm that drowned the king's ship-army.' He paused. I could sense even from where I stood, a pace or two away, that some huge force was aimed at him and he was countering it. He was shaking with the effort.

I tried to turn to Rollo, to see if he, too, felt that strange, paralysing power, but found I could not move.

Then the man who was posing as Father Clement began to speak.

'I may look like a priest of the church and the servant of a Norman king and his bishop,' he said. His voice was quiet, his tone kindly. It did not match up in the least with the power that I felt blazing through him. He glanced down at his black robes, running a hand over his clean-shaven jaw. 'This is a guise I can readily adopt, and in addition the ways of a priest are very familiar.' He paused, and a look of pain crossed his face. 'I was a wild child, for I lost my close family when I was very young and I was angry with the whole world. The remainder of my relatives could not deal with me and so they put me in with the monks, who tried to beat the spirit out of me and turn me into one of them. They did not succeed. I remain what I am: a son of the north, whose allegiance is exclusively to the old ways and the old kings.'

We were right! I wanted to shoot a glance at Hrype, but I could not move my eyes that far.

'I learned last autumn that King Malcolm had advanced into the north of England,' the black-robed man was saying. 'He has edgy neighbours, has Malcolm, for his own lands are only in the south and the east of Scotland. The north and west are ruled by the Scandinavians and the wild people he refers to as the godless Gaels. We are not godless,' he added vehemently. 'Our gods are numerous, and a man like Malcolm ignores and derides them at his peril. But his time will come.'

For the first time, emotion had crept into his voice. He waited – getting himself under control, I guessed – then spoke again.

'He made a mistake when he married that wife of his. Margaret changed the land, and for a small woman, she has made a dramatic impact. The Roman Church now takes dominance over the Celtic, and Benedictine monks swarm in her wake. Even the eight children she gave her king are called by English and not Gaelic names.'

There was a short pause, as if he were giving us time to assimilate the various sins of Queen Margaret.

Then he said coolly, 'I hate everything English, even as I hate the Church of Rome. My allies in the north-west told me of Malcolm's advance into Lothian. There would be a counter-invasion force; that was obvious. I watched and I waited, and as the snippets of knowledge came in one by one, slowly and steadily I began to see the whole picture. I knew what must be done.

'There is a skill, possessed by members of some families and passed down through the generations, back into the mists of the past and the dawn of the line. It is a perilous skill, hard-learned, and its practice drains a man until he is all but dead.

'On the twenty-fifth of September last year, a man with this skill stood ready. The ships bearing King William's army sailed right past him as he stood in the place of power, and the storm that he raised destroyed them utterly.'

His eyes went from one to the other of us, along the line that we formed as we stood before him. Then he spoke again, and he sounded as if he were chanting. 'I will tell you of the place of power. It was once revered and honoured by all of the people who understood the force of the natural world and the huge reserves of might that lie bound up in the crossing places, the margins, the half-and-half worlds of daybreak and twilight, river fords and marshland.

'I will tell you of the circle as it once was, with tall timber uprights and, inside it, an upturned oak stump, its trunk deep in the ground, its roots in the free, open air. Here an ancient people made a sacred place. The wide-spreading roots of the mighty oak were the platform where they laid the body of their greatest magician, giving it up to the sea, the shore. A huge fire was lit. The four elements were all there, and their spirits, summoned by the men of magic, came readily: air, fire, water, earth.'

He spoke as if he had been there. As if he had seen with his own eyes that body on its strange bier, the encircling wooden walls and the fire that surrounded them.

'The body was not that of a man,' he said, his voice barely more than a breath. 'The greatest magician of the people was a woman.'

The echoes of his words seemed to twist and float around us. Then, as if he had waited deliberately so as to gain the maximum impact, he picked up his tale.

'The man who raised the storm believed himself to be alone that day, but someone saw him. She was just a young girl, with a round face and a sweet smile. She was very afraid.' Briefly, he closed his eyes, as if remembering something. 'The man wore a cloak and carried a staff. His hair was long and uncombed, and his beard reached his chest. The power was on him, in him, and he scarcely appeared human.

'She knew the terrain better than he did, and she evaded him. But he followed her. He had diminished into human form, and he trailed her without her noticing him. She led him to Chatteris, to this abbey, where to his dismay she announced to the nuns that she wished to join them. Now you probably do not know that for the first few months, a young postulant is all but walled up here, having no contact whatsoever with the outside world. The only man she encounters is the priest. The magician knew that he had to reach her: he had to find out if she had indeed witnessed his storm-raising and whether she would tell anyone.'

He frowned, as if recalling the dreadful problem he and the storm-raiser had been faced with. Then he said, 'There had to be a way. I prayed, begged my guardian spirits and my ancestors for help, and they heard me. I learned that the elderly priest at Chatteris had just died and was to be replaced by a certain Father Clement, lately the priest at Crowland Abbey, which you may or may not know burned down last year. No,' he said, glancing at Hrype, 'I had nothing to do with that.' Then, with a swift grin, 'You don't care much for religious foundations, do you, cunning man?'

He knew. He understood what Hrype was . . .

'I went to Crowland,' the impostor said. 'Father Clement had already left. He had been summoned by his bishop, to speak to him before he took up his new appointment. Accordingly, he had gone to Bishop's Lynn, where I followed him. He stayed with the bishop for a day and a night, and the following morning he set out for Chatteris.

'He did not get far. I waited until we were well away from the little town, with the last of the dwellings far behind us. I waited until the track ran down close to the water; we had not long crossed the Nar, and the great Ouse meandered along to our right. I caught up with Father Clement and, in the guise of a lonely traveller eager for a chat and a bit of human company, I engaged him in conversation. We walked for some miles, and then I suggested we share my pot of gruel while it was still warm.'

Even if I could have spoken, I do not think I had words to say. I stood spellbound, unable to look away from the black-robed figure before us.

'He died easily. There was no pain, for the draught I gave him rendered him drowsy. He was smiling as I killed him. I tethered his limbs to hazel stakes and gave him to the salt marsh. Then I came to Chatteris. I discovered quite soon that the little nun was called Herleva, that she was a chatty soul who loved to giggle. Not very bright, but affectionate and popular. She had a friend, a slightly older girl who was also a white-veiled novice. The two spent as much time together as they were allowed, and it was clear that there was a deep friendship between them.

'I thought I was safe. Six months had passed, Herleva seemed happy and content, and it appeared there was nothing in her new life to remind her of the events that happened as she was leaving the old one. I was about to slip quietly away, when something happened. Herleva's friend had a visitor; her sister, I believe, although I did not meet her, or even see her myself, so I cannot be sure. But this young visitor was learning to be a healer. She was being taught other skills, too; I hid carefully and sat unobserved, listening as she whispered to her sister the nun, telling her of the wondrous things she was learning.

'She left, and the nun went to seek out her friend Herleva. She told her with awe in her voice of the things her sister had just been speaking about. I knew what was going to happen. I wished I could stop it, but I could not. I moved my position slightly so that I could observe the two of them. I can see them now: Herleva's frown, the downturned mouth, the disgruntled expression as she realized that her best friend's visitor had left a deep and lasting impression. She was jealous.

'The temptation, it seemed, was too much for her. "I once saw magic too," Herleva said, in a tone of such self-importance that you would have thought she had performed the magic herself. "It was just before I left home to come here," she went on in her light little voice. "I'd been up by the sea, saying goodbye to some of my favourite spots. I saw that a storm was brewing, and I took shelter in a hedge. I saw the storm grow and burst. I saw a fleet of ships that perished. I saw hundreds of men drown, screaming as they died. I saw the man who stood alone up on the shore and made the magic happen." '

He paused, running a hand over his face. Then, his expression oddly ironic, he said, 'She might have been about to say more, to utter the words that I dreaded to hear. She didn't. But I dared not take the risk; I had to act. She was sent out here, to tend the donkey in this field down by the water. I followed her. I said, "Cold this morning, Herleva." I held out my flask. "Here, have a sip of this. It's gruel, and it's hot."'
He glanced at us: Rollo, Hrype, me. As if to exonerate himself, he muttered, 'She suffered no pain.'

I sensed a mighty, silent protest form itself in Hrype and burst out of him. The impostor felt it too; he staggered back a pace or two.

Quickly, he recovered. 'She might have told her friend of her suspicions! I couldn't risk it. I sought out her friend – her name is Elfritha – and I said I was making a new mixture to warm and comfort the cold and hungry poor who flock to the abbey for aid, and asked her if she would be so kind as to sample it and tell me what she thought. "You have a friend, or perhaps a relative, who is a healer, I believe?" I said.

'"Yes, I have," she agreed readily, blushing and smiling with pleasure at being able to help. "My sister is apprenticed to our aunt, whose reputation is widely known in the fens around our home village."'

I felt a pain like a knife in my guts. It was all my fault! If I'd kept my mouth shut and refrained from boasting of my latest knowledge before my sister, then she wouldn't have told Herleva, and Herleva wouldn't have been driven to try and do better with an even more fantastic tale of her own. Herleva would still be alive, and Elfritha would never have been poisoned. And, even worse, my beloved sister had actually bragged about me, her very words making her more suitable to test out the false Father Clement's foul draught!

He was shaking his head. 'I do not know why she did not die,' he mused. 'The draught was made in the same way as that which killed her friend and my predecessor.' He shot a look at Hrype. 'What do you say, cunning man? Any suggestions?'

Hrype, with the power of speech returned, sounded hoarse. 'Elfritha is both sister and niece to healers,' he said, and his voice was icy with hatred. 'She has been given healing remedies since she was a child. It was your misfortune, false priest, to give your poison to someone who was used to the deadly ingredients, and so better able to withstand their impact.'

The impostor nodded, as if the explanation made sense. 'You are probably right,' he said.

He was concentrating intensely on Hrype. I wondered if that meant he had identified him as the main threat. I hoped so, for that would mean he was less concerned with Rollo and me. I tried once more to look at Rollo, and this time I managed it. He, too, was staring at me. He mouthed something, but the movements of his lips were so subtle that I did not pick it up. I concentrated on him, so fiercely that my head began to ache in protest. I bent all my mind to his, and then I knew what he wanted me to do.

I wasn't sure if I could. Turning my head slightly was one thing, but what I had to do involved far more than that. But we had to do something, and quickly. This man before us, dressed in his priest's robes, had already demonstrated that he had power, and it was highly likely that he had already sent out a summons to his storm-raising friend. We might just be able to overcome him alone, but if both faced us, we'd have no chance.

I tested myself. I tried to bend my knees, to let my shoulders slump. I managed both, after a fashion. Then I took a big breath and let my entire body go slack. I fell, in what must have looked exactly like a faint, and found myself lying on the damp ground.

He was distracted, as Rollo must have known he would be. Not for long, but it was enough. The moment his fierce, intense

attention slipped away from Rollo, Rollo raised his sword
and leapt on him, flattening him so that he lay on his back, and
then quickly straddling him, the point of his sword to the
man's throat. Hrype was only the blink of an eye behind him,
dropping to his knees beside the black-clad figure.

I thought Rollo was going to kill him. So, I believed, did
Hrype, for he reached out and took hold of Rollo's sword
arm. 'You cannot,' he said. 'In the eyes of the world, and, far
more importantly, in the eyes of the church, this man is a
priest.'

'Those who knew the real Father Clement will testify that
this man is no such thing!' Rollo's voice was hot with furious
protest, and he wrested his arm out of Hrype's grip.

I shut my eyes. I could not bear to see him kill.

But nothing happened.

After a moment, I opened my eyes again.

Hrype's silver eyes were fixed on Rollo's. Hrype said, very
quietly, 'Those who know the real Father Clement are not
here. You will have been arrested, tried and hanged for priest
murder before they even get here.'

'What do you suggest, then?' Rollo demanded harshly.

'We bind him and take him back to the abbey,' Hrype said,
untying a length of rope belt from his waist and handing it to
Rollo. 'We make our accusations, and we send for the sheriff.'

I had never thought to hear Hrype propose anything so
mundane. He does not normally have much time for the forces
of law and order.

Rollo had pushed the impostor on to his side – I wondered
briefly why he was making no protest – and Hrype was tying
his wrists. 'We will have to—' Rollo began.

Then the impostor suddenly gathered himself together,
lunged up at Hrype and hit him very hard on the side of his
jaw. Hrype went over like a felled tree and lay very still. The
impostor flung himself at me, and I felt the sharp prick of
steel on my neck.

'Yes, it's a blade,' he said, right in my ear. 'I should keep
very still, if I were you.'

Rollo stood before us both, his sword pointing at the false
priest's heart.

'Kill him!' I yelled. 'He's evil, he tried to poison my sister, and he doesn't deserve to live! *Kill him!*'

'Fierce words,' the impostor remarked, the arm hooked around my throat tightening and the point of the knife pushing in just under my ear. 'But useless, I'm afraid. If he lunges at me, he may indeed kill me, but you will die first. He won't risk that. The man loves you,' he added pleasantly. 'Isn't that wonderful?'

He could not see my hands, and I was feeling with my right one for the buckles on my leather satchel. I always carry the items a healer needs for simple treatments, and among them is a short, sharp blade. I use it to open up festering wounds, or to edge further apart the sides of a deep cut so that I can clean it properly. Once I even used it to slice into a lad's finger and extract a big splinter that had gone right under the skin.

Cuts hurt less when the knife is keen, and I also carry a small whetstone. I always keep my little blade very, very sharp.

I had the satchel open, and I had located the blade. I took firm hold of it and, meeting Rollo's eyes, made sure he could see what I intended to do.

Then I wrested myself to one side, as far as I could, and swung my blade up. I knew I made contact, for I felt his warm skin under my hand. Instantly, the knife point under my ear drove in, and I felt my own blood flooding out.

I swung my hand again and again, trying to make contact, but with each sweep the arc was less. I saw him above me, fury in his eyes, a long cut on his chin where my flailing blade had caught him.

He had his knife pointing at my heart, and I knew I was about to die. I held my little blade in front of me – if only I could hit a vital place, I might . . .

There was a roar from behind the black figure of the impostor. It was Rollo, demanding his attention.

Not knowing what his name was, Rollo had shouted out, '*Devil!*'

The impostor turned. He and Rollo faced each other, one armed with a knife, one with a short sword. But the one with the lesser weapon had magic in him.

Quite how much, I did not yet appreciate.

He stood looking at Rollo, and he began to laugh. 'You believe there are two of us, don't you? I, who with my background can readily impersonate a priest, and my companion, the wild-haired man of magic, the storm-raiser.' He lifted both arms and, in a language I did not know, screamed out some words to the wide blue sky. From nowhere there was a great rumble of thunder, and I felt the earth shake.

'You fools!' cried the black-clad figure. 'We are one and the same!' Then he lowered his left arm and pointed it at Rollo.

He might have been full of wild, unnatural power, but Rollo was younger, fitter and a fighter. He was so fast that I did not see the strike, only its result. The dark robes fluttered as the body hit the ground, and the unknown man who had taken the identity of Father Clement fell dead.

I looked up at Rollo.

He had just killed a man, and I knew for sure that the dead impostor was not his first victim. It should have given me pause. But as I stared up at him standing there over the corpse of the false Father Clement, his whole body still alight and glowing with blood lust – killing lust – I knew it made no difference.

I could try to justify myself and remind myself that Rollo had killed to save the lives of the three of us, not to mention taking vengeance on the man who had killed the real Father Clement and Herleva, and who had tried to poison Elfritha too. But that justification would have meant I was being untruthful with myself, and Edild always says that, no matter who else you lie to, you must never lie to yourself.

I loved Rollo. I had loved him since first I met him. I would go on loving him, no matter what. He was my friend, my protector, my responsibility; he had just saved my life, and I had saved his. He would very soon also be my lover; that was already certain. There was no going back.

In that instant I understood something about the man I loved. I understood, too, that I would never change him. If we had a future together, I was going to have to find a way to accept it. Accept *him*.

I knew it was not going to be easy, for I was a healer and my instinct was to save life, not to take it. But I also knew without a doubt that I would manage it.

Rollo came over and knelt beside me. He put a hand to the cut under my ear, pressing hard. Presently, he said, 'It's stopped bleeding. Have you a dressing in your satchel?'

I nodded. He seemed to appreciate that I was temporarily unable to do much for myself, so he took out a pad of linen and the small bottle of lavender oil that I always keep wrapped inside the linen.

'You should put some of the lavender—'

'On the pad. Yes, I know. You told me.' He sounded as if he were smiling. He wound a strip of cloth around the pad to hold it in place, tying it round my neck. Then, with one more look at me, he went to see to Hrype.

I'm the healer, I thought. *That's my job.* I tried to get up, found that I could and went to join him. Hrype had a huge bruise on his jaw, but his eyelids were flickering and he was regaining consciousness.

He struggled to sit up and looked around, seeing the dead body of the impostor. He glanced up briefly at Rollo, who nodded. Hrype murmured something, and Rollo smiled. It occurred to me that Hrype had probably said *well done*.

'What shall we do with him?' I asked.

Hrype had staggered over towards the water. I thought he was going to vomit – people often do after they've been knocked out – but in fact he was just having a look. He glanced around at the surrounding landscape and nodded. 'We'll do what he would have asked for if he could,' he said.

Then I knew.

They wouldn't let me help. They were, for once, totally united, and they absolutely forbade it. So I sat on the bank over the fen and watched.

Hrype made the honeysuckle ropes; Rollo cut and trimmed the hazel stakes. Then Hrype made a wound on the body so that it had received three. One from each of us . . . They carried the dead man out into the fen, so that I could no longer see clearly what they were doing. I guessed, though. They would have hammered in the hazel stakes and tied him down, under several feet of water.

It was very unlikely that anyone would ever find him.

POSTSCRIPT

We left Chatteris Abbey, Edild coming with us, for Elfritha was well on the way to regaining her health. Besides, we – and only we – knew that my beloved sister was no longer in any danger. I don't know what the nuns thought had become of the man they believed to be Father Clement. I was quite bothered at the thought of those women, one or two of whom I'd met and really liked, abruptly being robbed of their priest, but then I remembered that he wasn't a priest at all and I didn't feel so bad.

We went down to the waterside where the boatmen waited, Hrype and Edild walking together ahead, Rollo and I following. They, I guessed, would return to Aelf Fen. Edild had been away from her patients for too long, and, with me absent too, the villagers who'd had the misfortune to fall sick over the past few days would have had to see to themselves. Hrype, I knew, would be anxious about Froya. Even though he must have longed to disappear with Edild somewhere out in the wilds where nobody knew them, it just wasn't possible.

We asked around and soon found a ferryman who was bound for Ely and then on to Wicken, and he said he was willing to take passengers.

My aunt spoke quietly to me. 'You're not coming with us,' she said.

'No,' I agreed.

She smiled, very sweetly. 'Your sister is very impressed,' she said, nodding in Rollo's direction.

I felt myself flush. I just said, 'Oh.'

Edild gave me a quick, hard hug. 'Go and enjoy it,' she whispered.

'I don't think Hrype likes him much,' I said glumly.

'Hrype thinks a lot better of him than he did at first,' she countered quickly, 'and it's early days yet. There's no hurry.'

Rollo came to stand beside me, and we watched as Edild and Hrype got into the boat and it slowly pulled away from the shore. 'Give my love to the family,' I called, and she waved a hand in acknowledgement.

When they were almost out of sight, Rollo took my hand. 'Come on.'

I looked up at him. 'Where are we going?'

He grinned. 'Does it matter?'

We, too, took a ferry, and ours went just the short distance from Chatteris island to the mainland. There we wandered off into the warm late spring countryside, stopping in a small village to purchase some provisions. Then we walked further into the isolation of quiet fields, woods and little streams, until there was nobody about but us. Then we stopped.

I hadn't really thought that he would stay.

We had a magical two days together and one even more magical night. We said so many things to each other, told tales out of our pasts, made promises, much as all new lovers do. We exchanged tokens, I giving him a wristband crafted of fine strips of plaited leather that I'd made one dark night in winter; it was not much, for I had little. I fastened it round his wrist, and he touched it as reverently as if it had been encrusted with jewels. He gave me a ring. It was gold, rather heavy, and depicted a serpent with its mouth open devouring its own tail. He said it had belonged to his grandmother, who, like his mother, was a strega.

It was magic, he added nonchalantly.

'You know I have to go, don't you?' he said on our last morning together. He was holding my face between his two hands, staring down at me, his dark-brown eyes intent on mine.

'Yes,' I whispered.

'I have to tell him what we discovered, for he sent me to find out if a rumour was true, and now we know that it was.'

'Yes,' I repeated.

'He needs to know that the man who raised the storm is dead.'

'Yes.'

'He will be impressed when I tell him I couldn't have done

it without a simple-looking village healer girl,' he added. 'He'll probably think I'm joking. He likes a joke.'

'Yes.'

'Is that all you're going to say to me?'

'Yes.'

He paused, his smile deepening. 'So what if I said let's make love again? What would you say to that?'

'Yes.'

Parting from him wasn't so funny. It wasn't funny at all.

I went back to Gurdyman's house, where I now am. I don't know how much he knows about me and my Norman, as Hrype still insists on calling him, but when I get sad, Gurdyman is kind, and you can't ask more than that.

I am kept busy, for Gurdyman drives me hard and there is so much to learn. Sometimes I go and visit my family and friends in Aelf Fen, and I shall be going for a longer stay soon. The bad weather is coming, and Edild will need another pair of hands to deal with the sicknesses that invariably follow.

I shall miss Gurdyman, and the twisty-turny house, and my lessons, and the excitement of living in a big, busy, bustling place like Cambridge. But I'll be back here before too long, and in the meantime it'll be lovely to be home again. Zarina and Haward's baby was born back in May, and so far I've hardly seen him – his name's Ailsi – so that's something to look forward to. There are also my other niece and nephew, my sister Goda's children, and it's high time I got to know them better. And my parents will be happy to see me, for I'm sure they miss me.

I know that it doesn't matter where I am, because, as soon as he can, Rollo will find me. I just wish I knew when that might be.

Maybe I'll have to ask the runes.

AUTHOR'S NOTE

The Anglo-Saxon Chronicles records as follows for the year 1091:

When the king William was out of England, the king Malcolm travelled from Scotland here into England and raided across a great part of it. Then when King William heard of this in Normandy, he came back to England and immediately ordered his army to be called out, both the ship-army and land-army; but before he came to Scotland, four days before Michaelmas, almost all the ship-army wretchedly perished.

And in 1092:

In this year the king William travelled north to Carlisle with a very great army, and restored the town and raised the castle, and set the castle with his men, and sent very many peasants there with women and with livestock to live there to till the land.

NEATH PORT TALBOT LIBRARY AND INFORMATION SERVICES							
1	11/13	25		49		73	
2		26		50		74	
3		27		51		75	
4		28		52		76	
5	7/12	29		53		77	
6		30		54		78	
7		31		55		79	
8		32		56		80	
9		33		57		81	
10		34		58		82	
11		35		59		83	
12		36		60		84	
13		37		61		85	
14		38		62		86	
15		39		63		87	
16		40		64		88	
17		41		65		89	
18		42		66		90	
19		43		67		91	
20		44		68		92	
21		45		69		COMMUNITY SERVICES	
22		46		70			
23		47		71		NPT/111	
24		48		72			